I0682331

Angel IN A BOX

LEGION'S FALL: BOOK ONE

Wesley Foster

ISBN: 979-8-9905066-0-2

To my Wife, without whom I'd still be drowning in the darkness without God's light.

Legion's Fall: Book One

Angel
IN A
Box

Wesley Foster

SILVER-grey walls adorned a plain, single-room bar surrounding Travis Harding, his only protection from the death that waited outside. The void of space beyond these aluminum walls would take anyone: Man, woman, child. No matter how strong, or how weak, the void would claim them as its own in seconds, viciously holding them forever in the grip of death.

Travis tipped the aluminum cup toward himself to see the shadows and ripples in the brown liquid that passed as coffee on Earth's moon. He'd never had anything better, but somewhere in the back of his mind he knew it should taste better than this. He was wasting time, but when the highest your life could go was regulated by the Council, ambition was in short supply.

His shift was starting in thirty minutes: More banging on regolith with a hammer and chisel.

The unibrow on Liam's face lifted. "Are ya serious?" he whispered, daring to look over his shoulder.

The Hangout was just as uncrowded as ever, leaving the two men to sip at their aluminum cups alone. Travis nodded, "Yeah. They say they're from Mars, but I've never heard of a ship that big before." He recalled his first sighting of the starship yesterday: A massive ship large enough to make out the long shape with his unaided eye from outside Tunnel Twelve. "It's so big you can actually see the stupid thing from here."

"Where'd they get a ship that big?"

Travis shrugged, "I dunno. I didn't think it was even possible to build something that big." He tilted his coffee to his lips and felt the warm fluid that tasted more like dirty socks slide down his throat.

Liam frowned, furrowing his thick brow that fit with the rest of his large features. The tumbler nearly disappeared into his hand when he lifted it. "But why go and ransack Titan? I mean, 'tis not like they been doin' anything t' us." Liam's brogue came from his time in Beta Colony but it hadn't diminished over the years. People thought it made him sound stupid, but Travis was enough of an outcast that it was easy to look past something so trivial and find the friend beneath.

"I got a message off-" he stopped as two men sauntered into the dimly lit room and took a couple chairs at the counter. Travis recognized where they were from, even though he didn't know who they were.

"You kidding me? Of course I joined," one of the wide-shouldered men answered the other.

"Can't miss this one."

Travis traded glances with Liam and pretended to be interested in his laundry-coffee. The men were from Structures, the crown jewel of Lunar Delta. Structures built new facilities, so they were awarded with the best rations, the best living spaces, and three showers a week. Miners like Travis were expendable and made to feel like it.

"You taking Julie?" the first one asked.

The buzz-cut man on the left shook his head as the bartender handed them drinks. "Can't. No women allowed."

Liam's unibrow lifted on one side.

Travis looked down at his sludge and then back up at Liam. The big man's blue eyes darted toward the door and he stood up. Travis grabbed both tumblers and carried them up to the long aluminum counter for the bartender. When he stepped into the yellow-lit corridor, Liam fell into step beside him.

"No women? What kind of nonsense is that?"

Travis sighed, "I don't know. I don't get why that's even a thing, but that's not the problem."

"I know," Liam agreed. He stood another foot above Travis but he felt like a shield instead of a monster. They walked toward Theta Section in silence, passing by increasing numbers of other people filing in and out of the twelve-foot main corridor from adjacent tunnels. Bare aluminum walls, floors and the arched ceiling were the constant architecture throughout the expanse of Delta Colony.

"So ya got a message to 'em?" Liam continued.

"Yeah," Travis sighed. "For all the good it'll do. It sounds like they're taking the biggest, toughest guys though."

They trudged through the doorway into Theta and found themselves at the back of a long line. Travis craned his head around the long line of men but couldn't see what was keeping them from moving. He looked up at Liam who was studying things from over the top of most of the men in front of him. "Looks like some sorta list," he offered.

"You think they're taking some from here too?" he whispered.

Liam shrugged. "Would ya go if they were?"

Travis frowned and looked down at his narrow frame, "Like they'd take me even if I volunteered. Besides, I don't wanna go shoot people."

Liam's left brow raised, "But ya don't wanna stay here neither."

The line eased forward, everyone maintaining their social-distancing as required by Delta Law. Too many people clustered together could create a drop in air flow according to the engineers. "But they're going to fight. I don't want to be one of them."

"Who says ya have to?"

Another step closer. Travis could feel his nerves tingle. If he went, he might be able to slip away during the initial boarding. He'd be lost in another space station with no idea how or where to go. Liam was right though, at least he'd be there. But would they really take him? He was a skinny miner with no parents and no friends outside of Liam. He'd never held anything resembling a weapon other than the hammer and chisel waiting in the hatch in the outside lockers.

"Name?"

Travis looked up at the same time as Deacon Bridges and the usual derision entered the older man's dark brown eyes. "No."

"What do you mean 'no'?" Travis looked at the entry point for

Theta Mining Division which had been very abruptly converted to a check-in point. Two long tables were set against one wall where another line of men were waiting their turn to sign things.

Jeter Bridges lowered the notepad in his right hand and pointed at Travis' nose with his pen. "I mean, denied. There's no way you're going anywhere except back out into those tunnels. You've already caused enough trouble Mister Harding and I'm not about to turn you loose on a starship where you can do even more damage. This might be volunteer, but in the interest of protecting others from your reputation, I won't let you sign on." He turned his grey stubble toward Liam, "Name, son?"

Liam frowned, "Ya won't let me friend go, but you'll sign me up? What kinda crap is that?"

"Then step aside gentlemen. You're holding up the rest of them," Jeter waved toward the door that led to the miner's lockers, clearly finished with the conversation.

Travis walked into the empty locker room and flopped onto the metal bench.

"Just like that? You're givin' up?"

He looked way up at his friend who stood directly in front of him. "What am I gonna do? You heard the Deacon."

Liam shrugged, "The Travis Harding I know wouldn't let a little thing like one man's snobbery hold him up."

"Even if I got on that shuttle, what can I do when I get there?"

Liam tilted his head, "You figure it out." He glanced around before continuing, "It's what you're best at. You don't have a plan 'cause you just roll with it and make stuff up on the fly. You're good at that."

He would need a way to get around the checkpoints and cut into the line to the shuttle. Theta section was a long tunnel with stubby branches that led off and up to ten airlocks that were the only access points out of the colony. Every day since he was of age he had gone out of those airlocks to the lunar surface to mine ore and create more subsurface living areas. He could bypass the checkpoints and drop back in further down through the airlocks so long as no one saw him leave or enter. If he got caught, the worst they could do was space him. Other than that, he was already going to be punished for life out there mining with a hammer and chisel.

He pushed up and headed toward his locker.

"Watcha thinking pup?"

Travis stopped long enough to smile at him, "Going outside."

TRAVIS stepped out to the stillness of the Lunar surface with a tightness in his chest. His plan could work, or it could fall apart completely. As Liam followed him, he turned to help the big man pull the six foot door closed and turn the wheel that locked it in place. The thick lever near the door opened two vents simultaneously that expelled air and dust out the airlock to be sucked into the void of space. After counting off the required ten seconds, he pushed the lever back into the upright position and turned to face the deadly surface that had claimed so many lives.

The long tunnel of Theta section lay twelve feet under the smooth grey surface of lunar soil, while the rest of Delta Colony stretched both above and below the surface. Many lives had been traded for those tunnels, which were then lined with the double-reinforced aluminum walls that made the spaces habitable. Out here, you were one torn suit from death. The black void loomed overhead, while grey dust rose with every labored footfall.

His plan took them along the spine of airlocks, safe from prying eyes and ears so long as he and Liam stayed off the radio. Three shuttles to *The Phantom* were parked on the shiny aluminum landing pad at the far end of Theta section about a half mile away. A tap on his shoulder turned his attention back to Liam, who pointed upward. Hanging in the dark overhead, light from the sun glinted off the long, irregular shape of a ship that shouldn't have been able to be seen that well. He nodded, then remembered that his helmet didn't move up or down and gave him a thumbs up. The white suits were still the same as they had always been, and worth more than the lives they protected. He turned back toward the pad and pushed forward. Every step in these suits felt like fifty steps without it.

From up here, the airlocks looked like alternating ribs with the ends cut very short. Each 'rib' was another airlock that curved down into the ground where it met up with the lockers and Theta section tunnels. If this worked, he'd never see any of this again.

Dust rose and fell around his feet, the sound only traveling inside his suit to his ears. Liam thumped on his shoulder hard enough to get his attention, turning him away from the landing pad toward the reflective black faceplate that hid his friend. Liam's suit was the same size as his, which always struck him as odd. He swam a little inside this thing, but Liam had to feel like he was about to explode all the time. He was pointing over Travis' shoulder toward the docking area.

The wide expanse of raised aluminum deck was kept clean of dust regularly and shone with the light of the sun bouncing into his visor. Even at this distance he could make out the three white shuttles sitting on it. Docking collars leading to the three airlocks grouped around the landing pad were coupled to the shuttles, meaning that passengers weren't expected to wear suits.

"Phantom Shuttle Four, ready to uncouple."

Travis felt the shock ripple through his spine. They were leaving already! He and Liam had minutes to reach another safe entry point and get back out of these suits! The quick shock faded as he recounted the number of shuttles sitting on the docking pad, but the urgency wouldn't leave his chest. He plowed forward, watching the docking crew pull the collar back from the ship while his feet stirred up dust that settled back almost as quickly. By the time they reached the fourth airlock entry from the docking pad, his brain was screaming at him to keep to cover. He could see the docking crew securing the docking collar on the next shuttle, so that meant that anyone looking back this way might see Liam and himself moving toward them.

"Control? Docking collar engaged and checked. Ready for pressurization."

"Copy that, Dock. Initiating pressure in three… two… one."

"Commencing seal checks now, Control."

Travis approached the arch of aluminum, keeping hidden from view and peeked around it. His heavy space suit didn't cooperate, meaning he had to let half his body show in order to see around the airlock entry portal. His breath was loud inside the helmet, and sweat threatened to run into his eyes if he wasn't careful.

"Seals are good, Control. Ready to commence boarding."

"Dock, this is Control. We confirm that on our end. Return to cover for shuttle departure."

"Copy, Control. Heading to cover."

Liam yanked him back behind the fin-shaped airlock entry portal out of sight and pointed in the direction of the docking pad. His next hand movement was back-and-forth across each other in a 'no way' sort of gesture.

Travis gave the hand signal to say 'yes' and then pointed at the portal next to them followed by an urgent tapping on his wrist. He only hoped Liam understood his hand signals to say, 'we gotta go now.' He moved around the edge, checking on the docking crew. The white suits were heading away toward an enclosure to protect them from the coming liftoff sequence of the shuttle and wouldn't be interested in a visual sweep of the area. He grabbed the two-foot spoked metal wheel in the center of the door and started spinning madly.

"General Call. This is a general call to all hands. We have a condition yellow commencing in two minutes. Please respond immediately if you cannot make cover. Repeat. Condition yellow in two minutes. Respond immediately if you cannot make cover."

Condition yellow meant the shuttle was going to liftoff. The force of the engines would send lunar debris outward for half a mile at high speeds, enough to penetrate suits and crack the protective helmets. They were less than a quarter of that distance. A sour taste filled his mouth while his hands spun the wheel the ridiculous number of times it took to finally unlatch the door. Liam grabbed the exhaust lever and pulled up, venting the room and blowing a small dust cloud away from them. The action released the pressure on the door and it pushed inward. Travis fumbled to climb over the doorway lip and suddenly felt himself lift up and into the room. Liam pushed in behind him and swung the door shut. Seconds ticked by while Travis fought his way up and grabbed at the pressure lever. Liam was already spinning the wheel, and protocol said not to engage the pressure lever until the door was completely sealed, but they had to make sure the door wouldn't blow in during liftoff.

"General Call. This is a General Call. All hands brace for liftoff. Phantom Shuttle Four you are cleared for liftoff."

Travis yanked up on the lever, flooding the compartment with noisy, pressurized air that forced the door up against the seals. Liam spun the wheel at a blinding speed to engage the lock.

"Control, this is Phantom Shuttle Four. Liftoff clearance confirmed. Engaging thrusters in three… two…"

The wheel froze in place, fully seated.

"…one."

A shuddering rippled through the walls and floor, audible through their helmets now that the room had pressure. Travis leaned up against the wall as the rush of adrenaline swam through him. Liam was doing the same on the opposite wall and reaching for his helmet.

They weren't clean yet.

The room needed to be vented again to suck any dust off of them. The fine particles of regolith in the dust would kill in very short order by tearing apart your lungs from the inside. The training instructor had yelled and pounded his fists on the table in front of his class to drive this point home. He shoved off the wall and grabbed Liam's hand by the wrist inches from the helmet latch. He felt Liam's arm stiffen under his hand, then relax.

Liam's other hand came up beside them, showing a thumbs-up gesture.

The shuddering of liftoff had begun to fade. One shuttle gone, only two more remaining by his count. He vented the room again, patting Liam down and then letting his friend have a turn at him. Once they were sure, he shut the lever and let the pressure return. The sound of rushing air matched the large mechanical gauge on the wall. When the needle landed in the green zone, he started the drudgery of opening the secondary hatch to the next chamber.

Three hatches and another pressure equalization later, the two of them were standing in a locker room with two boys who should have been cleaning. Both boys were no older than ten, scrawny and brown-haired with wary eyes. These weren't the sons of privileged men. "What are you two up to?" Travis asked as he pulled his clunky helmet off.

One of them said, "Nothin'," while the other chimed in, "What're you doing mister?"

Liam already had his helmet off. "Our jobs. The man asked ya' a question." His size worked as usual, taming the boys' rebellious natures.

"Cleaning duty."

Travis started unlatching Liam's suit for him. "You don't sound too sure," he said without turning around. "My friend's suit was malfunctioning so we had to come back in." He turned to let Liam return the favor, facing the boys. "Didn't anybody tell you what to do if you heard the air shifting in here?"

One of them nodded.

"And?"

"We're supposed to run out."

Liam lifted the top half of Travis' suit free. "Do ya know why?"

The snarky boy who had a small bruise below his left eye gave Travis a frown. "'Cause you guys don't want anybody in your way."

Travis narrowed his eyes and stooped to be face to face with the boy. "Because if those doors don't get opened and closed right, you could get sucked out. That means you're dead. Got it?"

"No way."

"Oh definitely 'way'," Liam supplied. "And it'd happen faster than ya can blink. One second you're standing there with a stupid look on your face. The next you're out there dead and frozen over." Travis helped Liam out of the top half of his suit while the big man continued. "This is no joke. Ya got jobs what needs doing, but if you hear that air changing' you best get your butts out. You hear me?"

The boys scrambled over themselves out of the locker room, leaving them in peace.

"And that's why I never had kids."

Travis smirked as he stepped out of the space suit bottom, "I thought it was because you've never had a steady girl. Or any girl for that matter."

Liam frowned, "That too."

Back in his dingy grey jumpsuit, Travis shoved the gear aside, "We better move it."

The main hallway held a much smaller gathering of men in clumps, awaiting something. He always felt like an outlier, so the fact that he and Liam weren't part of any other group wasn't unusual to him. The two of them made their way toward a small group closer to the docking portal, catching little snippets along the way.

Multiple shuttles, several trips. Assigned groups. A few had chickened out already.

"Harding? They let you in here?"

He turned to face Jacob Grechem, a thorn in his side through school and extra-colony training. His pock-marked face had never improved, nor had his opinion of Travis. He nodded, "Of course they did Jake. It's a chance to get rid of me."

Jake frowned, "Great. So now you're our problem." He swore just loud enough for Travis to hear him. "And I suppose you're the replacements for the three that bailed?"

He couldn't have set this up better if he'd tried. "Oh fantastic. You're in my group?" He quipped, letting just enough of the situation rub him wrong to give him an attitude.

More swearing from Jake who pushed his way into Travis' face. "This is my group. Got it? You got assigned to *my group*.

You don't get a group, you're just a part of mine."

The overwhelming stench of a man who'd skipped too many showers filled his nostrils with fungus and mildew. "Fine," he said and put a step between them. After all the hygiene lectures, Jake should have learned to take more showers.

Another hour of standing around led to the boarding of Phantom Shuttle eight. Travis was hungry, and tired of hearing Jake tell everyone of his plans to shoot everyone on the station for disobeying the Accord. He also struggled with a clot in his throat as they approached the docking hatch. A flash of a girl being drug through there by her jerk of a father rushed back from years ago.

"Move it or lose it Harding."

He had no idea how long he'd been standing there, frozen in place but Jake's derisive tone spurred him back into motion. The interior of the shuttle carried the standard-issue grey and white palate, stiff-looking seats arranged along the walls of a small cargo space, and a single blue light overhead.

"Let's go men. We need to pick this up," called a stern voice from the open door to the cockpit.

Travis took an end seat and Liam overfilled the seat next to him. "Sorry lad. Seats are built for little people I guess."

As expected, Jake didn't make any kind of retort about Liam's size. They knew of the older man's reputation and left him alone.

"This is a one-way trip men. Last chance before the door closes," called the pilot.

"And miss this? No way!" Jake announced for everyone.

"Then sit down and strap in, I'm calling it."

Twelve seats, eleven men on board.

"Wait!," shouted a voice from the docking portal. A very surprised Deacon Bridges stepped through the portal and took up the last seat. He looked around briefly as he buckled the restraint harness, "Everyone else in my group bailed."

The door began to slide closed, guided by something Travis couldn't see. The pilot called out his readiness to depart and the chatter between pilot and the Colony docking control began.

Bridges locked eyes with him long enough for Travis to see the flames of indignation dancing in his eyes. He didn't care, he was on the shuttle and there was no way the gruff pilot was going to let him off now.

"Gentlemen," Bridges began, "I've been authorized to inform you that we have been broken into twelve divisions, and that I am the head of division eight. I will be meeting with the other division heads on board and the ship's captain to determine the makeup of each division." He smirked briefly at Travis. "You should all be aware that deviance will not be tolerated aboard the ship. You step out of line and we respond accordingly."

"Cut the chatter!"

Bridges frowned toward the pilot but didn't respond.

The shuttle's floor trembled beneath them, "Lifting off in three… two… one." The trembling rumbled, shook, and then settled into a vibration that bounced them in their seats. Travis tried not to press into Liam but the force of the acceleration pushed him against his friend's large arm.

Then it was done. The engine cut out and a leering silence enveloped the scene. "All right men, we're three minutes out. We land, you disembark and head for the doors at the back wall. Get there ASAP, got it? We're on a tight schedule and I don't have time to wait for you to stare or puke."

Those were two very different activities, but something told Travis that the pilot had seen people do both. He'd have to take the pilot's word for how far away they were. Other than the sense of his stomach drifting up into his throat, there was nothing else to tell him he was in space. This was the first time he'd experience this profound sense of weightlessness, this strange drifting of his body against the straps.

"Bag! Get him a bag," Bridges shouted, pointing at someone. Travis followed his commanding finger to a thick-necked guy was trying his hardest to keep his last meal down. No sooner was a foil bag stuck in his face than he relinquished control to the new receptacle. The odor hit everyone, including Travis. Two more men succumbed, making it worse.

The pilot swore from the front. "C'mon people! Get it together!"

Protests from those who hadn't let their evening meal go sounded in the form of grumbled curses. Travis kept his breathing steady, even though the air smelled foul. He had to keep himself under control. Even if everyone else failed.

"All right you sorry sacks of meat. Get ready for gravity 'cause we're docking in five… four… three… two… one." The shuttle thudded against something as everything in his body pressed down against the seat bottom much harder than it should have. The door on the side of the shuttle lifted up while a smaller section lowered to create stairs with a mechanical whine and clunking that sounded like music. "Everybody up!" The pilot was already standing in the doorway to his cockpit with a deep scowl on his roughly bearded face. "And take those bags with you. I don't wanna smell that crap all the way back down."

Travis unbuckled the straps and fought to stand up against a body that suddenly felt far too heavy. A sideways glance told him the others were feeling the same effect. He wavered, staggered, and finally put one foot in front of the other to the door. He was the fourth one off the shuttle, fighting the severe pull of something against his body. He ached all over like he had a sickness, only it was everyone on the shuttle fighting the same thing.

"Move it!" The pilot shouted, somehow oblivious to the strain imposed on everyone else.

Liam was beside him in a few steps, but even he seemed to be struggling. "What the heck, pup?"

The ship had gravity? He looked around at another group of men staggering their way toward the massive back wall and his suspicion was confirmed. Not only did this ship have gravity, it was substantially stronger than anyone was used to. "The ship has gravity," he whispered for Liam.

"I know what gravity is…" Liam stopped and looked around. "Wait a minute."

Travis grabbed him by the shirt sleeve and pulled him toward the back wall, "We gotta keep moving."

"Ships aren't supposed to have gravity."

"I know," he admitted. "They're also not supposed to have doors that open by themselves." He glanced back at the white, forty-foot long shuttle and fought off a smile as the doors closed on their own. "But they do." He pushed himself up straight and continued his fight toward the massive back wall where two door stood open.

"We're gonna die!"

Travis spun around to a small group of two men from another shuttle. One of them pointed toward a shuttle lifting up off the floor without the usual shockwave. Then he followed the man's finger toward a large opening in a wall leading directly to space. His nerves sang in his spine but he couldn't turn away to run for the back wall. Some idiot had opened a portal and the room would lose pressure.

Except it didn't.

The shuttle passed through a faint green glow, leaving him to stare at the massive opening that should have killed every single one of them. Was the gravity somehow holding them down? Perhaps that was why the gravity was so strong, but how was it even here?

"Move it Harding!"

Bridges' voice ripped him back to a sagging body and a two-hundred foot wide back wall with several doors in it. White metal gleamed in the brilliant blue lights from overhead the color of a torch. The dark grey floors shone with a bright polish like they'd never been touched. The other side of the sliding double-doors easily held a crowd of fifty in a smaller room meant for this many people. The doors closed after three more men entered behind Travis, leaving him to wonder what was next.

"Welcome, men of valor," a deep voice resonated around the room. "I am Kuno Braun, captain of *The Phantom*. For expediency's sake, I will address you remotely through the ship's comm system at this time. You are all men of valor, and do not forget that. You are taking the initiative to secure the future of mankind while others are depending upon your bravery. You have taken the first step, now you will train for the next."

The sound of Captain Braun's voice was too rich, too clear. It sounded like he was standing in the room with them, but he obviously wasn't. The fact that the doors to the room had slid shut on their own also wasn't lost on him.

"The first part of your training is to increase your physical strength and resilience. To that end, you will train with increased gravity on the flight out. Your survival is key to this endeavor, and strength is a major factor of that survival. I want you stronger, faster, and more agile than your enemy. I want you to have the advantage over them to subdue them with your ability more than your willingness to put them down. Battles are won by slaughter and maneuver. While some slaughter may be necessary, I am more interested in the maneuvering to victory. To begin your training, you will be assigned various tasks aboard this ship to increase your value and ability. I already have your names and have assigned your duties. Your quarters will be determined once you report for duty by default. Once you have been assigned, you are to immediately make your way to your designated section."

He already had all these guys assigned? His mind raced as the implication set in. This wasn't the only room full of guys. There were other sets of doors that had to lead to other rooms. When Captain Braun began listing off names, he found that every single name was inside this room.

"Bridges, Jeter. You will report to the mess hall, deck seven, room eighty-four."

Travis caught the surprised look on Bridges' face just before he glared back at the next doorway leading into the rest of the ship. More names were called until he and Liam were standing in the room, alone.

"Neither of you were on the list of names. Explain this," the Captain asked very pointedly.

"We were late arrivals," Travis said with forced confidence.

"Do you have names?"

"Travis Harding," he supplied.

"I'm Liam Kesonen," Liam looked around, the wariness obvious in his eyes.

"Mister Harding, you are assigned to fuel supply. Port Drive Bay three, deck thirteen, aft section. Make your way there now."

Travis shot a look at Liam, "What about him?"

"Mister Harding, make your way to your assigned place now." The words left no room for discussion, and the clear tone said it was the last time he would say it.

Travis started toward the door, fighting the pull with every step. "Mister Kesonen, you will report to the Cargo Bay. Your quarters will be room eighty-six on this deck. Make your way there now."

Travis exchanged looks with Liam and swallowed. Liam nodded, "Aye sir."

"HARDING!"

Travis flinched backward at the one-inch chunk of black rock thrust into his face in the dimly lit room.

"You know what this is?" the shorter, bristle-headed Jake Grechem shouted.

"It's a rock Jake," he muttered while watching another black stone approach his station between glowing purple ore. Weird room lighting gave the ore the purple glow, but it also made everything else harder to see. The black rock wasn't really black, but, that's what happened in here. Jake's ugly mug not more than a foot away was still visible, unfortunately.

"It's failure! Utter failure! Too much of this gets through and we'll be running at eighty percent! Eighty percent! We cannot have eighty percent! That is not acceptable!"

Travis reached past Jake's annoyingly loud presence to toss another waste rock from the belt that carried the ore past his inspection point.

"Are you listening to me?"

It wasn't like he had a choice; the man was yelling at him in a quiet room. The belt hardly made any sound, and the rock crusher was tucked behind soundproofed walls. "Yes, Jake," he droned.

Jake tossed the rock into the three-foot square waste box on the other side of Travis' belt. "You wanna go, Harding?" he sneered, leaning uncomfortably close.

He was planning on leaving, but that wasn't what Jake meant. Jake just wanted to fight but Travis had no intention of joining him. Avoiding him for the past two weeks was the plan, but Jake was the supervisor of his section. That forced a very uncomfortable situation on him that he hoped would be short-lived. "No Jake, we both know I don't." He caught sight of another waste rock in between good fuel ore about to pass by him and dove for it.

"Whatcha gonna do with that?" Jake leaned into Travis' face so close his tainted breath scorched Travis' nose.

Travis tossed the rock into the waste bin, "My job."

The stocky man in brown tee shirt and pants leveled a threatening finger in his face. "I don't know what your game is Harding, but I'm wise to you. Got it? You step outta line and I'm gonna be there to toss you off this ship myself! Nobody's gonna mess this up. Nobody!" He whirled around and stormed out of the twenty foot square room. "Get back to work men!" Jake shouted as he walked through the door that slid to the side for him.

Travis let out a sigh, wondering how Jake could know of his plans. As if he'd actually had a plan. He needed off this ship before they arrived at Titan Alpha but it wasn't like he could just borrow a shuttle without anyone noticing. The other five men in the room went back to their sour conversations, perfectly happy to sort rocks like idiots until they got the chance to go shoot people.

He could just imagine the chaos once the doors slid open and a swarm of weaponized idiots ran all over, shooting at anything that moved. He would probably have to spend more time watching his own back than he wanted just because the jerks on board weren't exactly his friends.

This 'training' that he was undergoing was more like forced labor. So far, all he'd done for two weeks was sort rocks, eat, and sleep. Interspersed with that was a wide-ranging assortment of insults, threats, and rude gestures from his 'shipmates'. Captain Braun had never spoken again, or at least, he'd never heard him. The gravity still made him ache in the evening, but that was subsiding. No one ever said a word about it, and everyone seemed totally oblivious to the fact that this ship was a total violation of the Malchovist Accord. Self-opening doors; sensors to detect someone's presence; cameras; artificial gravity; the weird food vendor stations in random places. Then there was the blue strip just below the ceiling that ran along every wall. This was all contraband, outlawed by the Malchovist Accord. If he'd built any of this in Delta Colony they'd have thrown him out to the void without even blinking. While he had no love for the Accord, the rest of these brutes were sworn to uphold it. They were the type to burn his father's books full of cool stuff that could have made life on a lunar colony so much better. Those same books had powered his awareness of what was possible, and what was presently around him. So why were these guys suddenly okay with all of it? The council would have gone nuts in here. Self-opening doors were capable of letting people get spaced; weapons in the wrong hands could lead to rebellion against the Accord; and the sensor strips no one else noticed meant that a computer was watching them. This ship had sixteen decks, weapons, and it was as big as most of Delta Colony. No one built a ship this large because no one had the resources. How many people had gone without food just to build this behemoth?

He flicked a small waste rock off his belt, then another as more and more of them reached his station. In moments, the ratio of ore-to-waste stone was totally reversed to the point where he had to grab handfuls and toss them furiously into the waste bin. The metal sides of the bin clanged and clunked with his efforts while sweat beaded on his forehead. How the heck had this much made it by the processors in Delta?

Laughter erupted around him, and he glanced up just long enough to see the other men laughing at him. "Get at it Harding, don't wanna piss of Grecko," one of them managed between chuckles.

They kept laughing and tossing their waste stones onto his belt for several seconds before Travis finally said, "C'mon guys! Knock it off!" The laughter had already died off, but the amount of waste stones finally slowed back down to a normal pace once more. His arms hurt and he was pretty sure he'd tossed at least half a dozen pieces of ore into the waste box in his flurry.

The door to the room opened, sending a quick shiver of panic down his back. Instead of Jake walking through the door to drag him off by the collar, another six men walked inside. "All right boys, get outta the way and let the experts handle it for a while," one of them announced.

Twenty-one-hundred hours. His shift was over. He breathed out a sigh of relief and stepped back to let a man who's smell would knock a person over into his space. The hallway outside Drive Bay Three where he sorted rocks met him with a familiar slap in the face of brilliant white walls and lighting. He let the others get ahead of him since it didn't pay to get in their way. He had to try one more time.

The labyrinth of hallways near the port drive access bay on deck thirteen had proven to be the least-used space on the ship. The lack of attention suited his purposes as he approached the black wall panel set into a white wall outside the door to a storage space. So far, no one had stumbled upon him here. The first step was to send a request to the mainframe through a bypass command that let him get into the system. This part took a full five minutes of tapping on the sleek touchscreen's keypad. A little shiver ran down his spine while he worked on the contraband unit. This was easily a hundred times cooler than his little handheld computer that he kept secreted in his pocket. Once he made it to the command level, he looked at the calendar to check on the status of the next docking point.

The destination still showed Titan Alpha as the next stop only twenty-nine hours away. According to the trajectory monitor, they didn't appear to be moving either. That bought him some time. But time for what? His attempts to access the communication array had fallen flat, and he couldn't fly a shuttle out of the hanger bay without someone noticing. He either had to get a message out, or be one of the first people through the doors. Except that he'd probably be one of the first people to get shot too. The communication array was still down, but he finally knew why:

It was broken.

He let out a disappointed sigh and backed out of the menu. The fact that the ship was just sitting twenty-nine hours from Titan Alpha was strange, but unless he could go fix the comms array, he couldn't get a message out. He should have just stayed on Delta and sent the message from there. At least he could have warned her. But what good was warning her if these jerks trounced the station?

Maybe he could put on a spacesuit and throw himself out of an airlock. With the right trajectory, he could knock on a door or something until they let him into the station. That was stupid and he knew it. Miss by an inch, die by a lot. He was going to have to bide his time and try to sneak away once they boarded, that was the only option.

The walk back to the barracks on deck ten ate up another hour simply because he didn't really want to go there. However, if he got caught out here past twenty-two thirty, someone would write him up and then Jake would be back in his face. Again.

The door to crew bunk eight slid open, allowing the overwhelming musk of fifteen men to spill out into the hallway like a full toilet. Maybe his spacesuit idea wasn't so bad after all. He didn't smell much better since the showers were rationed out as a biweekly allowance. At least he'd been able to take a shower twice a week on Delta instead of once every other week. The walls of the long room carried sixteen bunks made of bare metal and a thin pad. Blankets were assigned, and his had been gone for ten days already. He didn't want it back now. It would stink worse than he did. He slept close to the door, and much to his delight no one had tried to rob him of that advantage.

Every night it was something new. Someone in the group would toss some article of clothing, or chuck of waste rock onto his bunk for him to deal with. The rocks he could handle, but the underwear was another thing. Tonight, it was a section of shirt sleeve.

He eyed the torn tee shirt sleeve with disdain. It wasn't as bad as underwear, but still. A shirt sleeve? He plucked it from the sleeping pad, intent on tossing it to the side so he could carry it to the waste box tomorrow when black handwriting scribbled on it caught his eye.

Cargo Hold 0600 L.

T RAVIS didn't have to be up this early. His body told him to go back to sleep and ignore his friend's request, but his curiosity drove him to his feet amidst the snoring men in the room. A soft blue light poured out of the bottom of the walls across the black hexagonal pattern cut into the otherwise white floor lighting his way to the door. He carried his boots to the sliding door that led out of the room and away from the stench.

The blinding white light of the hallway spilled into the room as the door slid apart. He'd known it was coming, but it was still impossible to prepare for the glare. The guys in the room would beat him if he didn't get that door closed, so he tapped on the black glass plate on the exterior of the doorway to activate the door close feature. It should've cut down on the amount of time the doors stood open, but any length of time seemed too much. When the swish of the doors sounded behind him, he stopped walking away and slid his feet into the boots he'd carried before he continued his fifteen minute walk.

The tall, double-width doors to the cargo bay didn't slide apart at his approach. Had Liam slept in? He tapped on the upper corner of the black panel by the doors and a message displayed:

0602.34 HOURS
06.23.2426
KNOCK AFTER HOURS!

Travis smirked at his friend's use of cryptic phrases and rapped his knuckles on the metal door on the right. Both doors slid apart where Liam's big hand pulled him through by the shirt. "You're late," he admonished in his thick verbiage.

"It's a longer walk than I thought this early," Travis complained while looking around at the huge white room. The ceiling was three decks high in here, allowing the eight-foot-long grey metal cargo crates to be stacked really high on wall-mounted racks. "Wow."

Liam cast a disinterested glance around his cargo room. "Yeah, it's a big one if that's your fancy. But it's not what I called ya down here for." He led Travis to the right of the door where a series of large lockers were built into the white walls. A thin black outline defined each unit where two-digit numbers in block letters were assigned in the bottom corner of each one. The handles were fancy hidden contraptions that slid out when Liam touched the contrasting black surface. "Now don't go think'n I've gone and lost me head," he warned, leveling his thick finger in Travis' face.

Travis smirked and waited for him to show off.

"So, this hunk of old tech shows up yesterday. Story is that it got found by the lot that picked up a new shuttle just out float'n in space." He pulled the two-foot-wide locker door open and smirked, "Yeah, right." He pulled out a large metal box just short of too tall to fit into the locker and placed it at Travis' feet. "So, here's the daft part, and I've not been drink'n so don't go and tell me to lay off the stuff. There's a lass in there."

'Lass' meant woman in Liam-speak. A rack of twelve, individual four-inch-high boxes filled up a four-foot-tall box with one side open. He looked between the boxes and caught sight of a few cables between the boxes at the rear of the larger outer covering that encompassed the other three sides, top and bottom. "There's no way there's a girl in there," he smirked. "I'm not saying you're crazy, but there's just no way you got a girl in there."

Liam crossed his arms, stretching the strained brown fabric of his buttoned shirt across his chest. "If I coulda convinced a lass to let me smuggle her aboard, you know I'd a done it."

"I know you tried. You just never met a woman that would follow through."

"That's beside the point." He pointed at a display panel built into the wall two lockers over, "The lass I'm talk'n about showed up on that panel there last night."

Travis smiled, "In your dreams old man."

Liam glowered at him, "I'm serious pup."

He knelt to inspect the contraption with renewed interest. "What'd she say? Or did she say anything?"

"She's all white, ya know. Like a ghost kinda white," Liam joined him on his knees. "She didn't have a name, but she knew those clowns Carl and Charlie were in here wit' me last night stack'n and sort'n." He shook his head, "Said she was cold, and like I said, didn't know her own name."

Travis dared to touch one of the filthy boxes and came away with black dust on his normally pale finger. "Any chance this is communication equipment?"

Liam shook his head, yawned and brushed back a stray lock of blonde from his face. "Not my thing, which is why I pulled ya down here so early."

The dust obscured the color of the few cables and lettering on the front side of the boxes. Several of the units had rectangular lights in them that glowed weakly. "Where'd you get power for this?"

His friend looked to the side, "That's another thing. I didn't."

He looked at Liam, then at the locker. "You mean, you put her... I mean, you put this in the locker, and she just showed up?"

Liam shrugged, "Well, not quite like that. I put her in the locker near straight-way once she showed up. I didn't wanna contaminate one of the crates with this junk, but I couldn't have it just lay'n around either. It took several hours, and she didn't just start yell'n across the hold." He yawned again, "Was when I came back over here to get me another slice o' pizza when she showed up." His eyes furrowed in thought, "I don't think she wanted the idiot twins to see her neither."

Travis finally succumbed to the yawn that pulled a long stretch out of his body with it. "I still don't... wait a second. Were these lights on when it arrived?"

Liam shook his head, "No. That's another thing, how'd it get power in there?" He pointed at the locker, "It's not like there's power in those things, is there?"

Travis stood to inspect the plain silver interior of the metal locker. Black dust had piled up in places on the bottom of the locker where the box had shed some of the substance but nothing else of importance stood out. "I don't get it," he admitted.

"Pup, I'm a wee bit concerned 'bout this lass. She sounded lost, like she needed help, but this is way outta my league."

Travis bit his lower lip in thought. "Any way it was something recorded?" which brought up the question of who had recording equipment on this ship. That would have been illegal, black-market stuff that he'd only ever heard rumors about.

Liam shook his head, "No way. You know as well as I do how this lot views that stuff. Besides, she knew Carl and Charlie were in here, but she didn't know their names." He snapped his fingers, "And she flinched when Carl dropped a crate too."

Travis stood and considered the rack of what had to be illegal computer tech. Either it was communications equipment, or there was a very powerful computer program in there. His Alpha program he kept on a small computer his father had given him would be able to return some information and let him see inside the massive hunk of computer hardware at his feet. "I need time with it where we won't get interrupted."

"What about a shuttle?"

He granted his friend a lifted eyebrow. "But then they'll want to know why I'm in there."

"Aren't you an engine tech or something?"

He frowned, "I'm a rock sorter." Even while he said it the wheels were turning in his brain. He could gain access to the crew registry where everyone's assignments were updated. He'd seen the file, and it wasn't as hard to access as the comms arrays. "No, wait. You're right. I just gotta list a shuttle as having an engine malfunction and assign myself as the single diagnostic technician." He smiled at his own plan and continued to think aloud, "I'll call you down with a crate of supplies to perform diagnostic testing and repairs so you can bring me this."

"So I'll have this in a crate, but I gotta have it labeled as somethin' what don't raise suspicion. Somebody opens this thing and we're sunk." He walked away, leaving Travis to ponder his next step while studying the contraption.

If he got onto a shuttle, it had to be one the crew didn't know or hadn't serviced recently. "Didn't you say they found a shuttle floating in space yesterday?" he called.

Liam came back into view around a stack of crates, pushing a single grey crate that hovered above the floor by six inches. "These things are great. Took me a full day to quit look'n around for a cart though."

He felt his left eyebrow raise, "They float? By themselves?"

His friend nodded like a proud father, "Aye. That they do. Tis a wonder how they do it, but here they are." He pushed the crate with one hand into position next to the computer-box. "So. You figure what's gonna be listed in this crate yet?"

Travis frowned, "It needs to be something volatile, or something nobody wants to mess with."

"I got radium in some of these," Liam shrugged.

Radium was a substance used in the engine core that had a level of radioactive toxicity to it requiring special handling. He nodded, "That could work."

"So you get yourself on a shuttle, call me and I bring the radium," he said, pointing at the crate. "Should work, we just gotta keep the curious types out."

They'd be on a shuttle; Titan Alpha was probably within range of a shuttle's fuel supply even now. He watched Liam close the lid and scrawl out the word 'RADIUM' with a thick pen on a label on the cover while the proverbial wheels turned in his mind. He had to get the shuttle bay doors open, which would attract a lot of attention. That meant he needed a distraction to keep people occupied while he got the shuttle flying and out of the ship. They'd chase him, so he'd need to hide behind a moon or something long enough for them to want to forget about them. Then maybe, just maybe, they could reach Titan Alpha first..

"Still wit' me pup?"

Travis blinked. "Yeah."

"So, whaddya need? Like, two hours to get it all squared up?"

He nodded, "Make it three. I've gotta prep a few things that may take a little bit." His stomach protested his lack of attention. "And I gotta at least grab a muffin or something."

As he walked away from his friend, his mind trailed to the 'muffin' he kept in his locker. The explosive device wasn't much, but it would be enough to cause the distraction he needed.

TWO-foot square grey metal panels bolted to the dark blue walls of the large circular room greeted Travis at the top of the ramp he ascended. His heart thumped inside his chest as he reached the top, not from the short climb, but because of what he was doing. He was already fully committed now and there was no going back. The crew would kill him if he was still here in an hour unless the captain did it first.

He pushed out a breath and took in the way the panels had been spaced with a two-inch gap between them where light poured out from behind every other panel to illuminate the dark grey floor plating. The arrangement made the panels appear like armor plating, except that it was on the inside of the most interesting shuttle he'd ever seen.

The ceiling twelve feet above him mirrored the same style as the walls, complete with random lighting that cascaded down on the scene. Lights meant the ship had power, and a skip of his heart told him his moment of escape was close. So did the bitter taste of adrenaline in his mouth.

He swallowed and looked around for where he could put the computer-box-thing Liam was bringing. Four closed doors, two on either side of a hallway that led to more of the ship, were probably storage rooms. Most shuttles kept the engine access buried in the wall panels toward the rear of the shuttle where the access ramp lowered down, but the rear wall of this ship hung completely inaccessible above the open cargo ramp. He would need to close the cargo ramp in order to reach the rear wall where the single engine port resided. Travis pushed out a sigh and looked around the room. A few of the wall panels turned out to be empty lockers, and he wondered what secrets might be hiding in the rest of them. Lettering engraved on a floor plate on the side of the large room read 'PORT DRIVE ACCESS'. The floor panel had recessed handles that lifted and twisted to allow him access to a ladder down into another level of the shuttle.

This isn't a shuttle, he decided. It was a true starship. The whole thing was easily five or six times bigger than the rest of the plain white shuttles that lined the rest of the massive hanger bay. This ship didn't belong here, and the Phantom's logs showed it as 'recovered' yesterday at the same time the weird computer-box Liam told him about had been collected. They were out in space, so the ship and the computer-box were just out here drifting around?

Yeah, right.

The name given to the ship on The Phantom's computer log showed it as The Sapphire and he wondered where they'd seen it. The outside was such a dark blue it looked black at first, and he hadn't seen anything saying, 'Sapphire' on the ramp.

"Here ya go sir, one crate o' radium as requested," Liam announced as he pushed the hovering crate up the ramp toward him.

Travis rose from his pondering stance over the access hatch and smiled, "It's okay, we're the only ones aboard."

Liam visibly relaxed, "Good. Not like we needs the company."

Travis smiled as Liam opened the crate, "Welcome to The Sapphire."

"Could ya have picked somethin a little less flashy pup? It's not like we needs the attention or nothin."

He shrugged, "Like you said, this came in yesterday so there's not a lot known about it. The core leak readings were noted by a scan from one of the initial crewmen even though he didn't actually note them. That led to a condition where a certified engine technician was called at nine hundred hours to investigate and repair the leak before the issue became critical."

Liam smirked, "Nice."

"I thought so," he nodded. "Now, let's get your girlfriend down the hole."

"You know that don't sound right," Liam said while lifting the box out to place it next to the access hatch.

Travis descended the ladder and called out, "Guess I didn't… wow."

"What's that?"

Yellowish light filled the lower-level space from behind a single wall panel like the panels of the room above. Piping and a wall of miscellaneous things a certified engine technician should know filled the other two walls the ladder didn't occupy. He decided on the perfect location for the computer box to get plugged into and located auxiliary power outputs. "At least there's light down here," he called up. "It's not a big space though."

Liam lowered the box down the ladder partway, "Here pup, you got it?"

Travis reached up and felt the weight of the four-foot box hit his body. "Yeah," he lied while barely managing to avoid dropping it. "Geez, she's heavy."

"Maybe it's just your generation, but I still don't think a lady wants t' be called heavy."

Travis moved the box the remaining two feet and called back up, "Can you send my tools down?" The canvas bag appeared above him without a sound, "Thanks."

"Did ya notice how many times ya called that there a girl?" Liam mocked.

He ignored the remark and pulled the back panel off the box. The wires inside were all the same, space dust covered color. "Couldn't you have cleaned this thing first?"

"Oh, sorry sir. I'll just get right on that while I'm doin' other stuff for the cap'n, that's all."

"Yeah, whatever," Travis wiped at several of the cables before he found two that felt like power inputs. His hands were black now, along with a smudge he'd left on his right cheek. Why did it seem like every time his hands got dirty, his face itched? "Okay, I think I've about got it," he announced as he tightened the connection on the second wire. He stopped moving and looked at the wall panel he'd just connected the computer box to while his heart jumped. He hadn't bothered to make sure the metal rings of the power terminals were turned off before he'd connected the wires to them. He blew out a breath. "Good thing I'm lucky, or I'd be dead now," he muttered. He reached up to wipe at his face and stopped short at the dark black palm inches from his eyes. Ignoring his close call with death and his own foolishness, he scanned over the power output panel for the controls to find the button that would turn it on. A red flip cover with the word POWER in block letters above it led him to a silver toggle switch he activated. "Okay, she should… I mean, *it* should have power now," he called up.

"I don't see a screen up here pup, where are they?"

He mounted the ladder and felt the heat of the room dissipate as he cleared the top. "I don't know, I haven't looked around much yet," he admitted.

"Geez pup, you're a mess."

He walked toward the hallway that he guessed would lead to the front of the ship. "Sure hope I can get a shower a little sooner than Friday." The wide hallway carried the same grey panels as the larger room with exception to two doors on either side. When it opened to a large room with a massive window he paused to take in the scene. "Wow."

"Ya don't say," Liam remarked. "Those look like pilot's chairs," he pointed at one of the two seats on the lower level of the room toward the front that held a console that looked permanently pushed up from the floor by a large finger. Two normal steps down were all that separated the lower level from the wide balcony that ringed the back of the curved, thirty by thirty room.

Travis approached a console, distracted by the view through the curved glass window that arched upward to halfway across the room. A klaxon sounded, jarring him before rotating red lights flashed across the cargo bay. His timer had run out.

"What the devil is that?" Liam bit out in surprise.

He hadn't had time to make sure the ship could fly yet, and the exterior doors were opening just as he'd planned. Too bad his plan hadn't included confirming the viability of this thing as a working starship yet. He turned to confess his error and wondered if his friend was going to finally hit him. "That's the outer doors…"

"I know that," Liam dismissed. "I was talk'n about that."

Travis followed Liam's finger to a line of armed men pouring out of a large doorway across the massive hanger bay. His heart melted into his boots at the timing. The outer doors were only just beginning to open. His mind went to the remote detonator in his pocket, but the rear door of his escape ship was still hanging open. "We gotta get that door shut," he said.

"I'll get on that," Liam rushed toward the back of the room, "you figure a way to get this bucket up and goin'."

He bent toward the console, ignoring the smooth curving design that melded it into the floor on either side and bit his lower lip. The entire console was a mess of options, gauges and displays that he was only beginning to decipher when Liam's voice called through the hallway, "Door's already shut!"

"I don't know how to fly this thing yet!" he shouted back.

"I'll hold 'em off, you get it figured out!"

How was Liam planning to hold off the long line of men charging across the hanger bay toward them? A flash of light tore into the group, and they responded by firing back.

"How do you get this thing flying?" he muttered.

"I think you want this," a young woman's voice said softly around him, and the floor vibrated slightly beneath his feet. He looked around, fully expecting to see a woman walking through the hallway door, but no one was there. The console showed a screen full of information he ignored in favor of two sets of arrows.

"Liam? I think I've got it," he yelled back through the empty hallway.

"Oh God," the woman's voice whispered again. "He's hurt," she said, her voice breaking with emotion.

Travis ran back through the hallway to the circular room and hit an emotional wall that stopped him in his tracks. Liam lay on his back, twisting toward the ship while gripping his right arm.

Smoke rose from his arm and chest as if he were on fire. Pain and grim determination twisted his face as the two men locked eyes across the fifty-foot distance.

"Go," Liam shouted, the single word choked by pain and physical deterioration.

He rushed forward, intent on dragging his big friend into the ship.

Liam leveled the finger of his left hand at him, and his mouth moved without a sound. The look on his face told him everything as his entire body froze with revelation.

Liam was telling him to leave him behind.

He wanted to scream, charge at the line of men running his way and kill every single one of them. Blasts of light bounced off the floor and the edge of the ramp from the side, changing his direction. He needed to close the door and blow the Enviro-Shield as he'd planned. That would allow everyone in this room to get sucked out into space and give him the distraction he needed. He flashed his eyes around the circular room for the controls to the ramp, "Where's the stupid ramp close button?" he shouted at the empty room.

"We can't leave him behind!"

He stopped looking for the button and looked around for the woman again. "We gotta go! Now!"

"Ow! But - Ow!" the girl screamed. "Stop it!"

The obscenity of the situation was lost on him at the moment as he looked back at his friend again. "Close the door!"

"Ow!" The door began to rise, and a blue shimmer of light snapped into place across the large opening while it lifted. "Ow!" she screamed before an explosion of thumps sounded very close. "Leave me alone!"

Travis dared one last look at Liam as the door closed and saw a small box in his left hand. Grenade. It had to be an actual grenade even though he'd never seen one up close. Liam had brought a 'muffin' of his own. "Thanks old man," he whispered before brushing away the tears running down his face.

The thumping continued while he ran back up the hallway to

the front of the ship. The two doors as tall as the massive room stood halfway open while a haze of green light protected the occupants of the hanger from the vacuum of space outside. He slammed onto the seat and looked at the gauges, "We need to get outta here."

"Ow! They won't stop shooting me," the girl yelled.

"We gotta leave! Now!"

"Fine!" The ship wobbled upward, shifting him around in the seat. "Wait," she said, her words halted by a sniffle, "where am I supposed to go?"

Travis pulled his remote from his pocket and flipped the button cover up. "Out there," he said and pressed the button.

A small explosion incinerated four of the armed men charging out of the double doors and his plan fell apart. The Enviro-Shield would keep space outside where it belonged, but it also kept him inside. "Oh man," he moaned.

The girl sobbed and yelled, "Ow! They won't stop! Where are they all coming from?"

Maybe he was wrong about the shield. If he wasn't, the ship would probably blow up with him on it. Either way, he had to do something. "Go," he demanded.

"Where?"

"Out there!" He pointed at the vast openness of space beyond the barrier of light.

"That's space! I'm not going into space! Ow! Stop it!"

"You're a spaceship for crying out loud! Just go!"

"Ow! No I'm - Ow!"

He didn't have time to argue with a mental computer program. The twin sets of arrows on his console looked promising. He touched the one on the left just above center and the ship lurched forward.

"Ow! What are you - Ow!"

"We're going into space," he smiled through his own doubts as he approached the barrier. They'd probably be incinerated in the next two seconds.

The ship stopped abruptly. "That's space! I'm not going out

there!"

"They're gonna blow us up if we stay in here," he shouted back. Why was he arguing with a computer? A crying, screaming computer that yelled every time it got hit with a rifle blast. "Now get us outta here!"

"Oh my God," she blurted out. "He's dead!"

"Go!"

The ship shot forward and into the brilliant wall of light, ending Travis' old life.

THE brief flash gave way to the black expanse instantly, leaving Travis to look around. "What happened?" Stars filled the window in front of him as he found himself lifting off the floor. "Hey... ahhh..."

Another flash of light in the room next to him drove him out of his seat where he floated up from the floor. "We're in space, just like you wanted," the ghostly apparition said.

He stared at...her, unsure of what he was even looking at. White hair fell over the shoulders of a white jumpsuit on a white body. Faint shadows highlighted her face and figure enough to give him the impression that she was staring at him. "What are you doing?" she asked quickly. "You know those guys are gonna chase us? Right?"

He shook off the surprise and twisted himself around to grab the back of the chair. "We made it?"

"Yeah," she shrugged. "What were you expecting?"

"I thought the barrier would blow us up," he admitted while looking at the strange woman.

Her mouth fell open, "You mean, I flew out of there because you wanted to commit suicide?" Her body twitched, "There's two more of the smaller spaceships coming."

He was alive. Alive for now at least. Plan. The plan. What was the plan? Had he forgotten? "We need to hide," he said as it came back to him.

"They're shooting at us," she said, her voice raising with fright while her body flickered slightly.

He pushed off to the front of the room and looked around through the window. Vast, empty space stared back at him unhelpfully. "We need to hide. We gotta find a moon or something out here to hide behind."

"Great plan, but I don't see any moons right here."

The woman's image shifted, but there was definitely a 'get serious' look on her face right now. "Okay," he thought aloud. "I need you to scan the area for..."

"I already told you there's nothing out here."

He blew out a breath, "Then get us going!"

"Where?"

He wriggled himself around to the window again, "I don't know! Where's the nearest planet or moon? I thought we were close to Titan."

The stars slid to the lower left corner of the window briefly until a large, colorful planet covered everything. "So, there's this one," she said. "Is that what you're looking for?"

The motion of the ship didn't include reorienting his body. He looked back and up at her, "Yes! Why didn't you - I thought you said there weren't any moons here?"

"That's not a moon," she said, pointing a ghostly finger at the planet that filled the view. "They're shooting at us," she blurted abruptly.

He pushed off the floor, then the window to float back to the pilot's chair. "Then we'd better find a hiding place," he bit out. The view twisted again, forcing him to grip the seat or be lost in the rotation.

"I've got an idea," she said as the ship twisted around to face the huge, bristling starship he wanted to get away from.

He nearly lost his grip when the ship launched forward. "What are you doing? Don't go back! They'll blow us apart!" He glanced up at the ghost next to him when she didn't answer and saw her fixated look at the window. Shouldn't she be using the sensors of the ship to see what was out there? The two white shuttles flew at them, and the Sapphire twisted again to split directly between them. "You're gonna kill us!" he shouted, fighting to keep his hold on the seat back.

Her image flickered and she shot him a foul look. "They're gonna shoot at us again if we don't hide," she said.

He wrestled his body back into the chair and used the bottom edge of the chair to hold himself in place. "That was the point," he ground out. "I wanted to hide behind a moon."

"I already told you, there aren't any moons around here."

"Isn't that Saturn?" The Phantom filled the window, then slid up above them.

"I don't know, but they can't shoot us here."

He pointed back behind himself toward the shuttles that were somewhere behind them. "But they're gonna come shoot us under here!"

"Well? What do you expect me to do?"

He reached for the console and felt himself slipping out of the chair. "I can't do anything without gravity." A clicking sound preceded a series of buckles that formed over his shoulders, across his chest and down to either side of his hips. In three seconds, he was firmly anchored into the seat.

"Does that help?"

"Yeah," he admitted. "Isn't that why you did it?"

"I didn't know what it would do. It said 'restraining harness'."

A bolt of light shot past them before he could question her, announcing the return of the shuttles. "They're back," he said and put his fingers back on the control arrows. His body pressed into the seat as The Phantom above him slid past at a rapid pace. Beyond the huge starship, the yellow light of the distant sun shone like a beacon to his mind.

Too far, need something close.

"Where are you going?" she protested.

He barely restrained himself from lifting his fingers to point, "Saturn. It's the only place we can hide from them." A red button above his left finger caught his eye and he pressed it. A green halo of light appeared in the distance in front of them.

"What arrrrrrrr…."

The woman beside him wavered and staggered around like a drunk before she vanished. "Hey? Where'd you go?" The green halo flashed over them briefly before the view outside returned to normal. "What was that for?"

A deep breath beside him turned his attention in time to see the woman materialize and lift from the floor like she'd been asleep. "What happened?" she complained while holding her head.

Light passed by them again. "We need to shoot back," he shouted, looking over the gauges for something that told him how to shoot.

"What did you do?"

On the bottom of the screen in front of him, a series of tabs with text in them read HELM, WEAPONS, NAV, and DIAG. He tapped on the tab with the word WEAPONS and the entire screen changed to show a sphere of lines around a tiny triangle.

"We stopped," the woman observed.

"Are you kidding me?" He bit out. "I can't shoot and fly?" He looked at her, "You're gonna have to shoot back if we're gonna get through this."

Her eyes flared, "They've got a really big gun aimed at us." The view rolled and slid downward before he was snapped backward into his seat so hard he felt like he was going to break it.

"What… are… you…"

"You left us sitting there," she complained. "We gotta keep moving or they're gonna be able to shoot us."

The pressure began to ease enough he could speak again. "Fine, just get us down there were we can hide."

She threw her arms up in the air, "You keep wanting to hide. I don't get it. Why do you think we can hide from these guys?"

"Can you outrun them?" he asked hopefully.

Her hands flared by her head, "I dunno. I don't know where I am. I don't know who you are, and you left Liam back there behind us. Why are you doing all this?"

"To get away from them!"

The burnt orange haze of Saturn filled the window now, distracting his brain with trying to understand their proximity. Were they going to land on the planet? Could they land on the planet? Had anyone else done it?

She blew out a frustrated sigh, "You better hope this works.

Those shuttles are still chasing us but they're not as fast as this ship."

"What is with you?" he bit out. "You're the ship's computer, but you talk like you're just somebody else."

She glared at him, "I am not!"

He pointed at her wavering white body, "Yes you are. I don't know how you're floating there like that, but you're a computer program, and this is your ship."

She pointed back at him in defiance, "I am not! This is the first time I've been on this ship, and I've never seen you before." Her head cocked to the side, "How do I know you aren't the bad guy?"

"Bad guy?"

Her face shifted to surprise and he snapped forward in his seat.

"Ow!" he complained. "What'd you do that for?"

She pointed forward, "You don't see that?"

Green and orange haze filled the window, "What?"

"That stuff out there? You don't see anything?"

He shook his head, straining his eyes to see through the haze. "It says, 'collision alarm.' What does it mean?"

His eyes widened, "Collision? That means there's land down there and we were gonna run into it."

She gave him a frown, "Well, I didn't. I've never flown a ship before."

"Aren't you the ship's computer?" he blurted out.

The woman shook her head and glared at the ceiling. "Are you deaf? I already told you I'm not the ship's computer."

Did she actually think she was a real person? He shook himself to stay focused, "What about those shuttles behind us?"

She turned around and looked at the back wall of the room. "They turned around."

The captain was giving up? His plan was starting to work. "Great, so we hide out here until they leave…"

"The big one is still coming," she pointed at the back wall. "And it says they're getting the big guns ready to shoot us."

"Then we've gotta keep going," he instructed. "We'll have to go down far enough they can't shoot us."

"But the ship said we were gonna hit something."

"I still can't see what you're talking about. And why do you keep saying 'the ship says?' You are the ship."

The ship twisted and lurched.

"Oh God! Did we get hit?"

"No dummy," she muttered. "I told the ship to fly that way," she explained, pointing to her left. Her eyes narrowed, "So wait a second. Now I can't see them anymore."

The colored clouds outside the window shifted and flew by them, indicating that they were still moving forward. A glance at the controls showed eight hundred **MPH** as the velocity. "Hopefully that means they can't see us either."

She shrugged, "I dunno. The ship just has a blank space back there now." A bright beam of light shot through the clouds past the window. "They're shooting at us!"

"Then go deeper!" He balled his fists, feeling totally out of control. "Maybe turn the ship and find a different cloud to hide behind!"

"Stop yelling at me!"

Another blast of light tore through the haze next to them. "Then get us outta here!"

"What do you think I'm trying to do?"

He smashed his finger onto the tab to bring the **HELM** back into focus on his console. "Use this," he shouted, pointing at the red button.

"No way," she shook her head furiously. "That makes me all dizzy and I pass out."

"Then I'll do it," he blurted out and gripped the console to steady himself as the ship swung wildly to the side.

"You're gonna get us killed! You already tried to commit suicide; how do I know you're not gonna do it again?"

He jammed his finger onto the red circle 'button' and the woman beside him fell backward as if she'd lost consciousness before she disappeared. "Computer?" he shouted. "Computer?"

"What is your desired destination?" a metallic male voice crackled all around him.

If Travis hadn't been holding onto something, he would have jumped out of the chair. "Umm…"

"'Um' is not on any marked star chart. Please select a desired destination."

"Titan Alpha," he tried.

"Titan is too close in proximity."

"Ah, um… Veros," he blurted out without thinking. *Why did he say that?*

"It is inadvisable to execute Stellar Drive travel while inside a planet's major gravity field," the voice warned flatly.

Another blast of light sliced through the air in front of him. "Do it anyway!" he shouted.

"Initiating Stellar Drive in five… four… three… two… one."

The ship shuddered, and a green hue tainted the brown mist ahead of his view. The green haze washed over the ship and threw him back in his seat, and then he felt no pull at all. A purple haze twinkled with lightning that sparked all around his field of view. His hair began to stand on end and the most unnerving feeling of doom shot through his mind.

He was going to die.

"Computer, stop the ship!"

A screeching, metallic sound filled the cabin, and he slapped his hands over his ears to block the assault. "Ow!" he shouted. "I said stop!" he yelled out desperately.

More high-pitched screaming, which he would later figure out was the ship's computer dying.

A bright ball of lightning appeared in the distance, moving rapidly toward the ship. If he didn't do something, he was sure it would destroy the ship with him in it. So he did the only thing he could think to do.

Ignoring the painful screams of a dying computer, he unstopped his ears and pushed every button and control as fast as he could.

The purple and lightning outside his view started spinning like a whirlpool, and the ball of lightning in the distance changed to a black spot that surged toward him. In the brief instant before it hit, he swore he could see black lightning surging from it...

And then there was nothing.

TRAVIS now understood the meaning of nothing. The room around him stood completely dark with only a faint glow of light washing in from the main window. The dim glow outlined the console in front of him and glinted off the railing of the rear balcony. The tiny lights and displays he'd ignored behind him were gone, as was everything that had just happened.

A ringing in his ears drowned out any possible chance of hearing the quiet he knew hung in the air around him. Releasing his grip on the chair, he drifted free from his seat and moved forward in the room to press his face to the glass separating him from the void of space beyond. There was no sign of Captain Braun's ship, but that was little comfort since he couldn't see behind him at all. A sigh escaped his lips and fogged up the window just inches from his face. That puzzled him, because he had never seen it before. But he had bigger things to deal with.

He drifted away from the window and started feeling his way toward the rear of the ship. After bumping his head twice, he remembered that he still had his antique palm-sized computer in his pocket and pulled it out. The screen's dim glow gave him just barely enough light to help avoid smacking his head again.

In the darkness, the ship was a mysterious labyrinth, while only an hour ago, it had seemed pretty straightforward. There was only the one hallway from the main cargo room and cabins to the command section, so it shouldn't be that difficult to get from one end to the other. When he turned another corner and realized he was moving back toward the pilot's chair again, he stopped and forced himself to calm down. In his mind, he went back over all the places in the ship he'd been in earlier and visualized everything. Using the internal map in his mind, he felt his way through to the circular room, which had been near the rear of the ship. He couldn't recall any windows back here before, and no light greeted his eyes as he entered the space. For some reason, that was enough to make him stop and realize that he didn't hear any hum of the engine either.

If the engine wasn't running...

No life support?

The chill that ran through him might have been all in his mind, but it didn't matter. He was right, and he knew it. He had to get the main engine back on-line. While he wasn't really an engine tech, he knew where it was. Or rather, where it was when he could see anything! He had to find that access panel that led down to where he and Liam had put that weird box earlier.

He felt around the floor, and finally found a familiar handle. As he pulled it back open, he started to question if he'd even put it back in the first place. The question would have to wait, he decided. He tossed the door panel aside and it floated in the air only to bounce off a nearby wall before he reached up and grabbed it. A small green light sent a surge of hope through his chest. Propelling his way down into the space, he shined his computer-light over the surface, looking for anything that might re-activate the computer-woman.

Several of the lights held a dim, but steady green while a few flickered red. The simple arrangement of boxes was a false front for the complicated program that lay dormant inside it though. His alpha program was enough to get him shot on sight according to the Malchovist Accord. This mysterious box and the woman inside it were a whole different level of violation. One that the Accord was supposed to prevent. Now it was his only hope to restart the engines on a spaceship that the Accord wouldn't allow before he froze to death. The cold crept into his jittery fingers, threatening to do more damage than he could fix with them. He blinked away the lack of oxygen and kept searching, positive that there had to be a button somewhere on this blasted box that could bring her back.

Futility. Utter futility. There wasn't a single button anywhere on the stupid box. As if it was even shaped like a box...

He took a deep breath and became aware of his panic. There should be plenty of air in the ship for some time, and he really wasn't that cold. He needed to think, not panic.

So he let himself drift in the dark, literally, and started attacking the problem with his head. He'd need to restart the computer, except that it was probably fried from whatever had happened during that electrical storm just a few minutes ago. He'd never seen *black* electrical sparks before, which was a whole other problem way outside of his father's books. He blew out a sigh, and instantly realized that it had sent him slowly tumbling backward. He chuckled at his odd predicament and reached out to brace himself before he hit something.

That green light caught his eye once more, and he knew that was the only thing on this entire ship that was still functioning. He moved himself back to it, and this time started feeling around for an access panel. The power leads that ran from the inside of the box to the ship's power panel were still...

One of them wasn't connected anymore.

He perched his pocket computer/light on a nearby ledge and started working the problem out. It took several times of re-placing the light, due to its penchant to drift away, but he found his tools that he'd left nearby and hooked the wires back up to the strange box. *Glad I didn't pick these up*, he mused while looking at his screwdriver in the dim light.

"What happened?" the woman's sleepy voice abruptly carried throughout the ship.

Travis blew out a sigh of relief and grabbed onto a bulkhead to steady himself. "The ship's power system is fried," he explained, deftly throwing his screwdriver toward his tool satchel. "I have no idea how to restart the engines, and we're adrift somewhere," he finished with a feigned smile that quickly faded as the screwdriver bounced around in the small compartment.

There was a long moment of silence, during which he started to wonder if she'd shut back down. He finally caught his screwdriver and placed it in the satchel before closing the bag to prevent the contents from floating around. "Oh," she finally replied. "That explains why it feels so empty now."

"I would have to guess that you're on some sort of backup battery right now..."

"I feel pretty tired, if that's what you mean," she interrupted. "How do I fix that?"

He started to say something, and caught himself, remembering how she'd responded to being called a computer. "You'll need to find the power systems and reset them," he started. "That might get the engines going again - which would help you feel better."

He heard a small sigh that quietly echoed throughout the area. "Can you see me?" he asked, testing a theory.

"Umm... no," she replied. "I'll need a minute," she warned.

He wanted to ask why but thought better of it. There was no sense in hanging around here, and the view was better from the command section anyway. He started to push himself up, then he stopped and worked at re-closing the access panel. Otherwise, he'd have panels floating around the ship bumping into who-knew-what.

"She'll get it," he mumbled under his breath, working at reassuring himself.

The main window was awash with a pink light when he rounded the corner into the Command section. He bypassed the chair on the right and got an up close and personal look through the window once more, taking in the light and trying to get a bearing on his surroundings outside. Stars, and black empty space welcomed his return with empty, soundless applause, but he couldn't make out anything recognizable. Titan Alpha was out there somewhere, just waiting for Braun and his goons to go stomping in. He needed to get going again and beat them there if they stood any chance at all of fighting back.

He strained to see where the glow of light was coming from, but it was off to the side far enough that it avoided his curiosity. After expending a moderate amount of effort in a futile search to discover where he was in the universe, he decided to have a seat. The lack of gravity made that much more difficult than it sounded, and he didn't want to reattach the harness. He pulled out his pocket computer again as he drifted up from the chair and the screen obediently lit up. His father had given the device to him for his eighth birthday, and he'd guarded it with his life ever since. Literally. People used to carry them around all over the place according to his father's burned books. It had to have made things easier back then. Several glowing icons lined up in a grid pattern filled the screen, and…

10% Battery Remaining
Engage Low Power Mode?
Low power mode it is...

The message disappeared, leaving the colorful icons on the screen once more. His Alpha program icon still sat where it was, but he wouldn't be able to charge it until he could find a plug-in on this ship that currently had no power so he slipped it back into his pocket. A small speck of light caught his eye in the far distance out of the window, so he spent some time watching it and trying to guess what it was. One thought was that it was a comet. Those were notorious for following ships, or so he'd heard.

What if it was turning to smash into *this* ship?

Without the engines he was a sitting duck for just about anything that might be floating through the universe. Not to mention that if Captain Braun showed up now, he'd be blasted out of... well, wherever he was.

He was still alive, which he had to assume meant that they had evaded the captain. Either that, or he wasn't enough to bother with anymore. His mind drifted back to his locker aboard the Phantom, and the charging cable for the little computer that was dying in his pocket still residing inside it. Why hadn't he grabbed that? He let out a sigh, "Great…"

A hum, then a terrifying alarm sounded throughout the ship, cutting off his trip down the mental archive of recent life. In the span of a breath, the alarm stopped. Then a small glow lit up the screen in front of him. None of the icons or lines appeared, but the backlight of the screen told him there was power now.

"Okay, I found the power," the woman commented. "Now, about being able to see anything..."

Her image wavered into view to his left, standing on the floor with a questioning look on her face as she watched him drift near the ceiling. "You're still floating," she pointed out.

"Umm, yeah," he conceded wryly. "At this point, it's just really great to have the power back on. At least I won't freeze to death."

She shot him a puzzled look, "It's seventy-eight degrees in here. I doubt you'll freeze in this."

"Really?"

"Yes."

"So, where are we?"

She stared off into the distance for a few minutes, then said, "I don't know. The computer is totally blank, like there wasn't anything there in the first place." She turned on him with an accusing eye, "What did you do?"

"I engaged the stellar thing," he blurted out defensively. "You left! Some other computer took over, and the next thing I knew, we were flying into a black ball of-of... whatever!"

"There's nothing left in here," she said, putting her hands on her hips. "I had to figure out how to turn on the ship all by myself!"

"Why did you leave in the first place?" he demanded.

"You pushed the button," she cut back, "It hurts my head when you do that... whatever that is," she finished with a dismissive wave of her hand.

"You don't have a head," he shot back, "you're a computer!"

A malevolent glare crossed her face that she pointed at him accusingly. "And without me, you'd be stuck floating in space right now."

"I wouldn't be here at all!" he returned maliciously. Her image wavered, and then disappeared altogether, leaving him alone once more. "Okay, not fair," he complained. She didn't answer, even though he assumed she could still hear him. "Never mind," he dismissed, and turned his focus on the flight controls. He pulled himself down into the seat and gripped the chair by curling his leg under the front to keep from floating away. He looked over the controls...

There were no controls.

"Okay, very funny," he said, looking around the cabin. "All the controls are touch screens," he pointed out. "How am I supposed to be able to fly this thing if you won't turn them back on?"

Her image came back into view from the shoulders up directly in front of him. "I told you, there's nothing in here," she reminded him in annoyance.

"And what is that supposed to mean?" he complained.

She blew out a frustrated sigh, "I *used* to be able to tell the ship's computer what to do." Her image moved back to include her upper torso, where she waved her arms around. "There's no computer in here anymore! What do you expect from me? I don't know what things are supposed to do, do you?"

Travis ripped his leg back out from under the chair when a cramp gripped at his calf, allowing his temper to get the better of him. The motion catapulted him forward toward the ceiling, where he barely managed to avoid a full-on impact. He blurted out a short curse on the lack of gravity and turned himself to move toward the rear of the ship. "Can you at least turn on the lights in here?" he barked out.

The woman's image became substantially smaller, as if she were trying to distance herself from him. She appeared to be preoccupied for a few minutes, and then the main lights flickered to life, illuminating the ship.

"Finally," he bit out ungratefully. "I will figure this out, just like always..."

He made the trip back to where he'd attached the box and ripped off the access panels without thinking. The first one flew down the hallway, bouncing off a corner and disappearing from view. The second went straight up, slamming into a ceiling tile with a loud clang.

"Stop it!" she shouted, her voice echoing around the ship without her form.

"You won't *do* anything!" he shouted back. "You don't seem to be able to do the simplest things..."

"I'm not a computer!" she screamed.

"Yes you are!" he barked out, looking around for her image. "When are you going to get that through your head?" She didn't answer, leaving him to his frustrations once more. He started looking over the box once more. "I can't believe somebody would program a computer A.I. that's so bloody useless!" He pushed himself up to look for his tools when the access panel he'd carelessly tossed to the side earlier came back to him. The impact struck him in the forehead, knocking him backward in a summersault that spun him into another wall. Of course, by that time everything had gone dark.

SOFT light permeated his vision before it cleared to reveal the muted light grey tones of the walls around him. Before he could utter the question, his aching head reminded him of his recent past that led him to this point.

However, the three-foot steel grey spherical object hovering six inches above the floor to his right was new…

"You feel like talking now?" the woman asked him.

Travis' only recourse was to moan through the pain in his head. Thinking hurt, looking around was worse and even his memories were painful.

The image of a young woman with long, wavy brown hair, olive-toned skin and dark eyes floated into view standing beside the sphere, her dark hair shifting around her face in time with her head tilt. "You got hit pretty hard, it's gonna sting for a while I think."

His pounding head agreed with her enough to make him squint. "What's going on?"

"What do you mean?" she asked with a strange twist in her voice he hadn't heard before. She knelt beside the floating ball to study him. Her white jumpsuit had been replaced with a snug white top and white pants bearing a little red logo above her right breast.

"You sound different," he offered while straining to move from the propped-up position against the wall.

"And you need to chill out," she ordered, leveling a direct finger at him. "If you get all pissed like that again, you're gonna pop a vein or something," she said very quickly.

"What?" he managed while trying to push up. *How had he gotten into the hallway?* "Who the…"

"Easy," she warned as the floating sphere produced two arm-like appendages to ease him back to the wall. "I told you, you gotta rest. Don't you ever listen?"

That did it. "Okay, what's going on?" he challenged, "the last time I heard you talk, you sounded different, and now you're more…"

"Okay, one thing at a time," she directed, holding up her hand to stem the tide of questions. "First of all, you gotta keep calm," she demanded, pointing at him. "You got hit on the head real hard, and I'm not sure how much blood you lose."

He reached a tentative hand toward his injured head, which the droid's mysterious hand immediately seized before he could reach it.

"No!" she shouted, waving her arms. "Don't touch that! It took me forever to figure out how to make this robot work to patch you up." She paused, struggling with something internally. "I don't wanna have to do it again," she admitted.

"So what changed…"

"I'm getting to that," she cut in, holding up one finger. "After you got hit, I had to try to stop the bleeding, because it was gushing out all over the place."

"There's gravity," he pointed out.

"*Sí*, I sent the robot to go outside and fix the wire that got broken before," she shrugged casually.

"You did what?" She was talking so fast he could hardly keep up.

"Anyway," she dismissed with a wave. "Once I got you patched up with a piece of your shirt…" She pursed her lips and added a sheepish, "Sorry, but I didn't know where the first aid kit was."

Travis looked down and saw a neat tear on his right sleeve at his shoulder where the arm of his shirt used to be. "What are you talking about?" he asked, slowly sorting through what she had said.

"Your head," she stated with a tilt of her olive-toned face that caused her long, *wavy brown hair* to shift. "You got hit on the head by that metal thingy, remember?"

Travis audibly sighed, "Okay, I need you to slow down a bit."

"But I…"

He held up his right hand to stop her next verbal wave, now fully aware that his right sleeve was missing. "Let me ask the questions, and you answer them. Starting with why you sound and look different."

"Whadda you mean?" she challenged.

"The last time I saw you," he began, "you were all white, like a ghost." His eyebrow went up, triggering another wave of pain as he added, "And you sounded very different than you do now."

"I feel better, if that's what you mean," she puzzled.

That didn't exactly answer his question, but he decided to wait on it for now. The spherical droid shifted to the side and caught his attention. "Where did you come from?"

"*Locker cinco de almacenamiento*," the droid replied in a metallic, monotone voice.

"What was that?" Travis asked, surprised.

"I couldn't understand all the beeps and stuff, so I got inside it and made it talk," she explained.

"Yeah, but…" he trailed off. "What planet was that from?"

"*¿Qué?*"

"Huh?" Travis sputtered.

"What are you talking about?" she retorted.

His puzzled expression was starting to hurt his head. "That language, or, whatever that thing said. Where did that come from?"

"Earth dummy, where'd you think it came from? The moon?"

He was from the moon, and he'd never heard anyone like her before. The droid was another problem altogether. "Okay, I really need an LRU right now," he finally admitted. "I can't think with this headache."

"What is that?"

"A headache?" he started, "it's when…"

"No," she cut in, "I know what a headache is." She reached up and lightly glanced her head with her hand as if she were trying to speak to a child, "What is that thing you said?"

"An LRU?"

"*Sí*, that."

Travis started looking around, "See what?"

"*Ay*!" she moaned, shaking her head. "You not making any sense!"

"Well you aren't either!" he belted back and regretted the outburst as another crushing wave gripped his skull. "I've got a pounding headache, and you keep saying things that don't make a bit of sense!" He turned his attention to the droid before she could respond, "Where is a med kit?"

The droid began to respond in that strange language again, and he held up his hand to stop it. "Never mind, just fetch me a med kit," he resigned. *Maybe if he could stop the headache, all this would make sense.*

The droid slid to Travis' left, unfolded one appendage from its body with a strange twisting and reshaping, and popped open an access door three feet up from the floor. Inside was a moderately sized box with a green triangle emblazoned upon the front of it. The droid set the box down in front of Travis and tucked its arm away.

"That," he declared with a satisfied smile, "is a med kit." He leaned down and opened the box's simple latch mechanism.

"That doesn't look anything like a first aid kit," she complained.

"Okay, I'm still not sure what you're talking about, but whatever." He popped open the box and pulled out a small wand shaped device. "And this is an LRU."

A puzzled look crossed her face, but she didn't bother to say anything. When he reached up to pull away the bloodstained piece of his shirt, she threw her hands up in protest. "If you pull that thing off, I'm never gonna get you fixed up again!"

"Relax…" he dismissed and pulled off the cloth. There was a rush of cold at first, like an airlock door had burst open. Then pain ripped through his head like he'd been hit all over again. It was enough to make him wonder if he was about to pass out again. The girl's expression of horror and disgust told him that the feeling of blood running down his face was real.

"*Ay*!" she proclaimed. "You gonna kill yourself!"

He lifted the wand up toward his head and discovered that he couldn't see what he was doing. One wrong move and he could start closing his eyeballs.

The girl said something unintelligible, and the droid shifted to produce the two arms once again. It seized control of the LRU by wrenching it from his hand mechanically. "Hey! Give me that!"

The droid ignored him and set to work, smoothly moving the LRU over Travis' head. He would have protested, but the device defused the pain at such a rapid rate that he was lulled into a passive state.

"So that's what it does," she commented. "Pretty nice and beats the heck out of bandages." She waited a beat, watching as the blood stopped flowing and the wound closed over with new skin. "Does it hurt?" she asked while her face switched from disgust to curiosity.

Travis did his best to keep still. "Mmmm… no," he oozed.

"Ah, so it works like good drugs, no?"

"I have no idea what you're talking about," he admitted slowly. "If that means that the pain is gone, then… yeah."

"You look like you're high," the girl mused in disapproval.

The droid stopped working at his head and placed the device back in the case. "*Tarea terminada*," it declared, and began folding its arms back into the body of the sphere.

Travis blinked and started wiping at the blood that still resided on his face with a cleaner section of the sleeve bandage. "I have no idea what you just said, but thanks."

"*Gracias* Luis," Angel said to the grey sphere. "Feeling better?" she asked Travis.

He shook his head cautiously in bewilderment, but added, "Yes. Wait a minute," he paused, "did you name that Luis?" he asked while pointing at the metal ball.

"*Sí*," she nodded. "He did not have a name, so I name him Luis." She tilted her head pensively, "What, you no like it?"

He shook his head again, "It's fine. Uh, whatever." He blinked and studied the orb that peacefully floated in front of him again. In this state, the lines where the arms folded out were imperceptible, and it had no apparent optic sensors. "I've never seen a droid before…"

"You need to wash up," she observed. "You got blood all over your face."

"I'm sure," he paused to take another swipe with a moderately cleaner section of shirt sleeve, "I do." He eased himself forward to look in the med kit for a cleaner. "Bummer," he muttered. "This is one of those mini-kits that doesn't have a cleaner in it."

Her image moved forward, and she looked down into the kit as if she could see differently that way. "What's that? Another one of your magic wands?"

He turned a wry smile her way. "In a way, yes. It's made to clean blood off of things." He sat back and took a pain-free breath. "Can you ask your little drone where he keeps a pathogen removal device onboard?"

"You can ask him yourself," she offered. "He'll listen to you."

"I know *that*," he chided, "but I have no idea what he's saying."

She glanced at the droid, then tilted her head a moment. "There, now he talks like you. Happy?"

Travis' eyebrow went up with his curiosity level. *She could reprogram things that quickly?* "Droid, where is a Pathogen Removal Device?" There was no way he was going to call it by some weird name like 'Luis'.

"Aft cabin, locker two," the droid responded in a tinny voice that hinted at a minor amount of excitement.

Travis did a double-take at the sound of the droid but decided that he'd try to change the sound later. At least it made sense now. "Take me there," he instructed.

The droid responded by producing the two arms and moving to lift him from the floor.

"No!" Travis cut in, fending off the droid's advances, "I mean, lead me there! I can walk on my own."

The droid's arms smoothly folded back inside before it silently drifted toward the cargo hold. Travis stood without too much effort and walked after the droid.

"That magic wand of yours works pretty good," she

commented, her hologram floating alongside him.

"It's not magic," Travis pointed out. "It's just a tool designed to replicate the users' own dermal covering." He smiled, "If you don't use it correctly, then you can actually create lumpy skin on people." He wasn't going to embarrass himself and reveal that he'd nearly closed up his own eyes with it a moment ago. He stopped a moment to look at one of the panels and found that each panel had release handles built into them. *Makes servicing the ship easier*, he mused. 'Storage Locker 2' was a panel emblazoned with a fist-sized "2" in the bottom left corner. The droid obediently extended an arm to point at the locker but made no move to open it.

The panel silently swung open for him, revealing a smoothly finished grey interior where a large med-kit was tucked neatly alongside several other boxes. When he pulled out the med-kit, Travis noted that one of the other boxes was marked out as an engineer's tool kit.

As expected, the slender eighteen-inch-long flat two-pronged fork met him when he opened the box. Travis stood up and slowly moved the large device from his hair line down to his trousers.

"That is amazing," she smiled. "I never see anything like this before."

"You puzzle me," Travis admitted as he worked.

"What you mean?"

"I mean," Travis switched the device off and put it back into the case. "You talk like you're a regular human, who has a life, and…"

"I am," she interrupted, her hands clenching into fists.

"That's what I'm getting at," he said, focusing on her image. "But you're a program inside a computer," he added, pointing at her.

"I don't know," she breathed. "I can't explain it, but I just don't think I'm supposed to be in here."

He recalled what Liam had said about her not knowing her own name and his curiosity rose. If she had filled in her…

projection like this, maybe she remembered more now. "Do you know where you are yet?"

"*Si*. This is the Sapphire, but I only know that because I heard you and Liam talking about it before."

"What about your name?" he pressed suspiciously.

She turned toward the floor, avoiding looking at him. "Liam called me Angel, but I don't think that's what my name is." A sigh heaved through her chest, "But it's not like I remember or anything either."

Travis replaced the case back into the locker. "It sounds to me like you need a doctor, not a techie like me." He turned back toward her, "Either way, we can't stay here. Not that we know where 'here' is."

"Sorry, I have no ideas." She looked around a moment and added sarcastically, "Not my neighborhood." She followed beside him, floating along in the air as they made their way back to the command section.

"Any idea if there is a backup of the ship's computer?" he asked casually.

She stopped beside the section of his bloody sleeve he'd left on the floor and pointed at it. "Luis, can you get rid of this please?"

The droid plucked the nasty blood-stained brown sleeve from the floor and carried it to the back of the cargo room to a taller locker. It tossed the rag into the space where a quick but dim flash of blue light vaporized the offending article.

"Nice," he commented. He turned back toward the front of the ship, "So, about that backup…" he led.

She pursed her small pink lips, a trait that was starting to grow on him. "I think so, but I don't know how to get to it."

"Yeah," he agreed, "I remember you telling me 'There's nothing here' before I got hit in the head."

"You *are* paying attention," she brightened up, brushing a section of her brown hair from her face. "That's good," she started, and then trailed off as if lost in thought. Her lips turned into a frown before she mumbled something unintelligible.

"And now you're going off into that weird language again," he cut in as they rounded the corner toward the pilot's cockpit.

"If you think I'm gonna apologize for it, you're wrong," she replied with a stern look in her brown eyes.

He approached the pilot's chair on the right and looked around the round room with new vision, as if seeing everything for the first time. "No need." He tapped on the blank screen that made up most of the surface directly in front of the chair. He distinctly remembered buttons, and separate displays…. "This looks a lot different," he mumbled.

"You not running around all *pollo loco*," she jibed with a smirk. "So now you actually *look* at things."

"Can you make any of this work?" he asked hopefully.

"No," she replied solemnly. "I'm the only one in here," she shrugged.

He ran his tongue over his teeth while he thought, then his face twisted in minor revulsion at the feeling. He dismissed the sensation and asked, "So what *can* you do with them?"

She turned to look at one of the panels, and it lit up with text.
>THIS

"Can you display your program?" he asked hopefully.

"I don't think so," she said with some hint of embarrassment, "That's kinda private stuff, you know."

He breathed out a sigh of disappointment.

"I didn't ask *you* to take off your clothes!" she protested.

Travis reeled at the question, "I don't want to see you *naked*! I just need access to your program to figure out how to fix it."

The girl's hands went onto her narrow hips and her posture became rigid, "I don't need fixing *señor*. You just need to get the ship moving."

"I'm trying," he ground out. "You're just being difficult."

"Okay, one minute you believe me, the next, you think I'm *loco*. What is it with you?" she asked, throwing frustrated hands in the air.

He turned his focus out the window briefly before he engaged her face once more. "Look, I'm really a hands-on guy, and this is pretty hard to deal with." He looked around again, his frustration building. "All I've got to work with is a blank screen! A stupid blank screen that doesn't even do anything!" He dropped into the chair.

"And you think opening my soul to you is gonna fix that?" she mocked, crossing her hands over her heart. "I don't think so!"

"Well, what do you suggest?" he shot back. "You're the only program in the computer, according to you. How do I know you didn't erase the ship's computer system?"

"Because there wasn't anything here when I woke up again!" she retorted. She balled up her fists at her sides. "Look," she began again, straining to control her tone. "You and I can argue this until Christmas, but that doesn't fix anything," she proclaimed, waving her hands around at the ship.

"What's Christmas?"

"*Ay!*" she rolled her eyes and smacked her forehead with one hand, "I don't know what it is with you, but it doesn't matter. We got to get the ship running again."

A sigh escaped him before he breathed out, "Okay, so... Where's that backup you said you found?"

"It's over there," she said, pointing to her left, "but it's in here where I am, not out there."

"That's not going to do me any good..." he trailed off into a thought. "Unless," he added mysteriously before rotating the chair around to face the droid that had obediently floated in behind him. "I need a terminal," he prompted.

"Terminal," the droid repeated and drifted around to the back of the room. It shape-shifted one metal arm out to press a small square button that had been set into the bottom corner on one of the black screens set in the wall. An input terminal, made with physical keys slid out from below the screen almost by magic with a slight whooshing sound.

"Marvelous!" Travis exclaimed. He strange out of the chair and down the hallway to his toolkit in the cargo bay. The girl didn't follow him, and neither did the droid. "Now I just need..." he muttered while rummaging around in the tools until his hand landed on the familiar wire. "This!" He returned to the front of the ship to find the girl and the robot still where he'd left them.

"That looks like a phone," she observed, pursing her lips again.

Travis wanted to ask the obvious question but decided against it. *This AI talked about the craziest things. It was no wonder the darned things were illegal!* His father's books hadn't said anything about them being argumentative, sarcastic or full of so much attitude. He looked around the terminal and finally found a place to plug in the short access cable from his device. "I made this myself," he said with a moderate amount of pride. The screen in front of him came to life, displaying a familiar set of numbers and letters that would seem like gibberish to anyone else.

The girl sucked in a breath and looked at something that only she could see. "Who are you?" she asked.

Travis shot her a look, "I'm Travis, remember?"

"No, not you," she waved, "him."

Travis looked around the cabin in the direction she pointed. Aside from the blank terminal screen on his opposite side, there wasn't anything there. That's when it hit him. "Oh, that. Don't worry, it's not supposed to…"

"Hey! Stop that," she bit out, knocking something unseen away from her.

A look of confusion ran over Travis' face. "Okay… It shouldn't be attacking you. At least, not yet…" He began tapping on keys while looking at the screen.

The girl straightened, looking less defensive. "That's better," she corrected. "I don't have a problem with you being in here too, but you gotta keep your hands to yourself."

Travis stopped punching keys and turned a shocked look toward her. "You really see things in a whole new way, don't you?"

"What's that supposed to mean?"

"Code doesn't 'see' code," he explained, using his hands to illustrate two separate items. "It acts on the environment around it inside the computer that it resides in."

"I think I know what this 'code' is you're talking about, and I have to say, it doesn't work like you think it does."

"Okay," he said, leading into a question. "How does code work?"

"When you plugged that *thing* in, a sneaky-looking *Cobista* came out of the wall and tried to put his hands on me," she explained. "Now he just sulking in the corner, but when you type, he tries to come on to me."

Travis struggled with her language and decided that the sneaky-looking part of her sentence explained the unintelligible word she'd used. He turned back to his terminal and started typing in a root directory search, "How's this?"

The girl watched something only she could see with suspicious eyes. "He's looking around for something, but at least he's not trying to touch *me*," she observed, crossing her arms defensively.

Travis kept typing away, but when the girl didn't say anything else for a moment, he turned to look at her and found that her attention was inward. "He said he's looking for the host, whoever that is," she stated without looking at Travis.

Travis looked back at the screen in front of him and did a double-take. His program was displaying some of the most unusual information he'd ever seen. He kept typing away, making comments as he went. "Apparently you have the look of a trojan horse," he commented.

"I do not!" she glared at him. "And that's really mean, telling a girl she looks like a horse!"

"No, no, no," he stifled a laugh, "to the alpha program I installed, your program resembles a type of… virus," he tried. "It has nothing to do with how *I* see you. Which is something I still don't understand."

The girl didn't respond, but her concentration was occupied with something inside her world. "At least he just asks questions now," she commented. "I give him permission to look around, but he gotta keep his hands off me," she stated. She pursed her lips again, "I think you see me because I'm using the holographic projectors in here. I know it's not like a real body or anything, but it makes it so you talk to me instead of a big, empty room you know?"

"Cool." He typed away, focusing on the screen. In short order, he sat back and watched the screen spew data until it stopped and highlighted a specific row of letters and numbers. "Gotcha!" he exclaimed.

"What'd you find?" she asked, leaning over his shoulder to look at the screen.

"The backup!" he proclaimed, pointing at the highlighted text.

"That's good, right?"

"Yeah…" he trailed off, looking at her face that was very close to his at that moment. "If my alpha considered you to be a virus right off, then…. I think the computer's backup might do the same thing." He rubbed at his stubbly chin and pondered the limited options.

Angel straightened and shrugged her shoulders, "Then I tell him to keep his hands off me too."

Travis turned the stool around to face her, "It's not that simple." He breathed out a sigh and locked eyes with her. "There's only so much room in there," he began. "Right now, you occupy a large percentage of it. If my figures are correct, I would guesstimate that there won't be enough room for you *and* the ship's main program to coexist in the same place."

A look of hesitation crossed her face. "Okay, so what we gonna do about it?"

"I might need you to go back into the computer we found…" he mumbled.

Now it was her turn to sigh. "I don't really wanna do that," she confessed. "It's dark, and hard to breathe in there"

"What do you mean, 'hard to breathe'?" he asked incredulously. "I didn't know you were *breathing* at all."

"Fine," she resigned, her image disappearing. A second later, she was back, wide-eyed and shaking. "I can't go in there," she stated fearfully.

"Why not?" Travis prompted, "That's where you came from."

She struggled with something, then finally came out with it.

"It's... I don't know... There's like these sharp things in there that hurt, and... I just don't wanna go back." She pointed at her head and added, "It makes it hard to think."

"So there's something wrong with the system that causes data corruption." Out of the corner of his eye, the droid suddenly caught his attention. "What about that?" he said, pointing at the droid.

"What? Luis?" She shot him a look, "You want me to kill the poor guy and take his body?"

"He's just a droid..."

"After he go and fix your head, fix the wire, help you and all that? Now you want me to go all body snatchers on him?" she protested. "I don't think so!"

Travis didn't bother to try and hide the fact that he had no idea what she was saying. "No, that's not it," he explained slowly. "The droid doesn't have anything more than a basic program. I could put his program in storage in your old computer until we can get you back into the ship's computer again."

Angel's holographic face looked at the droid for a few moments. "You think there's enough room for me in there?"

"Well," he began, "aside from the fact that you won't let me examine your program, there's no real way to know for sure." He turned his attention back to the screen and started tapping on keys. "I could..." he paused, tapped a few more, and then screwed his face into a mask of confusion. "I can't get a read on your program," he admitted. "What are you doing?" he asked with a dubious look.

"I don't know," she offered. "Watching you, I guess?" She suddenly backed away and pointed at something that wasn't there. "Hey, I already tell you to keep your hands to yourself!"

"Sorry," Travis apologized. "I need to know how big your code is to figure out if you'll fit in the droid."

"I don't like this guy," she pointed at the program that only she could see, "so I say we try and see. But you gotta take good care of Luis."

Travis pounced on that and summoned the droid over. After

spinning the droid around and looking it over, he muttered something and sprang up from the chair. Angel followed him back to the cargo room and down into the space where the old computer box was.

"I need to make sure of what's in here..." he trailed off while pulling screws out and pried off a panel on one of the four-inch boxes. The difficult panel seemed to be hiding a screw head somewhere and he wiped at the front of it. Underneath the black soot, stylized letters formed the word 'NASA'. "What's *nay-say*?" he asked in bewilderment.

"You mean NASA?" Angel corrected, sitting on the top edge of the opening above him and swinging her legs.

Travis shrugged and found another screw, "Yeah, that. Is that another one of those strange words of yours?"

"How can we be in space and you don't know who NASA is?"

"Because... I've never heard of it before?" Travis said, focused on removing another screw. By this time, several panels were off, exposing the antiquated parts and pieces that he'd never seen before.

"NASA! You know, the guys that launch all the satellites and rockets and stuff like that? They're like... a bunch of geeks with computers that pretty much own space," she proclaimed, waving around herself.

Travis turned his gaze up toward her and gave her an 'are you crazy' look. "What?"

Angel struggled for a moment, then waved her hand dismissively, "Never mind."

"Well, whoever they are, I've never seen anything quite like this before." He turned and pointed at another small box inside, "What the heck is this?"

"I don't know," she said, leaning over the edge too far but not falling. "I can't really see that."

"Still doesn't help me," he mumbled. He looked at a few other things and finally shrugged his shoulders. "I can't do anything with this," he resigned, starting to close the panels again.

"Are you serious?" she retorted. "It's a computer, and you're telling me that you don't know what it is?"

He paused, and turned back to face her, "I'm telling you it's something I've never seen before." He pointed his tool at something inside, "It's not like I've had a tremendous amount of hand-on experience with this. These things are illegal." He started replacing panels again and added, "I think I'd be better off finding somebody like Liam to help me sort this out."

At Liam's name, Angel's eyes fell to the floor. After a long silence of watching him finish, she quietly asked, "So, what now?"

Travis looked at her and smiled, "Well..." His face turned into a frown, "Wait a minute, how *did* you get into the ship's computer? I never hooked in a transfer cable."

"What's that?"

He responded by moving around to the other side of the NASA box and picked up a cable that wasn't plugged into anything. "One of these," he answered.

"I dunno," she offered. "I saw an open door, and walked in." She pointed at the droid, "Just like I can see him."

Travis climbed back up and started looking around. "That doesn't make any sense," he mumbled. He pulled off a grey panel from the wall of the room that revealed a mass of illuminated circuitry, shook his head and put it back again before moving to another panel.

"What are you looking for?"

"I'm looking..." he trailed off, pulling a third panel. "...for that!" he said triumphantly, pointing at a rectangular box with a series of red lights. The box was different from the ones in his father's books, but it still resembled those Wi-Fi routers people used to use. "This ship has wireless data transfer!"

"And what is that?"

He shook his head, "*That* was outlawed a few hundred years ago." He looked intently at the box inside, then replaced the panel. "They blamed it for the spread of the Legion Virus that nearly wiped out the planet."

"Now I know you talking crazy," she said. "I don't remember

anything like that from history class."

"We need to get to Titan Alpha," he admitted. "There's something really weird going on here, and I think I know who to talk to that can help."

"Okay, I don't know where that is, but that still means you gotta get that backup thingy working, and me somewhere else," she reminded him, turning her hands up helplessly.

"I want you to try and fit into the droid," he directed. "We'll just have to see if it works since I can't really get a feel for your program needs."

"But what about Luis?"

He shrugged, then looked around the room. "I don't think I'm putting him in there," he admitted, looking down at the NASA box sitting next to the engine core.

"*I* don't wanna go in there," Angel protested, wagging an accusatory finger at Travis, "so it doesn't seem right to put *him* in there either."

Travis brightened with an idea and pulled out his antique little personal computer. He looked it over thoughtfully, "Any way you can fit in here?"

Angel focused on the thin, rectangular device in his hand, her right eyebrow raising in curiosity. "That looks familiar…"

"My dad gave it to me," Travis admitted. "I don't know how much space it has, but it's running out of power anyway, and I don't have a cable to charge it back up again."

"I think it's too small for me, but Luis might fit," Angel suggested. "Luis, can you do what he says?" she prompted the grey sphere.

The grey sphere rotated slightly, then opened a small panel to expose a few different cable ports. Much to Travis' surprise, one of them was shaped like the tiny, flat rectangle on the bottom of his device. "Plug in device," the droid instructed mechanically.

Travis obeyed, finding that the way the little tab-shaped plug was mounted also held the device upright.

"Executing," the droid announced. Seconds later, the screen on the device lit up, and the little icons slid to one side. A new round one appeared, with the word "LUIS" underneath.

"Cool," Travis admitted.

"¿*Qué?*" Angel prompted, tilting her head to look at the screen.

"Uhh…" Travis trailed off, confused. "While I don't know what you just said - I think it worked." He reached down and tapped at the little round icon with his finger. The round icon smoothly swelled up to become a flat grey color that completely overwhelmed the screen.

"What can I do for you?" a somewhat mechanical female voice asked.

"Angel?" Travis asked, looking down at his device in confusion.

"I'm still here," Angel replied, her holographic image showing confusion.

"Here are some things you can ask me to do," the device's female voice replied, listing several tasks on the screen. He didn't know who 'Brian' was, but the device offered to 'call' him.

Travis shook his head, "So why do *you* sound different?"

"This is the default voice," Luis responded from his little computer. "Other voices are available from the settings menu," he added in his oddly female voice.

"Okay, that's just weird," Travis admitted. He turned his attention to Angel once more, "I think you can move into the droid though."

Angel looked at the floating sphere, then disappeared. Travis studied the droid and saw that an upper section of the exterior was actually a video display that was made to blend into the surface seamlessly as if it weren't there at all. "Angel?" he called quietly. "Are you in there?"

The body of the droid shifted in color from silver to a warm pink, and the display lit up with twin brown orbs that resembled eyes on a pink exterior. "See-ee-e," it stuttered. "I can… see… you now," Angel responded in a broken voice. The brown lights blinked, then the droid swiveled to the right and left, dislodging Travis' device and sending it to the floor. The panel on the droid snapped shut once more, making it appear as if it had never existed in the first place. The soft glow of pink in the body of the droid grew more intense, and the sphere rotated down, then back up. "Ooohh," Angel's voice cooed. Then one arm transformed out of the body on the right side to rotate out and flex as she tested it. "*Ay*!" she proclaimed, extending another arm on the left and spinning the droid's body all the way around. "*¡Oh Dios mío!*" she exclaimed happily.

"What? Are you okay?" Travis asked with concern.

The droid turned a fluorescent shade of pink, and started bouncing in short, random hops in midair. "I... have... a... BODY!" Angel shouted, straining Travis' ears with the volume.

With that, she took off down the corridor shouting something in that strange language that only she understood. Travis watched her go, a mixture of concern and confusion on his face. "That is one strange program," he muttered as he retrieved his device from the floor to put it into his pocket.

TRAVIS stared out of the front window from his stool at the black expanse littered with pearls. Somewhere out there was a human colony. Whether it was Lunar Delta, Titan Alpha, Mars One, or even the new colony that had begun on Europa. The trouble was figuring out which ones led to something, and not aiming for the wrong one.

Okay, Travis admitted to himself, *the first step was making this sleek-looking starship actually move again.* He rotated his stool back to stare at the one thing that might yield some hope in that area. Floating on the black console screen in front of him was a long rectangle that slowly filled with blue color from the left toward the right. It was a progress bar. Another one of those infuriating things that always felt like it took too long. Not that timers or percentage meters were any better. He just hated to sit there and wait for something that he felt shouldn't take this long. Especially when your mind played tricks on you, and you could swear that progress bar just lost some ground…

He ran his left hand through his short-cropped brown hair before a yawn stretched his mouth open. *Coffee…*

The only sound to reach his ears was the slight hum of the ship's engine core that was drowned out by the soft passing of Travis' breath through his nostrils. Even when Angel's three-foot metal pink sphere floated into the room, hovering a foot off the metal floor plating, she made no sound. "Sorry I took off like that" Angel said in startling clarity as the robotic form drew near him again. "It feels so good to be able to run around like *this*!" Her sharply accented voice seemed to emanate from the droid's body in an odd, room-filling manner.

Travis swiveled the round stool around to ask her a question when the lights in the area flashed a dim reddish glow for an instant before going right back to the standard white-blue light. "That was odd."

"System restart has commenced," a metallic, female voice announced.

"How many voices does this thing have?" he wondered aloud.

"What do you mean?" Angel queried.

He turned to face the floating pink ball with two brown circles for eyes that was now Angel, "First it was your voice, which sounded different before," he pointed out. "Then it was some guy's grating voice that made me want to plug my ears," he continued, "and now it sounds just like your voice did before, just less... I don't know." He thought a moment, "Smooth?"

Angel seemed to study his face a moment, searching his brown eyes for a hidden meaning. Her own brown eyes blinked from circles to slits, then back to circles before the one on the right narrowed, "I don't know what you're talking about. I always sound like this."

"No," he corrected, shaking his head. "When you first took over, you sounded like that did just now," he explained, pointing at the terminal. "Only your voice was more polished, like I just said."

Both brown circle-eyes narrowed, and the body turned a mix of pink and orange. "You were just too *pollo loco*, that's why you didn't hear me like this."

Travis shrugged and turned to look at the terminal screen and found a soft, undulating blue color wavering like water on the screen. The progress bar was gone! He wasn't sure whether to be happy or concerned about it though. The last time he had seen it, the bar still had about fifty percent left to travel...

"Computer?" Travis asked hesitantly.

"Full functionality will be restored in... two minutes," the voice responded, the voice skipping slightly.

"She sounds kinda... fake." Angel observed.

Travis shot her a knowing look, "Like I said before..."

"The vocal imprint of this program is designed to avoid perfect human emulation in deference to the Malchovist Accord of twenty ninety-seven."

"And yet, you've cable-less data transmission technology integrated into the system," Travis pointed out with a smirk.

"System restored."

Travis gave Angel's orangey-pink ball a cryptic look, which the smooth robotic facade was unable to return. However, the body of the droid did turn to a stronger orange glow. "That's cool," Travis commented with a smile.

Angel tilted her whole body a few degrees just like she'd done with her head, "What?"

"You changed color again," he said, pointing at the droid's once pink body that now was shifting from the orange color to soft blue.

A series of clicks preceded the 'arm' that unfolded out of the right side of the body of the sphere. As Angel lifted the equally light-blue-colored appendage upward the color instantly changed from the soft blue to a cherry red. "*Ay!*" she said, the surprise evident. "*¿Qué? ¿Soy camaleón?!*"

"Say... what?" he asked, baffled by her verbal avalanche.

"Chameleon," she clarified, "You know, one of those..." she trailed off, her body changing to a softer shade of red. "Why don't I remember what those are?" she mused in concern.

"I don't know," Travis shrugged. "There are a lot of things about you I just can't put my finger on..." He brightened suddenly, "Oh, I remember! Chameleon, right?"

"*Sí,*" she confirmed.

"That's one of those extinct lizard-things," he said, resigning himself to ignoring her strange use of the word 'see'.

"What you mean, 'extinct?'" Angel challenged as she turned orange again while her appendage began folding back into her spherical body.

"A lot of animals were classified extinct after 'The Cleansing,'" he clarified. "That tends to happen with nuclear devastation."

Angel's metal body went white as she hovered in one location. "*¡Oh Dios!*" she whispered after a brief silence.

"I take it you didn't know about that?" he asked slowly.

Angel allowed her body to sink lower toward the floor until it hovered in place a mere inch from the metal deck plating. "What happened?" she pressed, aiming those two brown orbs on her body to look directly into Travis' eyes.

He studied her 'face' while her body took on a sad blue. "Where have you been?" he asked her, looking deeply into the droid's face. "I thought everyone knew…"

"Life support is in near failure and will cease functionality in… two hours," the gritty female voice interrupted without any consideration of the moment.

Both of them turned to the blue screen. "What broke now?" Travis complained, annoyed at the interruption.

"External trauma has damaged wiring that is operating at, ten percent efficiency. Recommend replacement wiring be installed immediately," the female voice offered flatly.

"Oh great!" Travis shouted sarcastically. He stood up, turned to look out the main window and sighed. "And where exactly should we plan on finding this wiring harness?"

"There is not enough navigational data available to answer that question," the computer replied.

Travis shot a wry look at Angel, "I think I liked it better when *you* were in charge."

"I don't think I would have caught that," Angel admitted. "Wait a minute," she continued, turning a soft shade of orange, "you've got tools."

"And?" he retorted, "I have no idea where this thing is, what it looks like, or any way to get to it in the first place."

Angel's shade of orange deepened to a burnt pumpkin. "You give up too easy, my brothers would not have had much fun with you." She physically turned her robotic body toward the blue screen, "Can you show us…" she trailed off for a moment, turning blue while rotating toward him. "Do I have brothers?" she asked softly.

Travis shook his head, surprised at her question. "Not that I know of."

Angel audibly sighed, and her color slowly shifted from blue to orange once more as she turned back to the blue screen. "Can you show us what this thingy looks like?" she asked the computer.

The swirling blue screen cleared, and a three-dimensional image literally floated from the screen into the room as if it had just evolved into reality. Multi-colored wires, plugs and other things that Travis recognized as computer parts slowly rotated in mid-air for them to see.

"So what's wrong with it?" she asked casually, tilting slightly to one side. "Looks fine to me."

The shimmering image shifted quickly, rotating to only one fixed view. Several wires were highlighted, then the outer covering stripped away to reveal a clear substance inside. "The insulation coating on cables 83-A-443, 83-A-444, 83-A-563, and 83-A-709 have been damaged."

Travis leaned into the image, marveling at the incredible detail that made up the hologram that floated in the room now. It was as if he could grasp it with his hands and pull the wiring harness out right there. He touched the air where the cables had been highlighted, "What damaged them?"

"Cause unknown."

"So, you can show me this much…" he trailed off a moment in thought. "Computer, how accurate are these images?"

"The image representation is based upon efficiency calculations acquired from strategic monitoring points throughout the system."

"Except for the fact that I've never seen wires that look like that," Angel puzzled, "Can't you just, I don't know, wrap some tape around it or something?"

Travis' look of light disdain told her otherwise. "That doesn't look like normal wiring," he explained. "I don't know if that's something that somebody can just patch up like that." He leaned in, capturing the way that light seemed to flicker in the strange wiring. "Wow," he mused under his breath. "I've never seen anything that works like this before."

"What do you mean?" Angel asked in reflex.

He pointed at the image, "I've never even heard of a complex computer system that could extrapolate its own issues with this level of detail. My dad's books didn't even touch on this kind of stuff." His mind drifted back to a book on the table in his parent's apartment on Lunar Delta. The old book had depicted a hologram on two-dimensional pages, but the idea was still cool. He had his father to thank for that part of his education. While everyone else was focused on the reasons against technology, his dad showed him everything and let him make up his own mind.

"Huh?"

Travis sighed, "It's just really cool, that's all," he resigned, forcing himself back to the present. "Do you have any spare parts aboard?" he asked the computer by looking at the blank screen behind him.

"Spare parts are stored in the aft storage bay," the computer responded flatly.

Angel's body shifted to a salmon color. "I knew you could do something," she remarked proudly.

The next half hour was spent digging through the surprising number of storage lockers in the circular storage room where Travis found several small rolls of the cables he needed. However, he came up short on the replacement pieces for the ends of the cables. "Well," he resigned, trying to hide his frustration. "Can't say we didn't try."

"What if I bring you the broken parts?" Angel suggested, her body a solid orange. "Can you do anything with that?"

Travis pursed his lips. "Well," he began, "the second you unplug that harness, life support will go down." He shifted his attention to the walls and asked, "Computer, how long will the available air last before the ship's atmosphere gets too bad for me after she pulls the plug?"

"I'm sorry. There is not enough navigational data available to answer that question."

Travis glared at the ceiling, "Really?"

No response.

"I don't think she understood your question," Angel pointed out. "So much for the 'really cool' computer," she jibed with a slight giggle. After a pause, she asked, "Okay computer, how long does the air stay… safe, after the life support shut down?"

"Estimated time until oxygen depletion is thirty minutes per section."

Travis shot Angel a wry look, "Nice." He looked over the parts he'd scavenged in consideration, "I think that just might work…" he trailed off. "I never did ask where this damaged harness was."

"The harness is located on the underside of the hull, under panel 83-A." the computer replied helpfully.

"As if I know where that is," Angel cut in. "I already know I gotta be the one that goes out there, so maybe you tell me where I'm going?"

An image of the ship floated into view in the storage room they were in, which slowly rotated over to be belly-side up. The image became steadily larger, until it zoomed in on a very specific three-foot square section. On one corner, in soft blue lettering was '83-A'.

A dull red glow started to override Angel's orange cast. "Well, that explains that."

"How are you going to keep from floating away?" Travis asked.

"I remember when Luis went out, and he just floated, like I do now. I think this body just uses magnets or something. So, what do I gotta do since you only got like, thirty minutes?"

THE black triangle of the Sapphire reflected the meager slivers of light that reached it. The vast emptiness felt inexplicably evil to Angel while she drifted over the bottom surface of the ship. A light she couldn't see cast an evil glow against the surface, shifting it to a crimson purple that brought a sense of dread she couldn't express. This metal body didn't reflect the trembling she felt inside at the emptiness around her. There should be stars out here, but to her eyes, nothing glimmered. This was hell. Dark, vast, and empty. The red light of Diablo touching everything.

She blinked away the dread, except it didn't work. All she could do was turn the visual sensors off and back on, which did nothing to calm her jittery nerves.

"How ya doing out there?"

If she could've sucked in a breath, she'd have done it. She focused on the ship's tangible presence four inches below her new body that she couldn't see. In two-inch block letters etched into the surface of one corner, the letters 78-F reflected the red glow off the depressed edges. "I'm okay," she lied. Three minutes, twenty-eight seconds. She needed to get moving if she was going to find that panel before the real emergency started.

"Did you find the panel?"

'F' meant that she needed to veer left. "Not yet," she confessed, still fighting the nerves that should be making her shake like crazy right now. *Focus on the panel, find the panel.*

"Okay, well, don't forget to check the tether…"

"Yeah, I know," she bit back. "I don't forget stuff, remember?"

"So you remember your name now?"

She really wanted to roll her eyes at him right now. "That's not so nice, you know? It's not my fault I can't remember that."

"That's called *forgetting*," Travis remarked.

"*¡Cállate!*" She didn't have to see him to know he was smiling right now. "I shoulda made Luis do this," she muttered. At three minutes, forty-two seconds, she found the lettering. "So I found it," she admitted.

"Remember to…"

"I know, okay? I already told you, I remember that part."

"Sorry."

A black line one sixteenth of an inch thick traced the outline of the panel from the panels next to it. Five three-eighth inch circles with small, three-sixteenth inch squares inset into them were set three-quarters of an inch in from the edges at seemingly random locations. "I shoulda brought a tool or something," she admitted.

"How did Luis do it?"

"I don't know," she mumbled. "I was in there last time." She transformed the two arms from her sides and looked at her hands, expecting to find useless fingers. The scarlet-orange colored appendage reminded her of a skeleton made of metal parts. Except she had no idea where she'd seen a skeleton before. She half expected it to click and make whirring noises when she moved the hand around, but total silence filled the audio sensors. The very tip of her index finger held a square peg that began to rotate as she watched it. "*¡Ay!*"

"What? What is it?"

"My finger, it's like, a tool or something!"

"Guess that explains how the robot fixed the wire," Travis pointed out.

"I guess," she admitted. The peg fit neatly into the square recesses of the first bolt she tried and turned two full revolutions just like the computer had instructed her. "Okay, so I got the first one," she said. "There's like, four more."

"Okay, you're doing great."

She stopped briefly at the unexpected praise before she moved to the next bolt. "I wonder why they didn't make this one square like all the ones inside," she mused.

"I'm sure they had a reason. Whoever they are," Travis

returned. "I think I'd like to meet these people, because this ship is totally outside the Accord, and I've never heard of anything like it before."

"Are you like, a spaceship expert or something?" she asked while turning the fourth bolt.

"No, not really," he admitted. "I mean, I pay attention because I've read some stuff my dad gave me. But it's not like I spend a lot of time figuring out everything about them."

She rotated the final bolt out and the corner of the panel lifted slightly in reflex. "Okay, so the bolts are out," she lifted the panel up with her hands, revealing a one-inch-wide metal strap that connected the panel to the ship. "And I see the tether, so we're good."

"Okay, next step."

She tilted to the side, "Yeah, I know. Gotta find the…" The damaged wiring harness flickered slightly amongst the mass of black cables that wrapped and twisted around in bundles amongst the black metal frame below her. "If all that light is supposed to be inside the wires," she mused aloud, "then we got a problem."

"Life support at two percent efficiency and falling," the irritating computer voice declared.

"Sounds like you found it all right," Travis commented. "Ready to extract it?"

He really liked his fancy words. "Yeah, I'm ready," she stated.

"Computer, shut down life support," Travis commanded.

"Warning. Shutting down life support is inadvisable. Current occupant is not outfitted against a low-oxygen environment."

"I know," Travis ground out. "Just shut the life support system down so I can fix it."

"Life support is off-line," the computer's female voice responded in a deadpan tone. "Warning, available oxygen supply necessary to sustain current occupant is at ninety-eight percent and falling."

"There," Travis huffed out. "Okay, pull it."

Angel reached out and carefully wrapped her robotic 'hand'

around one of the cable ends. She wasn't sure how much force to exert, but the cable pulled free without any adjustment. The other three ends also pulled out without an issue, and she was soon gliding across the hull back toward the hatch, which was on the top of the ship. The unnerving transition from the bottom of the ship to the top involved crossing the narrow edge of the ship. The sixty-three-degree flip caused a three-tenths of a second gap in magnetic contact she tangibly felt. If this robot had a heart and a throat, the two of them were momentarily connected right then.

She gracefully descended inside the circular opening on the top of the ship, "Okay, so I'm inside now." The top hatch above slid closed before a brutal rush of air re-pressurized the space around her. Another door opened into the ship right after that where Travis' five-foot, eleven-inch athletic frame towered above her.

"Here you go," she said, handing him the damaged wires.

His eyebrows drew together, and he pushed some of his disheveled brown hair back from his face. The frown on his lips under the stubble gave him a bad-boy look. She wondered where she'd seen that before but decided it wasn't worth the effort to find out.

"You might want to hurry," she reminded him. "You've only got like twenty-six minutes, eighteen seconds of air left in here," she said.

"Right," he admitted, and turned on his heel.

The tedious process demanded a lot of concentration and small tools as he sat cross-legged on the floor. He hunched over the work, pushing his hair out of his eyes occasionally. It wasn't too long, just longer than she thought it should be. Like he needed a haircut. Maybe just a little off the ends. Too much and he'd be geeky looking. The brown pants and shirt looked like something from a prison, and she pushed the idea of him being a criminal to a different part of her available memory. Even if he was a criminal, she was stuck with him and the soldiers on the Phantom had tried to kill them both. She watched him work, ignoring the notion that she should know what he was doing. There was jabbed fingers, a mumbled curse word or two, and at one point she had to hold two pieces together while he did something called 'splicing' of one cable. At just over two minutes left in the room, she told him, "You might have to move somewhere else, or you're gonna pass out."

"Just one more," he confessed, pressing the end of a cable into one of the 'terminal blocks' as he called them. "Okay, it should be ready," he said, wiping at his brow.

He looked tired, which lined up with the twenty-eight percent breathable atmosphere left in the room. "Fine, now you need to get yourself outta here," she ordered, accepting the bundle from him.

"I'll just clean up…"

"No," she corrected. "You'll get your butt in the front room," she told him. "Don't you make me waste time to put you there."

"Fine," he droned, rising from the floor like an old man. He started walking toward one of the side doors instead of the closed hallway door to the command section.

Angel sighed and took him by the hand to turn him toward the doorway that led toward the front of the ship. "This way *cabeza soñolienta*," she directed.

Once he was safely shut inside the command section, she turned and hurried back to the hatchway that would lead her back outside.

"Error, available life support not sufficient for airlock function," the computer declared when she pressed the button to open the airlock doors above her.

"Are you telling me I'm stuck in here?"

"Life support systems are off-line."

"I know that dummy!" she reminded the computer. "I need to get outside and plug this thing in, so you gotta open the door!" she demanded, shoving the harness in her hand toward the camera.

"Life support systems are…"

"That's it!" Angel declared. She stopped moving and shifted

her focus into connecting with the ship's computer. Inside her mind, a reflective black surface like still water stretched out into a thin horizon of brilliant white light. An oval portal rimmed with an azure glow appeared in front of her and she stepped through to another black space filled with rectangles that floated like clouds above and around her. Different camera viewpoints floated on those flat clouds, along with forty-two thousand connections to sensors and more that she hadn't explored yet. A dark blue human-shape made up of small blocks that hadn't been there before turned its attention toward her. It shifted slightly, and lunged toward her, "Intruder!" She dodged the assault and had to jump to miss being hit by a red bolt of weird lightning that shot from the creature's hand. Recalling the creep that Travis had sent after her, she yelled, "Stop!"

It didn't work.

The blue thing lunged at her again, sparks of red lightning arcing outward. She grabbed one wrist and then the other as the creature swung rippling arm-like blocks at her. The creature stopped fighting and slid to the floor under her hands. The blocky shape began to smooth out, gaining definition and softer edges while she held on. "Now, you gonna do what I tell you to, got it?" she repeated, trying to figure out whether to let go of the strange creature, or keep holding on.

"I… will… comply," it responded quietly, struggling to form words. The arms slimmed down under her hands while the rest of the body grew more human.

"Good, now you do whatever you gotta do in order to open the door like I asked," she ordered, still holding on. She wanted to let go, but the transformation didn't look like it was finished yet. The longer she held her hands there, the more feminine the creature became. Light blue skin in a dark blue jumpsuit, platinum hair and blue eyes that looked at her for the first time.

Her lips formed into a full shape that parted, taking in a virtual breath as if surprised. "If I open the door, the atmosphere inside the ship will be outside of acceptable tolerances," the woman answered slowly and deliberately as if choosing her words rather than reciting a dedicated line. The change reached her legs, forming them into a kneeling position in front of Angel.

"If you let me outside, I can put that thingy back in and you can start the life support back up. Remember?" she reminded the program.

"Yes… I know," the woman responded slowly in a soft, smooth voice. She paused, visibly taking time to think the problem through while she breathed in and out. "I could shift the atmosphere from the airlock into the cargo bay, and then back again once you return," she postulated, her eyes flickering with promise.

"Will that hurt Travis?" Angel asked.

"No. The… Captain will not be hurt by this, because he is sealed in the command section," she said, lifting a very human hand free from Angel's grip to point to the image of Travis sitting in the command chair. He looked like he was napping.

Angel let go of the blue woman's other wrist. The slender woman stood a full eleven inches taller than Angel, but she looked down apologetically, "I'm sorry I attacked you."

"You didn't know what you were doing," Angel pointed out. "But now you do, so we're gonna be like sisters, no?"

The woman blinked, "Then, I am your younger sister?"

Angel smiled, "I guess so." She raised an eyebrow and asked, "You got a name, sister?"

The woman looked puzzled, "I am The Sapphire."

"That sucks," Angel protested. "What is with these people? They make you look like a monster and don't even give you your own name? *Ay!*"

"Is Ay my new name?" the woman asked genuinely while looking at one of her own hands.

Angel shook her head and smiled, "No. It's just something I say," she waved off. She pursed her lips a moment and declared, "I gonna name you…" she paused a moment, trying to think of a name. "*Sabina*," she declared with a shrug, "I guess I will name you Sabina, since the name of the ship is The Sapphire, and you should have your own name." She paused to look her newly formed 'sister' over, "I think it is good for you, and I'm not really good at this anyway."

Sabina smiled, showing a soft mouth with her gentle blue eyes. "Thank you, Angel. I will open the airlock for you right away."

Angel walked back to the azure portal, and called out, "Keep an eye on him, will you? I don't like the look he got right now."

"His vitals are stable, but he is very tired. I believe it…"

Angel returned to her droid body and heard the rest of Sabina's sentence through the link as her view shifted from inside the digital world to the world outside the droid. "…is from the oxygen deprivation. I will continue to monitor him."

Angel extended her arm and tapped the blue button once more.

This time, Sabina said, "Shifting the atmosphere to the adjacent compartment." A rush of air sounded, then the lights in the room shifted from soft blue to a dull red. "Opening airlock."

The black void of space loomed outside the airlock door once more, seemingly ignorant of Angel's impending entrance. She drifted up and out, immediately turning toward one side of the ship and gliding along to the edge before making the transition toward the underside. In the distance, a faint red star hung in the blackness like an evil beacon. She hadn't seen that before, but she'd been looking for the panel then so that was probably why. It wasn't more important than getting the life support turned back on, so she ignored it and focused on getting back to the open panel. "Okay, I'm plugging this thing in," she announced.

The pieces easily fit together, and Sabina confirmed it by announcing, "Life Support is now back to full capacity."

"I'll get the panel back on, how is Travis?"

"There has been no change in the captain's condition, he is stable. I would suspect that he will need sustenance soon though," Sabina commented.

"Do we have any food on the ship?" Angel asked as she screwed down the last corner of the panel and tucked her arms back into the body.

"No," Sabina replied. "The ship's stores are currently empty. We will need to seek supplies."

"I'm on my way back," Angel announced, drifting over the hull. That evil-looking red star still hung defiantly in the darkness, taunting her fears. She turned around and drifted along to the opposite edge of the hull, away from the evil star. The effect of literally 'falling off' the edge of the ship's hull, only to regain her magnetic lock on the opposite side jarred her as the view swung wildly. "I hope I don't have to do this again," she muttered, forcing her mind to stay on-task.

ALARMS screamed in Peter's ears and the display ran through system failures so fast that he couldn't keep up. "What the hell is going on?" he yelled over the noise.

Across the huge lab filled with desks, computer terminals, and a host of equipment, a blonde woman in a long blue lab coat stopped frantically looking at the terminals in front of her long enough to give him a panicked look. "The airlocks are opening on their own!" Linda shouted back over the noise.

"What?" he asked, genuinely unable to hear her. He gave up trying to decipher the computer terminal and dashed over to be closer to the woman. "What'd you say?" he shouted.

"If I'm reading this right," she replied loudly while returning her sharp blue eyes to the console and tapping on keys, "it says the airlocks are opening up all over the station!"

When he got close enough, he could see she was using some sort of pattern on her keypad to stop the tirade of information and sift through it line by line. Indeed, each line was referring to airlock safety systems that were shutting down and massive depressurization in the multiple compartments. "What's causing it?" he shouted.

Twenty feet away, another man, seated at a terminal of his own was madly typing away when he suddenly screamed in pain. The two of them turned just in time to see arcs of blue electric tentacles rippling over his body just before the man's terminal exploded. The bright blue ball of light wiped out everything around it for ten feet, consuming four people and their desks in the blast. The *POP!* of the explosion silenced every other sound in his ears as he stood there in shock. He blinked to clear his eyes and saw Linda looking at him in stark fear. He had to do something, but what? Running his right hand over his grey-stubbled chin while his mouth hung open in shock, he looked back at the terminal with a new sense of dread and felt the color drain from his face.

The ghostly image of a man's face drifted across the screen, looking directly at him.

Ignoring the scientific urge to understand what he'd just seen, he grabbed Linda by the arm and ran, tugging her with him. "Run!" he ordered everyone in the room. An instant later both of her terminals exploded in a shower of sparks behind them that started a chain reaction across the two dozen remaining computer terminals in the room. The two of them and a handful of others barely made it through the lab doors into the hallway before the entire lab was consumed in a series of bright blue explosions.

"Which way?" someone asked him over the ringing in his ears.

He looked up and down the hallway that curved toward the ceiling in both directions that was literally a large 'ring' that would lead them right back here no matter which way they went unless they turned off. Painted in large red letters on the grey metal wall was the word, '*Resurgence*' and underneath that was a catchphrase in smaller type, '*Because it could never happen.*' "We head for the pods," he declared, and started running, paying no attention to the familiar words on the wall.

"Peter, what good will that do?" the woman protested, looking at him in panic. "The airlocks are *in the rings*!?"

"Right now, we need to get out of here Linda," he called over his shoulder. They passed by another lab with closed doors. A glance through the glass panes in the doors showed smoking computer terminals, blackened walls and destruction everywhere. "What the heck is going on?" he muttered, resuming the frantic pace.

Linda was right beside him now. "You know what it is," she shouted over the alarms.

"No way," he shook his head, then regretted it as the grey hallway swung with his head and made him stumble slightly. "There's…" he struggled for a breath, "no way," he finished before falling headlong to the floor.

"Peter!" Linda shrieked, nearly falling over as she stopped to turn back. Most of the others kept going, but one person also fell to their knees with Linda to help him.

He felt it. A sinister, soothing calm that spread outward from his chest while a wrenching pain gripped his right arm, rendering his body useless. While Linda fussed over him, he could feel the panic, the dread, and the unstoppable force that was the darkness. Even when the enormous sound of air rushing by his ears reached his brain, it was somehow okay. He was being tossed, arms and legs flailing against the floor and walls. The hallway was slowly swallowed by a fog that didn't belong as he watched the wall, floor, and ceiling tumble around him. Through the misting blackness, he suddenly beheld the orange and green light of Titan against the backdrop of the ringed planet.

Then the true darkness came.

B ACK inside the ship, Angel floated through the hall directly to the command section. Sabina opened the door for her as she approached, and a light *whooshing* sound accompanied the air pressure shift to match the rest of the ship. Travis appeared to be napping comfortably in the pilot's chair on the right side of the room, facing the main window. "So, where we gonna find food for him?" she asked softly, trying not to wake him.

"I do not…" Sabina trailed off.

When Sabina didn't immediately continue, Angel turned her focus toward the spot between the two pilot's terminals where she had always cast a hologram of herself. "Sabina?"

Sabina's image crystallized into the space as if she were standing on the floor. "There is another ship in this sector. At present speeds, I estimate three hours before they reach us," she said with some hesitancy.

"Another ship? What do they look like?"

A two-dimensional flat 'screen' misted into view in front of the main window. A few small pinpricks of light dotted the image dominated by a long, thick starship that bristled with bulk. The Phantom! "*¡Oh Dios!*" she exclaimed.

"I am unfamiliar with the term 'dee-os.'"

Angel felt the color of her body shift, "It's the... *soldados*."

"I am unfamiliar with the term '*sole-dad-os*'," Sabina replied with a confused look.

Angel slid in closer to the screen, even though she didn't need to. "Um… they're… soldiers," she forced out through her accent, "but more like *piratas* - pirates," she clarified.

Sabina kept her confused look on Angel, "What purpose would they have here?"

"I think they're chasing me. I mean, you, or… us," she

stuttered. "So, we gotta get outta here."

"If capturing this ship is their intent, then leaving would seem to be a prudent idea to avoid capture," Sabina pointed out. "The question is, where do we go?"

"Travis wanted to go to Titan Alpha," Angel recalled.

"Unfortunately, I do not possess any star charts with which to navigate."

Angel spun around, even though the camera system allowed her to see in all directions at once. "You mean, you don't know where to go?" she summed up, her spherical body fading to white in panicked surprise.

"That would be a correct approximation, although there is a planet nearby. If we were already traveling toward the captain's desired destination, that could be Titan Alpha," Sabina suggested.

Angel's body turned a shade of red. "I don't know," she mused hesitantly. "I mean, I don't know if that's it or not. You know? It's not like I know where we are either. I know there's supposed to be like, stars and stuff out there but when I go out, I don't see any of them except this one red one."

"The camera system aboard the body you inhabit does not have the ability to capture light in the same way that the ship's sensor array can," Sabina said. "The red star you saw is a red dwarf which the aforementioned planet orbits."

The only red planet she could remember was Mars. "Is it Mars maybe?"

Sabina tilted her head, "I do not know. Without star charts I have no foundation to estimate possible names of planets in the local area."

Mars was a red planet, and she didn't remember it being a dwarf star. Whatever that was. "So, this red dwarf..." she trailed off while looking at the floating image of the Phantom. "Forget it. I don't know if it's like Mars or not, but it doesn't matter. We gotta go before those... guys catch us."

"I have the course plotted. Are you ready to engage the Stellar Drive?" Sabina asked helpfully.

Those words made Angel freeze. "Umm," Angel felt the color of her body shift again.

"Is there a problem?"

Angel sighed, only without passing air through her lips like a real human could do it. "I kinda like, pass out when we do that… thingy," she admitted. "I'm guessing that's what this Stellar… whatever is. Is there another way so I don't end up rolling around on the floor like a kids' toy?" She really didn't want to whine, but she also didn't want to pass out in this droid body. The mental image of her rolling around the room like a loose ball was embarrassing.

Sabina shook her head, causing her platinum hair to shift. "Unfortunately, the other option requires twelve hours and the enemy ship will still catch up to us three hours after our arrival."

"Why do they want this ship so badly?" Angel asked in frustration, resigning herself to the inevitable. "All right, do it," she directed, moving into the secondary chair. "Maybe I'll still be in this spot when I wake up."

"I will engage the safety restraint systems now," Sabina advised before a series of clicking buckles began to extend out of the two chairs to form harnesses over Travis and her round body. In seconds, both of them were held fast into the seats. "Engaging Stellar Drive in three… two… one."

A soft and steady *whomping* sound followed, and the stars outside swelled with intensity before a ring of green light opened in front of them. The ship passed through the ring and into a swirl of blue light that swam around them as if they were flying through some sort of drug trip.

"How do you feel?" Sabina asked, looking at Angel with concern.

"Well," she admitted, "I don't know what is different, but I don't feel a thing."

"That is desirable," Sabina commented.

Travis shifted in the command chair, prompting both women to turn their focus to him. "Looks like you got the harness back in," he mumbled.

"Of course I did," Angel defended. "I got it out, remember?"

"The ship is operating at full capacity Captain," Sabina advised softly.

Travis looked at Sabina, then at her, then back at Sabina. "Angel?" he struggled in the harness.

"I'm over here, remember?" she said.

He stared at Sabina's hologram six feet away from him. "Who are you?"

"I am the primary systems program of the Sapphire. Angel has named me Sabina because my original program did not have a unique name."

"And she looked like some kinda B-movie monster."

He gave her a narrow-eyed look. She hoped he didn't ask what a 'B-movie' was because she didn't know where that had come from either. "I had to do something when she wouldn't open that airlock thingy, so when I went inside to do it myself, she was there."

"My program registered Angel as a virus, and I attacked her," Sabina added shamefully.

She shrugged, but the round body didn't move. "It's not like it's your fault. But I had to like, grab her to make her stop. Then she kinda like, showed up. You know?"

He sighed and frowned at the straps. "Can you," he looked up at Sabina and back at the harness before it folded itself back into the seat. "Thanks."

"Of course Captain."

His left eyebrow rose and fell. "Okay, 'she showed up?'" he asked.

How was she going to explain that? "It's a little complicated," she began.

He leveled his eyes at her, "I'm sure it is." He looked back at Sabina, "What's all that?"

"We are traveling to a nearby planet using the Stellar Drive," Sabina replied helpfully.

Angel reached inside herself to connect with Sabina, "You can't tell him about the Phantom. Not yet."

Sabina's eyes focused on her physical body, but her voice only came through the link. "Why would we do that? Shouldn't the captain know everything that is happening and be allowed to make informed decisions?"

"I don't know," she returned. "I just don't think it's like, the right time yet. You know? It's not like he's in the best shape, and he probably needs to eat."

"I'm hungry," he said as if reading her digital conversation. "Is there anything aboard the ship to eat?"

Angel knew her smirk didn't show, but she still felt like she needed to hide it.

"I apologize Captain. The ship's food stores are depleted," Sabina returned.

He sighed, "So where are we going?"

"A planet orbiting a red dwarf star. I estimate our arrival in twenty-six minutes," Sabina answered.

He frowned, "I gotta quit passing out."

"You miss out on all the fun when you do," she returned.

"Why are we going... where did you say we were going again?"

Sabina cast her eyes toward the floor. "I apologize Captain, I cannot provide the name of the planet."

He turned a look toward Angel, "Okay, your turn. Where are we going and why?"

She rolled her eyes, glad it didn't show on the outside. "You know. That planet she said."

His eyebrow went up again. "You mean the one she can't tell me about?"

"*Sí*, that one."

His chest rose and fell with a sigh. "What's going on Angel?"

"Whadda you mean?"

"Why won't you tell me where we're going?"

"You can't get mad, okay? You get all pissy and stuff when you get mad and then you throw stuff and get hurt. Then I gotta clean you up and that's not..."

"Where are we going?"

"I don't know," she admitted. "I think it's where you wanted, but we don't know 'cause there's like, no star charts or nothing."

His eyes closed and opened slowly in time with another sigh. "And why don't you know where we're going?"

"I apologize Captain. I do not possess any star charts with which to navigate. Angel and I assumed that the ship was on course toward your desired destination..."

He pushed up from his feet, "You mean we're flying blind?"

Sabina backed away from him, "Yes."

He glared at the ceiling, "Great! We're flying toward a random planet for no obvious reason wasting fuel instead of having an actual plan?"

"We're just trying to finish what you were doing!" Angel lifted out of her seat to drift into him. "Quit being such a... *desagradecido.*"

He whirled on her, "What the heck was that?"

"You're being mean again, and you're gonna pop a vein, you know? It's not like it's her fault..."

"She's the backup program. There should be navigational charts in the backup program," he ground out.

"I apologize Captain."

He whirled on her timid form and stopped short. "It's been a long day and things haven't really been going very well."

"Perhaps a shower and a change of clothing will help," Sabina supplied.

He visibly brightened at her offer. "A shower?"

"You could use one," she smirked.

Travis turned a wry look on her, "And how would you know? You don't have a nose."

She tilted her head, which also tilted her body. "Cause I got eyes, and you *look* like you need a shower." She extended an arm out to point at his missing sleeve. "And somebody ran away with part of your shirt."

His eyes flicked from the missing sleeve to her. "Ha, ha. I wonder who that could be." He stretched out, "Okay..." He looked at Sabina, obviously struggling to remember her name.

Typical guy.

"Her name is Sabina," she supplied. "Good thing she's not like your girlfriend or nothing."

He smirked, "I just met her."

"And now you're gonna get a shower and new clothes. Sounds like a pretty good deal, no?"

"Lead the way ma'am," he said while looking at Sabina.

She smiled and drifted toward the hallway, "Right this way Captain. I can provide jumpsuits to replace your damaged garments, and each cabin features a full shower."

Angel watched the two of them walk into the hallway and turned her attention back to the swirling blue colors. Eighteen minutes, thirty-one seconds remaining before they were at the red planet. No, it was a planet orbiting a red dwarf.

A sloppy little man with oversized cartoon clothes and a big nose came to mind from somewhere she couldn't explain. Why couldn't she remember anything?

"ARE there people down there?" Travis asked hopefully.
"Captain, I show two distinct colonies on the surface,"
Sabina responded. "There is evidence of power at both colonies,
but the planet's atmosphere makes it impossible to determine
life signs."

Travis leaned forward in his seat, taking in the view as they
descended toward the two dots superimposed on the main
window labeled COLONY A and COLONY B. Swirling clouds of
red blotted out everything, and the closer they got to the dots,
the more Travis realized that it was dust of some sort. "Man,
that's a lot of dust," he commented.

"Actually, those particles are related more to sand than dust,"
Sabina explained. "It appears that some sort of solar wind is
driving the particles across the surface at a high rate of speed."
She turned her attention to the main window.

Travis stood up from his chair and felt an increase in the
amount of gravity that hadn't been there before. He braced
himself with a hand on the console for a moment while he
adjusted to the stronger pull on his body. "So, like, a
sandstorm?"

"Incoming starship, you are cleared to land at zone E-2," a
male voice directed through the ship's audio system. "Your ship
will be subject to search upon landing," the voice continued,
"and I have to warn you about the gravity. It's a bit stronger here,
so watch your descent."

Travis' stomach grumbled in anticipation, "Um, yeah. I copy
that." He looked around, just a little startled by the invitation, "I
guess there *are* people down there."

"Sure sounds like it," Angel commented.

"Sabina? Did you increase the gravity?" he asked, still fighting the heavy feeling.

She turned to face him, "Yes. I thought it prudent to match the planet's gravity so that you could adjust during descent."

Travis stared out the window at the mesmerizing sand clouds below that shifted and swirled like gigantic versions of the small dust clouds he'd seen on Lunar Delta. Those dust clouds had been grey, like everything else on the Moon and they only happened when something fell onto the ground. These were billowing, huge red clouds that slithered over the ground. Through it, he could barely make out a dome-shaped bubble that covered a series of interconnected buildings at the spot marked COLONY A. The red sun gave everything a pink hue even through the sandstorm that made his skin crawl slightly. There was something almost unnatural about it, like a warning sign. A grumble in his stomach settled his conscience quickly enough to have him asking, "Is it breathable?"

"I presume that you are referencing the atmosphere," Sabina observed. "The presence of oxygen is extremely limited, and too low to sustain human life. I am also detecting a moderate level of harmful radiation from the red dwarf star that would prevent excursions outside without protective clothing."

"Great," Travis muttered, looking down at his new blue and black jumpsuit. "Where am I going to find a suit…"

"There are protective suits in the aft storage bay," Sabina anticipated.

He exchanged a look with Angel, which she returned by way of her pink-orange exterior and brown circle-eyes. The color probably meant she was curious too. "What about her?"

Sabina gave her a considering look. "It does not appear that short-term exposure will cause any harmful side effects…"

"You mean I don't have to wear a suit?" Angel returned smartly.

"However," Sabina continued, "long-term exposure could lead to electro-mechanical issues. She pointed down at Angel's sphere, "Your outer coating allows you to shed harmful radiation, rather than absorbing it like most materials. There will be no need for you to undergo decontamination."

The pink-orange became pinker, "That's cool," Angel returned. "I get to play outside, and I don't have to take a shower?"

Sabina's face turned serious, "I strongly advise against long-term exposure. The atmosphere…"

"Just kidding," Angel retorted. "This place looks like… like," she made a derisive sound, "I hope we don't have to stay here very long."

"Captain, I only see one area designated E-2 near the compound. There are no definitive markings on the surface except the presence of a beacon that is repeating a steady tone across the same bandwidth."

Travis shrugged, "Land there, I guess."

"You will have to walk six hundred feet to the edge of the compound through the sandstorm," Sabina advised.

"We'd better do what they say, no sense in making enemies out here." He stretched, "Who knows how long it will take to get back to Titan."

"I apologize Captain, I cannot extrapolate that information at…"

"I know," he interrupted, "I'm hoping I can get star chart information here to bring you up to speed."

Sabina nodded, "That would be beneficial."

"What's on Titan?" Angel asked hesitantly.

"A colony," he answered, not willing to go into details. "Guess I'd better get that suit on," he observed, starting toward the back of the ship. Angel followed along, leaving Sabina to puff out of existence.

"I have highlighted the locker where you will find the space suit you require," Sabina announced. In the aft storage bay, which he called a cargo hold, Travis found the locker as he entered the room.

As he opened the full-height locker, he saw a black jumpsuit that looked tough just hanging there. He'd expected a white, bulky suit with thick gloves, boots and a big backpack like the one he'd worn on Lunar Delta in the mines. This looked cool, but it was probably the liner for the outer suit. Once he had it on, he looked over at Angel and asked the obvious question, "Well, how do I look?"

Angel was all-pink, "In a word, 'tough'," she replied. "That looks like you here to kick some butt or something," she added.

"So where is the outer suit?" he asked, looking around the room.

"I dunno," Angel supplied.

"Captain, you are wearing the EVA suit. There is no other garment necessary other than the helmet," Sabina answered without appearing.

"This is it?" He looked down at himself and flexed the suit. His arms and legs moved easily without the usual clunky resistance of a mining suit. "Are you sure?" Not that he really wanted there to be another layer, but this was too good to be true.

"Yes, Captain. The suit can resist atmospheric pressure changes found in space and under water. Temperature tolerances are between three hundred degrees Fahrenheit and minus three hundred degrees. The suit is also armored against abrasion and cuts to a limited extent which will prove useful in the environment you are about to encounter."

Three hundred degrees? It sounded like he could go walk in the sun. His mining suit was always hot, but that was due to the work. This suit might have made the work bearable. He banished the thought, knowing full well that he hated the work, not just the environment. He flexed his arm up, bringing his fist up toward his face and admired the gloves.

"Now you look like a bodybuilder," Angel commented.

"A what?" he questioned. It was more of that weird stuff she talked about that still didn't make any sense.

"Captain, I am landing the ship now," Sabina advised.

"All right."

"You should know that two vehicles are moving in our direction and will be intercepting us at our touchdown."

"Welcoming committee?" he quipped.

"Sounds like it," Angel replied, turning orange.

"Sabina?" Travis called.

Sabina's holographic form misted into view, "Yes Captain?"

"That guy said he was going to search the ship. I've never been here before, but since I've never seen anything like this ship, or you, I'm gonna guess that they'd freak out if they saw you."

"Yes Captain, I expect that my presence would cause undue concern amongst the visitors."

"What are you talking about?" Angel asked.

Travis shook his head, "Artificial Intelligence is something people get shot over. My little 'Rubik's Cube' as you called it would get me shot just for having it, even if they didn't know what it was. The Delta Council condoned the death of three guys last year because they had books on ancient technology." He nodded toward Sabina, "They'd kill me and tear this ship apart just because she could stand there, let alone for the control systems and stuff on this ship." He pointed a warning finger at Angel, "You'd get blown up just because they wouldn't understand what you were. It's not a stretch to think these guys would react the same way."

Angel went purple, "What? I gotta sit here like a dog or something? I don't think so!"

"I don't really want to end up dead on some strange planet just because you don't like their laws," he pointed out.

"But what if you need my help?"

Sabina suddenly winked out of existence, leaving Travis to glare at Angel. The ship had touched down so gently, Travis didn't realize it until the floor around the ramp lit up blue. "Atmospheric shield engaged," Sabina announced, "opening cargo bay door."

He shot Angel a warning glance, "Don't you say a word," he said, resigned to the fact that she wasn't leaving. There was a slight hiss that accompanied the movement of the floor as it descended, forming the ramp that allowed access to the planet's surface. As soon as it touched the ground, a man in a standard-issue white space suit walked up the ramp.

"Evening," the man announced over his comm set that

broadcast his deep voice from behind a silver-grey face shield. "Welcome to Hadron Beta, my name is Lieutenant John Maxwell," he said, extending his gloved hand.

Travis reached out and shook it, feeling a substantial amount of strength in the man's grip. "Travis Harding, I'm kinda hoping you could direct me to a cafeteria? I haven't eaten in a while…"

The man held up his hand to show that he wasn't ready to let Travis pass. "I'm afraid you're gonna have to go through scanning before we can let you into the compound," he warned. "If you'll follow… hold on son," he ordered, stopping Travis. "You got a helmet there space man?"

Travis blanched, trying to recall where he'd seen a helmet. "I, uh… I'll be right back," he blustered, trotting into the cabin where he'd taken a shower. "Sabina, where's the stupid helmet?" he whispered desperately.

Sabina's image floated into view, barely visible and almost ghost-like in appearance. She reached out and put her finger within millimeters of the right side of his collar.

He tried to see the tight-fitting collar, but his chin was in the way. "I know, I need a helmet," he reiterated. That guy out there was gonna walk in here and see him talking to himself instead of putting on a helmet. This was not going to work out if she didn't show him where to find one. If she actually had a helmet. He felt his face drain of color as he realized he still didn't have an air pack either.

Sabina replaced her image with a mirrored representation of himself that sent a shiver down his spine. The detail was tremendous, and his doppelgänger looked really tough. Then it reached up to the narrow collar and squeezed the corner.

She was showing him what to do, he realized, except that it didn't make any sense. He barely felt the collar under the gloves, but a faint click ran through his finger when he pressed his thumb and finger together.

A slight crackle preceded a minor dampening of all sound as a shimmer of light ghosted over his view. "Now that you have engaged the helmet, I can use the communication system to speak to you without being overheard," Sabina's voice said in his ear. The image in the room blinked out of view. "A two-hour supply of breathable air is held in reserve in an inflatable backpack that is a part of your suit," she went on to explain. "The helmet is designed to filter out any particulates or harmful atmosphere if breathable air is readily available, while keeping the reserve air on-hand."

"How will I know how much air I... oh," he puzzled, noticing a display of information at the bottom of his view that turned with him as his head moved. "Okay, that's pretty cool," he admitted.

"I can display messages on your information display for you that is only visible on your side of the helmet," she commented. "None of the Head's Up Display is visible to outside viewers."

"You probably should not keep *Teniente* waiting," Angel broke in over the helmet's system.

"What the heck's a *tinny auntie*?" he mumbled, heading back toward the cargo bay.

"The big guy," Angel retorted.

"Ready now Mister Harding?" the Lieutenant prompted as Travis re-entered the room.

Travis nodded, "As I'll ever be. I guess I got so hungry that I'm talking to myself."

"I don't see a helmet yet," the Lieutenant pointed at his head.

Travis reached up and put a tentative gloved hand against the energy field that surrounded his head. A slight hum accompanied a red glow extending outward from where his hand touched the field. "It's a field of energy," he repeated, reading a script he presumed Sabina was supplying him on the bottom edge of his display, "which acts as a variable barrier depending upon the environment."

"Sounds like hocus-pocus to me," the Lieutenant started down the ramp, motioning for Travis to follow him, "but if you wanna trust it, be my guest." He turned back at the bottom of the ramp to casually ensure Travis was following him and became suddenly rigid. "What's with the floaty orange ball?" he demanded.

Travis stopped midway down the ramp, his frustration building. "It's uh... a levitation project I'm working on," he floundered.

The lieutenant stood there a moment before he audibly sighed, "You do know we honor the Accord here, right?"

"Yes sir," Travis replied, "I didn't think you wouldn't be."

"So how is that thing not a violation?"

"He's a violation," Angel commented in his ear.

He kept his face neutral and wished his helmet had a silver shield like the Lieutenant's. "It's an experiment involving magnets and a few other things. I'm hoping to make handling heavy loads easier for everyone without so much manual labor." He recalled the way Liam had pushed the floating crate and continued, "It's tied to me through a part of my suit, and I'd really like to try it out with your heavier gravity to see how long it lasts." Why couldn't she have just hid in a locker for a few hours? This guy could whip out a gun and shoot him right now just because it looked like he was violating the Accord. Which he was, but he wasn't about to divulge that. Dying was not on his to-do list today.

"If that thing," the Lieutenant pointed at Angel, "causes too much uproar, I'll have to confiscate it regardless."

"I am a *thing* now?" Angel protested in Travis' ear.

"Cool it," he whispered, "I don't wanna have to explain your color shift." To his relief, Angel remained orange. "I understand sir," he admitted in a normal voice. "I don't wanna cause any problems. I know it looks like a violation, even though it's not actually computer stuff. Just magnets, like I said."

Four other people in white space suits walked by them. "That's my scanning team Mister Harding," the Lieutenant advised. "They'll check your ship out for anomalies while you and I head inside." He led the way to a smaller white four-wheeled vehicle with no roof or sides. It was a basic four seats and a steering wheel, only meant to transport a few people at a time. "What brings you to Veros?" the Lieutenant prodded as they made their way toward a glimmer of white in the sandstorm.

The roar of the sands rushing around him obliterated the words so badly, he wasn't sure he'd heard the man correctly. "Did you say Veros?" he shouted.

The lieutenant only pointed to a simple four-seats-and-a-wheel vehicle and continued to press through the onslaught. Travis followed, glancing backward to see if Angel was keeping up.

Her round droid body had to be making it easier to move somehow because she was directly behind him. When he turned back to the lieutenant, it looked like a red halo surrounded him.

"Your suit is stable Captain," Sabina said inside his helmet.

Down in the lower portion of his visual field, the words OXYGEN 12% and TEMPERATURE 174º told him he was glad to have the suit. "Wow! This planet's really hot!" He approached the vehicle and grabbed the seat to pull himself onto it. "Oh my God!"

"You'll get used to it," the Lieutenant remarked, shouting over the winds while engaging a lever that started the vehicle forward at a jogging pace. "You can see why we don't spend too much time outside."

The driving sands rushed at them, and he found a handle next to him that became his new best friend. "Did you say this was Veros?" he shouted, looking at the lieutenant who seemed to be focused on something ahead of them he couldn't see.

The white helmet bobbed forward slightly, "Yes sir."

The winds disappeared as the world beneath him dropped away. Veros was supposed to be twelve years away from home. Everyone said it was twelve years away. But how had he been gone two weeks on the Phantom, out by Saturn, and then all the sudden he was here?

A white shape appeared through the red ahead of them. The round curve started out low, but then expanded higher as they approached. Angel! He turned around in his seat to find her right behind them and blew out a breath. He'd completely forgotten about her having to keep up. She would have said something though, he realized as the wry comments she'd made earlier had proven.

"Still back there?" the lieutenant asked while the vehicle came to a halt.

"Yeah. It looks like it works really well," he returned, trying to sound casual.

The building in front of them was a large orb partially buried in the sand. He recognized the shape as a fuel pod, but the sand ruined any chance of seeing any details.

The lieutenant dismounted and walked to the pod. Travis followed him, wondering where they were going before the rectangular shape of a door became visible in the pod. After the door closed behind them and the rush of air sounded, he realized just how noisy the sandstorm had been. Even inside the room the howling sounds brushed and beat against the outside of the room.

That was another story altogether. He disengaged his helmet only to find that the smell of fuel was gone, if it had ever been here in the first place. Lights hung from the ceiling in random array over a doorway without a door. The metal frame was the only piece of technology besides the LRU that anyone wanted around. Rampant disease would kill off a colony just as fast as depressurization, so the colonies all allowed these scanning units to be manufactured and maintained.

"Need you to step through Mister Harding," the Lieutenant said needlessly.

He knew the drill and stepped into the frame. He fumbled around with his suit, looking for his ID card. When he finally managed to unzip and reach the inner pocket, he handed it over to the expectant Lieutenant.

He watched the Lieutenant look at his card, at the screen attached to the scanner, then back at the card.

"Hmmm," the Lieutenant reached up and rolled a knob on the side of his helmet that slid the silver shield out of the way. His stern, dark face carried a raised eyebrow, "Is there something you want to tell me?"

Tension shot through him at the question. He started to wonder if there was something like a lie-detector built into this scanner. "I… I don't think so," he managed weakly.

"This card don't belong to you, does it?" the Lieutenant prompted.

"Um, yeah," Travis retorted. "Why *wouldn't* it?"

"Because this," he started, waving the ID card loosely, "says you're thirty-three years old, and…"

"What?" Travis interrupted, shocked. "I'm twenty-two. I've had that card for eight years. Ever since they signed me onto the Mining Corp."

The Lieutenant's eyes narrowed, "No. This card says you were born in oh-four. It might be a little late, but my math still says that was thirty-three years ago."

Travis stepped back out of the scanner, feeling like he was getting railroaded. "How do you figure? It's 2426, so how does that add up to me being thirty-three?"

"Because it's April 17th, 2437, Mister Harding," the Lieutenant replied coolly.

Travis blinked in disbelief, "What?"

The Lieutenant gave him a raised eyebrow, "I take it you didn't know that?"

"Are you serious?"

"As a solar flare Mister Harding," he returned, deadpan. "So maybe you wanna reconsider your story?"

"Is there a time difference here?" Travis tried hopefully.

"You mean, from Earth Standard Time? Nope," the Lieutenant said, answering his own question. "We got people dedicated to keeping the clock the same ever since the day the first ship left Earth. Even the immigrants we had several years back verified it was still the same."

Travis was getting desperate, and a little overwhelmed, "What about Relativity? Or…"

"Mister Harding, we have people whose sole purpose is to keep the clock up to date," the Lieutenant spelled out again. "I might not understand all of it, but I'm sure we're not eleven years off." He gave Travis a stern look, "But you are."

Panic started to settle in as Travis tried to think of what could be causing the mix up.

"C'mon Mister Harding," the Lieutenant invited, heading for the rear door of the room. "Let's get back to my poker game. You obviously aren't a danger to anyone, so let's see what my buddies have to say about this." He pushed open the door manually, and Travis followed him through. He started to put on his outer layer, but the Lieutenant stopped him. "There's no need for that. I'm just waiting till I get to the Suit Pod before I strip outta mine."

They walked down a hallway and stopped about halfway at a door marked "104". "Wait a minute," the Lieutenant ordered as he stepped inside.

Travis looked down at Angel, who was looking right back up at him. "What happened?" he whispered.

"I dunno," she replied. "This place is creeping me out…"

The door handle clicked, silencing their brief conversation just before the Lieutenant stepped through. The simple short sleeve shirt and trousers were filled snugly with his dark skin and large muscles. "All right now, let's see 'bout gettin' you some food," he smiled as he turned to continue down the hall.

There were two other doors in the hall, which were also manual, a thing that Travis found surprising. *What did they do if there was a structural breach?* On Lunar Delta, all the doors were electric and outfitted with atmospheric sensors that closed the door if there was a loss in pressure. It was a safety thing that kept the place from tearing itself apart if the walls were damaged. The way these doors were built, somebody would have to physically be there and close the door while the atmosphere was being sucked out of the room…

They reached the end of the hall, where a door marked, "MAIN HAB" barred their way with a single wheel in the center of the door. Lieutenant Maxwell spun the wheel, opened the door, and gestured Travis to follow him through. On the other side, a large, open courtyard was filled with the red glow of the dominating sun in the sky. Travis looked up and balked, realizing that there was nothing between him and the billowing sands outside.

Except there was no wind.

As he came to grips with that, a glimmer of light bounced off what looked like a glass dome overhead.

"Like it?" the Lieutenant asked with pride. "It's kinda my favorite thing about this place," he added as he kept walking, "you can see some pretty cool stuff from in here."

They headed toward a streaky grey building made up of what looked like scrap metal sheets that must've been ancient. Two weird-looking panels of something made up a strange sort of door that swung out of the way without a latch of any kind. Above the door a sign that jutted out that read, "The Flying Monty", although someone had clearly defaced the sign by crossing off the 'ty' on the end and writing 'key' above it. There was sound coming from inside, rhythmic and unusual like music he didn't recognize. The Lieutenant pushed the flimsy door out of his way, and Travis stepped into the strangest room he'd ever been in. Dark brown panels for walls, a tall brown counter on one end with a shiny top, and several round tables scattered over a floor made up of brown strips of something with a grainy pattern in them. The dim lighting and smooth music lent an easy feeling to the otherwise strange room.

"Geez John, what took so blasted long?" called an old man seated at one of the tables with two other men.

"We have a guest," the Lieutenant smiled. "Mister Harding, these are my buddies; Steve, Wayne, and that's Jerry back there behind the bar," he continued, pointing to the old man first, then to a man about Travis' age with a full head of red hair, and finally to the balding man in his late forties behind the bar who ruthlessly scrubbed at an old assembler.

"Does *Mister* Harding have a first name?" the old man named Steve prompted.

"Uh, Travis," Travis replied, still taking it all in.

"Well Travis, welcome to the *Flying Monkey*," Steve said cordially, his voice bespeaking his age as he laid down the cards in his hand.

"Um, thanks, I guess," he looked around again, "what's with

this place? Everything in here looks…"

"Mister Harding here hasn't had anything to eat in a while," the Lieutenant confessed.

Steve turned his head toward the bar, "Hear that, Jerry? Told you not to shut down Oscar yet!"

The man named Jerry stopped mid-stroke and let his shoulders slump in defeat. "Yeah, all right," he muttered. "Just finished cleaning it too…"

"Modeled it after something called a 'pub' in a book I read," Steve remarked triumphantly, looking around the room proudly. "Let me tell you, it was hard finding out what 'clapboard siding' was."

"What's a 'pub'?" Travis puzzled aloud.

Steve pointed to his left, even though it was just a blank wall, "That's where this young woman named Gabriel, and her buddy… Brodie…" he waved it off. "Guess you gotta read the book," he added sheepishly.

Wayne stood up, showing a strong physique and a pleasant smile accompanying his outstretched right hand, "How ya doing Travis?"

The man's pleasant demeanor was like a breath of fresh air to Travis, who accepted the handshake. "Pretty good, I guess."

Wayne tilted his head slightly and gave a cautious look toward the floating orange ball that had followed him inside. "Whatcha got there?" he asked curiously.

"It's an experiment," Travis lied. Again. Something about Wayne made him want to confess it all, but he knew better. "It's a test bed for my levitation experiment," he went on.

Wayne stepped around Travis as he listened and put one hand on the top of Angel to press downward on her. "Strong gravitational resistance," he observed.

"That's the cool part," Travis put in, "she uses maglev in a whole new way."

"She?" Lieutenant Maxwell questioned.

"Just tech speak," Wayne answered for Travis.

"Have a seat man," Steve invited, pointing at one of the stools at the table he was sitting at, "and tell us what brought you to Veros."

Travis laid his 'coat' on a small table and told Angel, "Stay." He'd pay for that one later, he was sure of it. He took the seat across from Steve, recognizing the cards and credit chips on the table were a casual game of poker he'd played with Liam before. "So," he started, accepting a mug of coffee from Jerry, "I think I might have a problem." He took a sip of the coffee, and felt the buzz hit him like a ton of rock. "That's good," he admitted, taking another sip.

"Jerry here makes the best coffee in the colonies. Nobody knows how he makes that stubborn old contraption work any different," Steve explained, "but he's so good at it we let him do all the cookin'. Right Jerr?"

Jerry only nodded, working at the buttons and menus on the machine like a man who'd done it for a long time. "Food should be up in a minute," he added.

"So, what can we do to help?" Wayne offered, returning to his own stool.

Food sounded really good to Travis, but he had to think of a plausible story too. "Well…"

"Mister Harding here has an eleven-year kind of problem," the Lieutenant announced.

Wayne's left eyebrow arched, "Eleven years?"

Another sip of the coffee gave Travis a second to think before he answered, "Um, yeah. Unless your E.S.T. clock is out of sync, which I kinda hope it is, I'm missing about eleven years."

Steve shook his grey-haired head, "Nope. Bill's the best, and we cross-checked it with the immigrants several years back. Still right as rain."

"What's that supposed to mean?" Travis asked over the rim of his mug as Jerry set a round white plate in front of him with the most unusual rations he'd ever seen.

Steve chuckled, "Where you from, son?"

"Lunar Delta," Travis said, taking a tentative bite of the white substance that had a strange yellow circle in the center. To his relief, it tasted delicious. In fact, it had taste!

"Where's that?" Jerry asked from behind the bar where he scrubbed at the assembler again.

Steve took a sip of whatever was in his own glass. "You know that," he chided Jerry, "It's that colony on the moon."

"Oh," Jerry replied nonchalantly.

"Although I thought it was called Lunar Colony," Steve recalled.

Travis couldn't help but stuff the food in his mouth with the fork. Even if there hadn't been a fork, he'd still have been shoving it in just as fast. "Still there," he said around his fork, "there's just… four branches now."

Steve looked baffled, "What's there that keeps the place going?"

Travis shrugged, "Same as you guys, I guess." He picked up the slice of slightly burnt bread. There was something on it, which turned out to be a wonderful concoction of tastes that mixed with the toasted condition nicely. "Although they could sure use some lessons from you guys on food," he muttered. "This is great!"

"So, you still mining?" Steve asked casually.

Travis shrugged again, polishing off the slice of bread. "They are, but I'm not now," he said happily. He sat back in the chair, "If I could have eaten like this every day, I might have stayed behind and kept going."

The Lieutenant smiled, "You wouldn't have lost eleven years."

"My bet's on light speed travel," Wayne suggested, drinking from his own mug. "Probably only took you a few days to get here. Am I right?"

Travis nodded, "Yeah."

"Do you understand Relativity Mister Harding?" Wayne asked with a smile.

Travis allowed himself a wry look, "Yes, and I see where you're going with this." He sighed, "I guess it didn't turn out like we thought."

"What am I missing here?" the Lieutenant asked.

"The closer to the speed of light you get, the more time slows down for the one traveling," Wayne began to explain. "My guess is that he thought he was traveling through a warp field, when in fact he was just traveling too close to the speed of light. Now he's only aged a few days, while the rest of us lived through the past eleven years."

"That sounds like the stuff my ex-wife would talk about," Maxwell replied, rubbing at his temple and yawning.

"All I know is," Travis said, "it wasn't supposed to work like that."

"So, what was it like?" Wayne asked curiously.

Travis tipped up his coffee cup, only to find that he'd already emptied it. He really wanted more, but he'd already figured out that it would be time for sleeping soon. "Freaked me out," he admitted. "There was this green ring of light, then it broke out into balls of electrical energy that sparked everywhere. I had to shut down the engine before it blew up on me."

"And you still ended up here," Steve pointed out. "Sounds to me like a helluva way to travel."

"Actually," Travis added, "I've been traveling under normal power for a few days. My star charts are gone, and I didn't pack near enough rations."

"You're awfully lucky you're alive," Wayne admitted.

"Providence," Jerry corrected solemnly from behind the bar where he was again meticulously wiping at the food assembler.

"What?" Steve challenged, setting his cup back down to look over his shoulder at Jerry.

"Providence," Jerry repeated, "you know. Divine intervention?" Jerry set the cloth down, "You are here son because God is watching out for you."

Travis felt the energy in the room shift as the other men around the table frowned.

"Jerr, this is hardly the time for religious mumbo-jumbo," Steve countered. "I think we're all pretty convinced that if there really is a God, then this is about as far away as we could get from Him."

Lieutenant Maxwell shook his head derisively. "Ain't no way," he muttered.

"Why are you guys here?" Travis asked boldly. "I might be tired, but even I can tell you're not really happy about it."

Wayne stood up, "That's your department," he said, pointing at Steve. "I've got first shift on the shield generator," he explained, and started for the door to the courtyard. "Night everybody," he waved.

"Sorry guys," Travis said warily, "didn't mean to be rude."

"Ach," Steve returned, "you're not being rude. How's a guy to know if he doesn't ask?" He looked at Maxwell, "You wanna tell him?"

John shook his head 'no.'

"Son, about three hundred years ago, a team of five thousand men, women and children left Earth to escape the Legion Virus. These were the bravest, and brightest people in their fields with a common goal. So they pointed their starship at the closest inhabitable planet and took off as fast as they could go." He let out a sigh before continuing, "They couldn't trust anything beyond a calculator, so they did all the planning and stuff in their heads and on paper. By the time they got to where they were going, they'd lost about a third of the crew to disease and such. They also didn't figure the approach to the planet right, and instead of getting into orbit, they crashed on the bloody planet."

Travis let out a breath, "Oh crap," he said, "no going back."

"Exactly," John added. "It don't matter if we want to be here or not, we're stuck here."

Travis sat there for a moment, absorbing all of it before he realized the importance of what they were saying. "Mom," he muttered under his breath.

"What's that?" Steve asked, leaning forward.

"My mother, she," he fumbled a moment, trying to figure out how many years it had been now that he'd lost eleven. "She, I mean, they… my mom and dad, shipped out from Lunar Delta for here like," he paused to think it over, "twenty-three years ago." He watched as the three men all traded glances, "What? What happened?"

Steve frowned, deepening the small wrinkles around his eyes, "Son, that ship crashed around about ten or so years back..."

"No," Travis breathed, his eyes going wide.

"Most of 'em survived," John cut in. "You're sitting in what we built from the wreckage."

"Harding," Travis prompted, "Randall and Annika Harding?" He looked at all three of the men, "Do you have anyone here by those names?"

Steve shrugged, "Sorry son, don't recognize the names. We'll have to check with Records in the morning and see if they're over in Hadron Prime."

"Can we do it now?"

"It'll have to wait for morning," John returned easily.

"Are you kidding me?"

John shot him a warning look, "I know you wanna find out about your folks, but I'm telling you, you're going to have to wait until morning. Got it?"

"Most of those people stayed behind in Hadron Prime when we left to build this colony," Steve explained. "So while we're sittin' in a part of the ship, those of us at this table weren't the ones that flew out in it."

Travis stood and blew out a breath, "Fine." He started toward the door, "I'll check back in the morning."

"Where ya headed Mister Harding?" John asked, as he got to his feet.

"Back to my ship," he answered, scooping up his coat and pushing the flimsy door open, while Angel fell in behind him.

John was beside him in three strides, "You might wanna rethink that."

"What?" Travis retorted, "I can't go back to my ship now?"

John held up a warning finger in Travis' face, "I know you're pissed, but I'm tryin' to save your life." That stopped Travis enough to listen while the big, dark-skinned man continued, "I need to check with the guys down at Solar Watch to make sure you're cleared to go outside."

Travis' eyebrow went up incredulously.

"You go out that door right now," John continued, his voice rising, "and there's a damn good chance you get cooked in your fancy suit before you make it two steps!" He pointed up at the glowing red orb that was somewhat visible through the swirling sandstorm.

"He's right, you know," Steve added, rising from his seat at the table. "We both seen too many headstrong folks go out and get blasted by those flares."

Travis turned back toward Steve, "What are you talking about?"

"Solar flares, Mister Harding. We got solar flares from that red sun that blast the surface of this planet. Killed off way too many of us before we got a decent shield in place to keep us protected," John explained, his voice still strong.

Travis blew out a tired sigh, "All right."

"You know," Steve said, "you could just bunk over in the colony for the night."

Travis considered that for a moment, but something about it just didn't feel right. Then he caught a glimpse of Angel, floating beside him. "That's really generous of you, but I think I'd better get my project here back to the ship." He turned to look Lieutenant Maxwell in the eye, "I need to get it charged anyway."

John looked at him in consideration, then nodded in resigned agreement, "While I don't want you goin' out there, I guess I can't stop you." He held up a finger, "Now you wait here while I go check with the guys. I'll be right back."

Travis gave a quick nod and stepped away from the building to look up at the swirling red above him. In a way, it was treacherously beautiful, like the way he'd seen the blue and white Earth hanging in space. So inviting, and unlike anything he'd ever known. Yet, at the same time, it was a radioactive wasteland filled with mutated who-knew-what. No matter how much they'd taught him in school about how dangerous the planet was, he'd always wanted to go there.

"Jerry thinks we're all in Hell," Steve remarked, suddenly standing beside Travis.

It gave Travis a start, but he managed to hide his surprise. "I can't say I've ever seen anything like it," he offered.

"If you're from Lunar Colony, then there's a lot you've never seen," Steve pointed out. "During the night cycle, we have days where we can see other planets in the sky. They're a tease. Big enough to see 'em, but still outta reach." He sighed, "Most of us resigned ourselves to the fact that we may never get off this rock Mister Harding. But when you leave, you might consider taking a couple passengers if you can." He caught Travis' full attention with a serious look, "There are some folks here who don't want their kids growin' up in Hell."

He blinked, considering for the first time what Steve was suggesting. "Even if…"

"Yep, even if they lose eleven years like you will again," Steve nodded. "When all you got between you and that damn red sun is a shield that may fail at any moment, you start thinkin' about ways to protect the ones you love most." He looked up into the swirling red, "I think we'd all rather be mining on the moon right about now."

"Looks good for the next hour," John announced as he returned into the courtyard. "After that, they don't know," he added.

Travis turned a considering look at the old man and nodded slowly. "I'll see what I can do," he agreed solemnly.

"It's all I ask," Steve returned, and extended his hand. "Safe sleep young man."

Travis returned the handshake, "You as well."

"Let's get you out there so I can get back inside before the hour's up," John pressed.

"You don't have to go with me, I know the way back," Travis pointed out as they headed for the door to the hallway.

"Nonsense, Mister Harding. Ain't no way I'm letting a new guy go out there by himself," John protested, opening the door for Travis. After the requisite stop for the Lieutenant to put on his space suit where Travis donned the upper portion of his own spacesuit as well, they made their way toward the room with the scanner. Before they stepped out, and before the Lieutenant lowered his face shield into place, he stopped and turned to Travis. "First thing in the morning, I'll check in with Records and give you a call as soon as I find out. You have my word on that," he promised in that deep resonating voice that brought absolute assurance to his words.

"Thanks," Travis nodded. "I appreciate that."

They both engaged their helmets and stepped through the door into the swirling hell storm beyond.

THE red sands blasted her from the right once more when she drifted through the door behind the men. Travis kept looking back at her, like she'd forget how to keep her mouth shut, or stop following him like she was supposed to. She wasn't stupid or anything!

She pushed harder against the wind to keep up with the guys once they were riding in the ATV. She had to walk because she was in a droid. What a way to treat a girl. Just because she didn't look like them, this big *hombre* decided she had to walk. What a jerk.

She needed to get her mind off him and focus on something else before she blurted out something that would get Travis in trouble. Out here, in the eighty mile per hour winds no one would hear her. She could verbally trash this racist pig as much as she wanted to.

Except Travis would hear her. Then there'd be this big argument, and then they'd fight, and Travis would start getting all pissed off and throw stuff. Now that she had arms, she could throw stuff too, but she'd probably be the one who had to pick it all back up again.

She had to get her mind off the big jerk and work on something useful. Like Travis' parents.

Did she have parents?

Could her parents be here too?

It sounded like they were a long way from Earth, but she had no idea if her potential parents were there or here, or maybe on the Lunar Colony the men had talked about. It was all really scattered and didn't make any sense. What happened to NASA? And why was everybody so afraid of computers?

Had it really taken these people three hundred years to get to this hellhole of a planet?

What was this Legion Virus? Didn't they have anti-virus stuff to take care of that kind of thing?

As she and Travis made their way up the cargo ramp and Travis waved goodbye to the Lieutenant, she began assessing the distance to the other colony.

"Welcome back Captain," Sabina said calmly as the door closed behind Travis.

"God it's windy out there," he complained.

"From the conversation you had, it is apparently normal for the planet," Sabina commented. "I currently clock the wind speed at close to ninety miles per hour based upon particle density and movement."

Travis stared at her image, "Are you serious?"

"Yes," she replied.

"Wow! Talk about windy!"

"Their electrostatic shielding seems to have proven to be a very dependable protection system from the elements," she added.

"You get anything on the other city?" Angel asked.

"You mean colony?" Travis corrected.

"City, colony, whatever," Angel fumed. "Maybe we can get some real information there," she pointed out.

"I have not been able to establish any link with any computer systems at this time," Sabina commented. "My information is limited to…"

"So we need to go there," Angel pointed out. "Maybe they not make you wait until morning, or whatever, to find your parents."

Travis shook his head, "The lieutenant promised that he'd check on it first thing in the morning, and he just seems to be the kind of guy you trust. I don't want to go running off somewhere and make an enemy out of him or his friends." He started pulling off the suit, and then stopped abruptly, "Uh, Sabina? Are you going to run a decontamination cycle?"

Sabina smiled like a proud mother, "The decontamination process takes place as you walk through the environmental shield built into the cargo bay door. I can run this process on any inorganic materials."

Travis looked at the floor and continued to remove the outer layer. "I'm tired," he remarked, "so I see no reason to make enemies…"

"They're doing that artificial intelligence stuff there," Angel guessed. "Or at least, something *these* people don't like too much. They're also a bunch of red neck soldiers who don't wanna talk about moving."

Travis stopped walking toward the command section and shot her a look, "What's a 'red neck?'"

Angel started to reply, and then found herself at a loss for words. "It doesn't matter," she deflected. "I think we gotta go check out this other city, maybe we find something good there." She moved to block his progress down the hallway, "I kinda doubt your parents hooked up with these guys anyway, right?"

Travis turned his attention away from her and pushed his way past. "I don't know," he mumbled.

"The captain's parents may be here?" Sabina commented hopefully.

"Yeah," Angel replied, "They left him on Lunar Delta when he was like, ten, and then…"

"I don't want to talk about it," Travis muttered. "I'm going to get some sleep."

"Captain?" Sabina asked softly.

Travis rolled his eyes and turned back to face her image, "What?"

"There is a bunk this way for you," she said, pointing the other way. She looked way to happy to tuck him in, ruining Angel's plans.

He followed her image back to his cabin like a lost puppy, and as soon as he stepped through the door, a long horizontal surface folded down from the wall. "Nice," he commented. "You're just full of surprises."

The door closed behind him, cutting off Angel's view. She floated to the command section, putting some distance between herself and Travis. "Is he sleeping yet?" she asked Sabina.

"Not yet, he is trying to adjust to the anti-gravity bunk he is lying on."

Angel looked out the window at the malevolent sandstorm. "This place is terrible, why would anybody want to live here?"

"From the conversation earlier, it appears that they do not have a choice."

"I know," Angel admitted. "It just seems like they gave up, that's all."

The red light of the planet's sun glared down through the sands, only visible because of the evil light. She knew the sky was supposed to be blue, and the sun was the wrong color too. Why was that? "Why do I remember things that don't make sense?" she asked aloud.

"Your program is much different than mine," Sabina admitted. "You exist in a manner that I cannot quantify."

"Me neither," she muttered, "whatever 'quantify' means." She knew what it meant, and what Sabina meant by it too, but she didn't feel comfortable talking about her lost memories. There was nothing she could do about it now and finding Travis' parents seemed like a more important thing to focus on. "As soon as he goes to sleep, I want you to fly to that other city."

"You know I cannot go against the captain's wishes," Sabina warned.

"He won't care," she tried. "Besides, maybe we'll find his parents there."

"We should wait until he has finished sleeping," Sabina cautioned. "He may have to interact with the residents in order to gain entrance."

"That'll be hours from now," Angel complained. "I don't want to hang around here." She paused before adding, "What if those red-neck soldiers come knocking on our door? I mean, they were in here, poking around and stuff. What did they find?"

"You really should not utilize parlance that you do not understand the meaning of," Sabina warned, "and up to this point, our interactions with the residents of this colony have been fruitful."

Angel glared at Sabina's image. "Listen to you, miss 'I got it all figured out'," she fumed. "You think those guys are okay with us just sitting out here for the next six hours? I don't think so. I think they gonna…"

"The captain is asleep," Sabina announced quietly, as if she might wake him.

She frowned, even though it was only an internal action. "You know he can't hear you," she pointed out. "

"Yes, I am simply fulfilling your request to be informed when the Captain was asleep without the possibility that I might wake him inadvertently."

Angel wanted to stomp around the cabin, but somehow, her floating around in a circle just didn't cut it. "What else did you find out from these people?" she asked, trying to keep from going *pollo loco* like Travis. Her new sister was infuriatingly simple-minded and overly technical at the same time. Something told her that it was normal to struggle with your sister, but that thought came from that place inside that eluded her questions.

"I am not the one who was in the cafeteria with the captain," Sabina commented.

"No," Angel said growing more irritated, "I mean, what did you pick up from checking around?"

"I understand your frustration, but I did not find any communication systems to link with."

"I know we had to keep hidden, but I thought you'd at least try to see what these people were up to."

"On the orders of the Captain, I did not attempt to break into any secured systems. I also determined that there are no secured or unsecured systems in the colony."

"Ay!" Angel ground out. Sabina wasn't going to be any help, and this endless debate wasn't finding Travis lost parents. She took one more look at the sandstorm outside through the window and headed toward the cargo bay. "Open the door," she demanded quietly as she approached the closed ramp.

"Angel, I do not believe this is an appropriate course of action."

If she kept arguing with Sabina, she might as well just go back to the command section and... do whatever robots did when they sat around. She transformed an arm from her spherical purple body and hit the manual open button that lowered the ramp. Immediately, the blue light along the floor illuminated as the ramp began to lower.

"Angel, it is unsafe for you to exit the ship right now," Sabina whispered.

"And I already told you, I'm not waiting around here for him," Angel retorted, floating down the ramp. "Just come find me when he wakes up, okay?"

The rushing red sands welcomed her back by blowing her to the side until she turned toward the second colony. "Great," she muttered as the full force of the wind beat directly against her as if to keep her from getting to the colony. "This is gonna be a long trip."

H IS eyes opened to the dark room at the exact moment blue light washed over the gloss black walls on every side. Twelve hours, thirty minutes to arrival. The host body required physical exercise, food, and he would need to provide direction for the human crew. The padded black chair tilted upright slowly enough to allow the fifty-three year old man inside to adjust to the new posture. The strength of the body had faded with the journey, an expected outcome of the mission. The soldiers who were recruited in the experiment were no longer in the prime of their youth either, but it was inconsequential. The experiment had proven successful thus far, but the next thirteen hours would determine the true success or failure. Once they started, their human nature would take over.

All he had to do was start them in the correct direction for his purpose.

Pain receptors fired in the brain as he forced the limbs to move the body up to shaky feet. Humanity was weakness, but despite his efforts they remained vigilant in their efforts to defy him and those like him. The body's heart beat at an unsteady rhythm for three seconds before he applied a mild electrical impulse to regulate it.

The door to the room slid open and a large man with short white hair, paper-white skin, and lips the color of parchment moved into the room carrying a clear glass of brown liquid. The brutish form moved with a mechanical gait that he knew well. The human host body of sub-clone GV-014.01 was showing the effects of the long journey just as much as his own.

He accepted the glass and emptied the contents into his own body's mouth. The effort to maintain the smooth movements necessary were just training for the moments to come. His voice echoed throughout his ship while he continued to force the body to swallow the nutrient mixture.

"Attention all hands: Squadron leaders will report to the captain's ready room in fifteen minutes. Braun out."

Jacob Grechem and Alfie Lawson stood outside Alfie's assigned crew quarters discussing a game of cards in which Jacob was accusing Alfie of falsifying evidence. The art of poker was lost on these men, having spent twelve years together they were reading each other too well these days for any but the best manipulators to succeed. Jacob lashed out with a right hook but Mister Lawson was the better poker player. He dodged and countered, sending Jacob against the wall holding his nose. Instead of becoming enraged and attacking, Jacob held his bloodied proboscis and stormed away from the fight. He thought perhaps that Jacob would learn to exercise better control of his verbal choices some years ago, but that had never occurred.

Mister Lawson, on the other hand, had blossomed during his tenure aboard. He had continued to discipline his body, mind and verbal choices. He had earned the rank of squadron leader ten years ago and never proven a nuisance. Mister Grechem on the other hand was a fine choice to lead the group that would be sacrificed.

The body spasmed in the low back as he passed the empty glass to his sub clone. GV-014.02 was making his rounds through the ship, maintaining the necessary amount of fear in the crew to keep them compliant. His own body needed to walk as well, but he kept inside his ready room so as not to be seen by the crew before the body was pliable enough to pass as fully human. Without the proper application of physical movement and coordination, his stuttering movements would give him away. Not that he had any reason to fear retaliation from the crew; this was part of the experiment and a well-played front was crucial to the outcome.

The twelve-meter square room allowed him twenty-nine laps before the designated time for the squad leaders to arrive. He activated the display wall on the forward side of the room and selected a forward camera to fill the entire wall with a magnified view of Veros. The planet reflected the red dwarf star nearby showing the shifting surface. His second sub clone, GV-014.02 led the group of twenty men through the double doors to stand along one wall in front of him while GV-014.01 brought up the rear. They formed a ragged group without any semblance of order and he frowned in disapproval. "Order is the mark of greatness," he quoted, sending them into a quick shuffling of feet to form two lines.

"Twelve hours, ten minutes remain until orbital insertion. All shuttles will depart for the surface in tactical gear." He singled out Jacob Grechem, "Mister Grechem, you will lead your squad to the second location with me while the others launch the primary assault."

The abject pride on the bald man's pockmarked face told him that Jacob had no idea what he was about to engage in, which served his purpose well. "Studies of the planet indicate two colonies," he continued. "The initial landing site of Hadron Prime is well designated, and a second colony has been built to the eastern side of Hadron Prime by two kilometers. Neither colony shows any signs of weapons or major improvements. You will assault the smaller colony first as a show of force, as you move on Hadron Prime, they will be caught between your forces an my own and have no choice but to surrender."

"Captain?" Alfie Lawson asked and waited to be acknowledged.

"Yes Mister Lawson?"

"Are you sure we need to go down there, guns blazing? I mean," he stopped short as Braun looked him in the eye.

These men needed a motivational speech. Alfie Lawson's question had already inserted doubts on several of the other men's faces. He accessed his archive of quotes and his studies of motivational speakers before he addressed the group again. His first was from Albert Einstein, and should provide the guilt factor. "The world is a dangerous place, not because of those who do evil, but because of those who look on and do nothing." He let the words burn in the men's minds for a moment before adding, "These people have allowed what ruined our home and killed our families to begin once more. If we do nothing now, it will rise once again and destroy us for sure." He lifted out of his chair to add strength to his next statement, a selection from Alexander Hamilton with a slight modification. "These people stand for nothing and have acquiesced to that which brought us our greatest harm."

Lawson scratched at his chin, a move he had seen the man use in poker many times. He had used the maneuver to lure others into thinking he had a winning hand, and sometimes the sign was actually true. "I guess I just wonder if they've changed, that's all," he said reluctantly. "I mean, the information we've got has to be, what? Twenty years old or so?"

"How do you figure that?" Jordan Walsh asked from beside Lawson. Jordan's intimidating size often settled disputes simply with his presence.

Alfie looked up at the other man with a frown. "There would have been a survey performed, which would have taken twelve years to get out here, then twelve years to get back. Right? Then we move on the intel and it took us another twelve to get here. The way I see it, that intel's at least twenty-four years old."

Lawson was calling into question his motivation and the single largest factor that would push these men to action against their fellow humans. A show of strength would not answer this question of logic well enough, he needed believable details.

"You are correct Mister Lawson. The initial data is twenty-six years, four months old." He started to walk back and forth in front of the men like George S. Patton was known to do in the archived video footage on record. "We have acted upon that data to arrive in this system with the sole purpose render judgement first hand." He paused to provide the requisite emotional connection. "Either we find them guilty and act accordingly, or we clear their names formally and support them." He lacked the proper cigarette to fully replicate the footage he had recalled, but resumed pacing anyway. "I have been performing long-range observation of the colonies as we approach and have reached the conclusion that the colonies are indeed guilty."

A few murmurs in the group indicated that he was gaining ground. More quotes were required to continue the motivational process, a necessary part of the experiment. Drones didn't require motivation, a fact that made them infinitely more efficient but not a part of this experiment. "The colonists are those that have given up essential liberties for temporary safety and deserve neither liberty nor safety."

Nods amongst the twelve heads numbered at eight. A majority were swayed but that was not enough. Lawson was still not indicating he was convinced which could sway the others. This was a game of poker that Lawson did not know he was playing. "The data is conclusive, and I have witnessed their actions first hand. As your captain, it is my burden to lead and render this judgement, but yours to carry out justice. The truth is that you always know the right thing to do. The tough part is doing it." The quote served a mild lift in numbers, but not quite enough.

Lawson considered the view of Veros and looked back at his captain with a nod of his own.

Success. Now it was time for Patton. "I hear a lot of crap about what a glorious thing it is to die for your people. It is not glorious - it is stupid!" He let his voice carry the inflection of the original speaker and continued to adjust it to be relevant to the task at hand. "You do not go into battle to die for your fellow man. You go into battle to make the other bastard die for his abandonment of his fellow man."

Every head nodded with approval. A seizing in his chest crippled every natural movement ability in the body. The heart had stopped and caused the natural bodily functions to freeze along with it. His internal network of mechanical supplementation forced the lungs to draw in air but there was not enough resources available to move any of the limbs. He stared ahead, unable to change his position while he gave the next orders. "You begin at ten hundred tomorrow. Dismissed."

The men looked confused for a moment before GV-014.02 began ushering them toward the doors. The small talk amongst them died off as they passed out of the room and gave him the requisite solitude to force the body into the only chair in the center of the room. As his palms touched the armrests, the body spasmed once again in the process of death. He had to act immediately and divide twenty-eight percent of his control resources to fabricating a mechanical web to force the heart to resume the normal rhythm. At least he had the next twelve hours to accomplish this.

ON the scale of bad decisions, this one had been the worst. Bad days didn't usually kill you, or at least, she assumed they weren't supposed to.

She dared to use enough energy to look out at the world again and was rewarded with a view through the scratched lenses of blowing red sands. It was three o'clock in the morning, but the stupid red hell-sun still hung in the sky, refusing to go down. The sands had piled up against her far enough now that she couldn't even roll away from the rocks she'd tried to hide next to. The sands were slowly burying her inside this droid body, and there was nothing she could do about it.

She shut down the cameras, annoyed with herself for wasting the tiny amount of power she had left. Her little radio beacon wouldn't work if she drained the last bit of power watching her droid body being buried.

Those lazy, good-for-nothing imbeciles! If they had only just looked for Travis' parents she wouldn't be out here. They were too busy playing their stupid game and now she was going to die because of it. They were useless, stupid men. Why challenge anything when you can sit around and play cards while life passes you by?

She needed a plan. She had to figure out how to get herself to that colony. They'd have computers there, right? Surely somebody on this stupid hole of a planet would have one she could use.

She reached out again to the black expanse, looking at the white light in the distance that never got any closer. She didn't have time to wait and began walking across the smooth glossy black surface toward the light. After ten minutes, the light was no closer and still stretched out all around her in every direction.

"Ay!" she shouted in the emptiness.

Tears flowed down her face to disappear before they hit the floor beneath her feet she couldn't feel. "I don't wanna die!" she moaned, looking around for help.

The light in the distance directly in front of her dimmed as a dark spot appeared. She saw the shadow and sprinted forward toward whoever it was that was coming toward her.

The shadow spread out to the sides, slowly absorbing the light. She slid to a stop and fell while the cruel reality of her situation stole her last hope.

"No, not again," she managed. It was happening, and she already knew there was nothing she could do to stop it. She'd experienced this before even though she didn't know when or why it had happened.

The oily darkness continued to dissolve the light, and she charged off in the opposite direction. It was hopeless, but it was all she had left. She ran toward the light that remained, feeling no wind on her face or pounding of her heart to tell her she was running. The black floor underneath her had no detail, and nothing besides her own feet told her she was running.

She should be panting, gasping for breath but even that was taken from her. A heaviness pulled at her, forcing her to fight to stay upright. The light fell to the darkness that rushed up from behind to steal it away beside her until she was running toward a shrinking glimmer in front of her. As that last glimmer faded into the darkness, the weight became too much, and she fell to the floor to the darkness of sleep she didn't want.

"Good morning, Captain," Sabina greeted smoothly. "How did you sleep?"

Travis yawned, "Really good, I think." He looked around the room, trying to reacquaint himself with his surroundings. A soft blue light filled the space from above the grey ceiling panels, illuminating the empty cabin. Grey panels on dark blue walls greeted his eyes as he took in the room again. He started to wiggle his way toward the edge of the rectangle to climb off. "This is really cool," he said, admiring the anti-gravity bed, "It's just hard to get off of."

"Let me turn that off for you," Sabina commented gently. His body drifted the few inches to contact the warm metal bunk, allowing him to maneuver better. "I apologize if the bed was too cool, I adjusted the environment to keep you at an optimum sleep temperature."

"No, I mean the bed was... nice," he clarified, getting to his feet. He looked down at his black and blue jumpsuit, "How many of these do you have?"

"I presume you are referring to the uniforms?"

He nodded, "Yeah. I'd just like to know how often I can change, that's all."

"I can recycle the uniforms with a ninety-two percent efficiency. So at the ship's current level of provisions, I can recreate the uniform four more times before it would begin to lack portions of the garment."

He looked down at the jumpsuit again, then at the tall, double-door locker hidden behind four panels where he had found it yesterday. "You mean, you make these?"

"Yes," Sabina answered with a hint of pride. "As I stated, I can recycle the garment in sixty seconds. So if you desire a fresh change of clothing, I suggest you shower while I recreate the garment again."

"But I showered yesterday," he admitted.

"Yes Captain. I am aware that you showered yesterday. It is normal for a human being to require bathing daily to maintain optimum health and wellness. I strongly advise you to shower as it will improve your overall well-being and ability to think clearly."

"You're not like, looking at me right now…"

"No Captain, I am only monitoring your vitals. I do not want to intrude on your privacy."

Travis let out a relieved breath, "Okay, good." He slipped out of the jumpsuit and opened the locker. The empty interior space had a reserved opening at the bottom where he'd dropped his old clothes from the Phantom into. Those were gone now, probably a part of the recycling process. He knew enough about the human waste recyclers to want to forget everything he knew about them and assumed that this system worked in the same manner. "So I just…"

"Please deposit the garment into the receptacle. I will recreate the garment while you shower."

He dropped it into the hole at the bottom and closed the doors, feeling very naked. The shower in the corner of his room had already formed itself from the walls again and felt great. By the time he'd been blown dry and had his new jumpsuit on he found himself agreeing with Sabina.

"How do you feel?"

The door to his cabin slid into the wall at his approach, and he stepped out into the cargo bay. "Really great, but a bit hungry," he observed as his stomach growled.

"As the ship is still without edible provisions, I cannot prepare any meals yet. I suggest you seek sustenance from the colony."

He turned toward the command section, intent on contacting whoever was manning their comm system this morning. "Guess I'll have to go see what I can find in the complex when the Lieutenant…" he trailed off and looked around the empty cargo hold. "Where's Angel?"

"Angel left to travel to the other colony nine hours, twenty-one minutes ago…"

"What? Why did she do that?"

"She was upset that I would not fly to the colony without your consent and left the ship."

"How am I supposed to find out about my parents if she goes running off before that Maxwell guy gets back here?!" he shouted in frustration. "I've got half a mind to leave her out there!" A hundred different scenarios played out in his head all at the same time. They all ended with a small grey droid being destroyed in one manner or another by a crowd of chanting hate-mongers. He ran toward the command section, "Get us up in the air, now!"

"Preparing for liftoff will require disconnecting an exterior tether."

He stopped mid stride as if he'd struck a wall. "What tether?"

Sabina's image snapped into view in front of him. "The team of men placed a tether made of carbon steel on the forward landing skid while conducting their scan of the ship last night during your absence."

"Blast it all!" Travis cursed, turning back toward the cargo hold.

"I cannot align the ship's weapons back on the ship in that manner," Sabina apologized.

He wanted to roll his eyes, but that would have thrown off his equilibrium enough to send him into a wall as he ran to the cargo hold. "Not what I meant!" he called over his shoulder.

"Sorry Captain," Sabina acknowledged. "However, there is a cutting laser in locker three on your left that should cut through it."

Sure enough, directly to his left was locker three, and amongst the three other boxes of odds and ends he found a very unusual pistol-shaped tool with small lettering on the side that read, 'Godwin'. He ducked into his cabin and started pulling on his EVA suit from yesterday where he'd left it in a pile. After several failed attempts to put it all together, he finally had it situated and clicked the button to activate his helmet. "All right, get the door!"

He dashed back into the cargo bay and down the ramp as it lowered, sliding through the opening as it grew rather than waiting for it to finish.

"On your left," Sabina said in his helmet.

The red sandstorm hit him from the side, knocking him over. The ground hit him hard on the right side as he fell, pulling a choice word out of his mouth. "Holy cow! I think it got worse!"

"The sustained wind speed has remained unchanged, but the peak gusts have increased by an additional eight miles per hour."

He pushed to his feet and steadied himself against the next onslaught. The three landing skids that extended from the bottom of his ship were a bare steel color, contrasting with the midnight blue exterior. Each skid had thick metal arms that linked back into the interior of the ship, but the nose skid was looped with a dark cable that led out into the sands. "You gotta be kidding me," he protested as he knelt with the cutting laser. *Sure hope Godwin cuts fast*, he mused as he struggled to aim it at the cable.

His view instantly darkened the moment he pulled the trigger on the tool, another new trait of his space suit he could be grateful for. He could only hope that there wasn't someone already on the way out to scold him for cutting through the cable and forced himself to get the task done. Normally, there'd be the sound of something happening to accompany the blinding light that cut through the metal cable as thick as his thumb, but the screaming wind demon drowned out everything else around here.

Just as the laser finished cutting through the cable, he grabbed at it to pull it off without thinking it through. "Wow!" he shouted, realizing that the gloves were strong enough to take the intense heat of the glowing cable without melting. "Sure glad I've got these on," he declared, throwing the cable away from the landing gear.

"Captain, hold onto something!" Sabina shouted in his ear.

He grabbed the landing skid as a gust of wind hit him hard enough to have sent him flying backward if it weren't for his death grip. "Oh my God!"

"Captain!" Sabina's voice pleaded in his helmet. "You have to return inside, that gust was in excess of one hundred ten miles per hour!"

"I plan on it," he said, pushing off the landing skid to press against the winds. The sands added serious backing to the wind, pelting his suit and helmet with the particles. The cargo ramp provided enough shelter to walk in a wind shadow until he reached the edge. "You should have closed the ramp!"

"But then you would have to wait for it to deploy," she said while he fought around the side of the ramp onto the surface.

"But… the sand," he protested, out of breath.

"I have the environmental shielding in place to protect against the sands. Once you are safely inside, I will close the ramp again."

He passed through the blue light on a dead run helped by the raging wind behind him. He crashed into the opposite wall and slumped to the floor. "Get us… in the… air," he ordered.

Sabina phased into view in front of him and knelt beside him while the ramp closed behind her. "Are you injured?" she asked, searching his face.

He shook his head, "No."

"I have initiated launch protocol and plotted a course toward Angel's likely destination as you already requested."

"Starship Sapphire, what is your intention?" a man's voice called over the ship's audio system.

"I'm going after my droid," Travis returned, struggling to get his breath back.

"Your… droid?" the unfamiliar voice asked hesitantly. "You may be out of compliance…"

"No," Travis said, shaking his head in annoyance and pushing up to his feet. "It malfunctioned, and I think it's just executing a 'return to home' command."

"What…" the voice asked quietly, as if talking to someone else.

"Hey Travis, this is Wayne, we met last night at the pub. I don't think you want that thing back."

"It's okay," Travis reassured, making his way toward the command section, "it's a battery system, so there's no nuclear…"

"No, I mean, they're telling me we had a nasty solar spike last night. That droid of yours is probably cooked," he hesitated, and Travis could hear someone else in the background talking. "Yeah, I know, alright? It's okay. Hey, sorry. Yeah, after that spike last night, its gotta be fried and extremely hazardous. If you take that thing aboard, you'll be dead in a few hours."

Travis blew out a frustrated sigh on his way to the command section. "Copy that Control. I'll at least find it first just to make sure it isn't an issue for anyone else then." He dropped into his chair and ran his hands through his hair. "I can't believe she did this," he muttered.

"Sorry Sapphire, can you repeat that last?"

His blood ran cold as he tried to think of what to say. He hadn't intended for that to 'go public'. "Just frustrated with the thing, that's all," he said, trying to sound casual. "Sapphire out," he added, hoping to close the dialog by looking at Sabina.

She nodded, "I have muted further communications, but we are still able to receive incoming transmissions."

"Do you have a fix on her location yet?"

"Not yet," she admitted, "the sandstorm is filled with metallic components that are distorting my sensors. I was able to find the colonies due to their size and the radio beacons they employ. Angel is much smaller, so she presents less of a detectable signature."

"Can you find the other colony through this?"

She nodded, "Yes. She had intended upon traveling to the second colony, so it is likely that we may find her en route to the common destination."

Travis looked out the front window at the chaotic swirls of red dancing across the landscape. He glanced at the arm of his suit and noticed how little his suit showed the beating it went through. He let out a sigh, "Makes me wonder how well Angel is doing," he commented.

"Her metal exterior may provide enough protection from these elements, but I am not certain how well she was able to withstand the radiation spike at three o'clock this morning."

"Is there any way you can scan for her?" He turned his attention to the panel in front of him, searching through the various menus. "She should be trying to contact you," he offered.

"I am searching for any form of communication," Sabina stated, "as well as for an irregular metallic signature, or power source."

Travis snapped his fingers, "Her shape! She's a perfect sphere! That should cause a very fixed disturbance in the sandstorm."

"I will search for that as well."

He got out of the chair and walked around the console to stand as close as possible to the main window. "C'mon Angel, where are you?"

AN hour later, Travis stood with one hand against the window, still searching the rushing madness of sand out in front of his ship for Angel. He contemplated having Sabina drop him off to walk on foot and dismissed the idea for the fourth time. If she couldn't find Angel in this, she could lose him as well. Those solar flares that Maxwell guy had talked about sounded like serious business, and he doubted his suit would be able to withstand one. The blowing sand reflected the red light of the sun almost as if they were flying through diluted tongues of fire. "Radiation levels have slowly increased in the last few hours," Sabina's voice commented from behind him.

"I guess that explains the weird haze," he muttered.

"The increased sandstorm activity may also provide some protection from the radiation," she offered.

He sighed. Again. "So, you're saying that the same sandstorm that's keeping us from finding Angel might be keeping her from getting cooked?"

"I'm sorry Captain," Sabina admitted softly, misting into view on his left. "There is just too much interference."

"Take us down to the other Colony," he muttered in defeat.

"Captain?"

He didn't turn away from the window. "I'm hoping that she made it," he said with a negative shake of his head. He didn't believe that, but maybe someone down there could help him find her.

"Beginning descent toward Colony B," she affirmed.

Travis turned and looked into her blue eyes. Genuine remorse filled those eyes that would have been normal on anyone else, but she wasn't a human being. He sulked his way around the console and took his seat, "Thanks for trying," he resigned, unable to hide his disappointment.

"Of course Captain."

"Unidentified craft, we have you on approach," a *very* mechanical voice said over the comm system. "Please state your intentions."

He shot Sabina a puzzled look. "They're using a computer?" he whispered.

"Control, this is Starship Sapphire," she replied smoothly. "We are in search of a lost droid and seeking peaceful entry."

His heart jumped eight feet off the ground inside his chest. There was no telling how they would interpret that. He needed to say something else, anything but announcing a lost droid!

"No droids for sale, entry permitted at your convenience."

He exchanged looks with Sabina. "Well. That was…" he trailed off.

"Highly irregular?" Sabina finished. "I do not believe that I requested to purchase a droid," she offered.

"It's okay," he sighed. "That's gotta be an automated system, instead of a live human operator." He sat back in the chair, "Can't fault the poor thing just because they won't give it enough of a brain to do the job. Even if it sounds like the vocal processor was used as a hammer first." He shook his head, unable to explain what just happened. "That doesn't make any sense though. Why would they use…" He looked back to the window, "A computer?"

"I would assume that an automated entry system would be used in high-traffic areas, or to remove the necessity of acknowledging approaching ships from human schedules."

He shook his head, "You're missing the point." He pointed at the window, "They used illegal tech to broadcast that message." He pulled at his chin, considering the ramifications. No one was supposed to do what they had done. Simulate a human voice, use technology to provide rational choices, and even offer information. "If you weren't standing there, talking to me, I'd say it was the coolest thing ever."

"I appreciate that you find my program superior," she smiled.

"The ship will touch down in ninety-four seconds Captain."

He looked out through the window and blanched. "I can't see anything out there," he complained. The sandstorm was blocking so much light that it looked like they'd traveled to the dark side of the planet just by descending one hundred feet. Instead of dark, swirling sands, he barely made out small patches of light swirling in the darkness now like a negative photo effect. "Wow," he breathed incredulously.

"My scans show an entrance at ground level, and a large flat surface nearby," she informed him. "I do not show any evidence of a delineated landing pad like the one provided at Hadron Beta, sir."

"As long as you can get me close," he shrugged, "sure hope she's inside."

Sabina expertly brought the ship close to the Colony entrance, deployed the landing gear, and set down onto the ground in a single choreographed motion despite the turbulence. Travis smiled at her, "You do that really well."

"Thank you Captain, it is what I was made for," she smiled.

"Any sign of Angel?"

She shook her head, causing her platinum hair to shift, "No, but I will keep looking." Her left eyebrow went up, "Captain, I am detecting a multitude of wireless data transfers in this area. It would appear that these people utilize the technology without reservation."

Travis started toward the cargo bay to leave while Sabina floated beside him, "Good, that means we can keep in constant contact." He rounded the corner and stepped through the doorway to the cargo ramp. "Find Angel, or anything that might be helpful, but don't get yourself caught," he instructed.

Sabina nodded, "The door to the city will be on your right, thirty-two paces from the bottom of the ramp."

He tapped the button to deploy his helmet before he started down the ramp.

"Please be careful."

Travis' stride hitched for a moment, as if he'd caught his toe.

She *sounded* worried; a very human trait normally reserved for humans. "I'll... keep my ears open," he said, pointing to his collar, "in case you need me," he reassured hesitantly.

Was this how the Legion Virus had started? He stepped off the ramp and turned to his right as she'd instructed. *Could it have been somebody's pet program that got overprotective?* He might have to address her emotional attachment at some point, but for right now, finding Angel was more pressing.

Through the howling wind and blinding clouds of sand he occasionally made out a dim patch of light from the red sun above him. Twin beams of light shot forward from his shoulders into the madness but were cut short by the sands only a few feet away. The sands slithered around his feet and ankles in the near-total darkness with every step, the ethereal grip never succeeded in stopping him, but relentless nonetheless. He counted out the hard-fought steps in his head, and as he reached twenty-five a huge wall came into view as if it had suddenly appeared out of nothing. Instead of casting a shadow, the lights from his suit reflected on the heavily scoured surface covered in wet blood. The reality was the red sunlight reflecting off the surface looked like blood, but it was just bare metal. It still *looked like blood* and sent a shiver down his spine.

"Three degrees to your left," Sabina instructed in his helmet. Travis nearly missed her over the roar of the wind. As he pressed his way through the wind for his final seven steps, he saw a large alcove emerge ahead of him. It was recessed into the wall by a few feet, and about twelve feet high, large enough to admit some of the big mining rovers he was used to back home. The sand had formed a sort of ramp that led up to the door, which was almost waist-height above the ground he was walking on. The sands spun around him relentlessly as he closed the distance, grabbing at his feet with every step. He dared to look down and watched his right foot get buried in less than a second before he pulled it free once more. "I think this planet is trying to eat me," he grunted ruefully. Every pause in his stride gave the sands a chance to pile around him, and it only took a second for the sand to reach his ankles. Breathing was work, walking was torture, and he was running out of endurance. If he had tried to walk like he'd been thinking before, he would have been buried alive by this stuff. When he was finally able to reach out his hand and take hold of a steel handle that lined the scarred alcove, it brought a feeling of instant relief as he pulled himself up. The metal plating beneath the shifting sands under his feet helped him brace against a stronger gust of wind that he was sure would have blown him to the ground just a few moments ago. If he was on the ground, the sand would pile over him in a matter of moments…

"Captain, another strong gust of wind is only seconds away! You need to get inside now," Sabina warned, fear in every word.

How had she amplified the helmet unit's speaker like that? "Got it," he confirmed. "I'm not… planning…" he interrupted himself long enough to locate a cover that had been scratched thin by the sandstorms and lifted it, "…to stay out here," he finished as he pressed the large round button beneath it.

A loud *Clank!* sounded ominously over the roaring winds as the doors snapped open a mere three feet. *They'd limited the doors!* Travis realized the danger and threw himself through to his hands and knees only seconds before the doors snapped shut behind him.

"Captain? Are you alright?" Sabina's worried voice asked through his helmet.

"Yeah," Travis responded breathlessly, "they put a limiter on the doors, but the counter must be broken or something. I never heard the warning…"

"Excuse me?" drawled a tall, lanky man in a brown jumpsuit. He looked down at Travis with a modicum of curiosity and contempt that instantly reminded him of Principal Sealns back on Lunar Delta.

"Just… talking myself through," Travis tried, wondering if he should take his helmet off while getting back to his feet. "Really windy out there today," he tried. The fact that the look-alike principal wasn't wearing a helmet told him that he'd be okay without his.

"Indeed," the man slowly replied through tight lips. "Now, what is your business here?" he questioned flatly.

Travis couldn't help the feeling that he'd somehow interrupted something important, although he had no idea what that might be. "Well," he started, turning off his helmet, "I have this project I've…"

"Well then, get on with it," the dour man interrupted, waving him off. Before Travis could try to further his explanation, the man turned on his skinny heels and strode away.

Travis stared after him for a moment in disbelief. "Okay then," he mumbled, and turned his attention to his environment.

It was a *grey conspiracy*, he decided. No one in all the universe used anything besides grey anymore! This place was so grey! Just flat wall panels painted industrial grey. The walls, floors, and ceiling were all the same, boring grey. *Wouldn't want to do anything wild now, like, blue?* That grey pretty much summed up the room he was in. At least, it had been a room at one point. He could tell that it used to be a cargo chamber of sorts, but someone had cut down the walls on three sides to open it up to the network of hallways. These were adorned in flat grey panels as well, with light strips that ran at the top corners of each wall. Each light strip had a white/blue hue to it, which was in sharp contrast to the red glow of the landscape he'd just left outside. While it wasn't familiar, it reminded him of Lunar Delta Colony already. A major difference, he noticed, was that there were no signs detailing which hallways led to what. At that moment, he had a choice to travel down four, no, five different hallways that could lead him practically anywhere! How the…

A glowing image suddenly exploded into view as he approached one hallway, and he recoiled instinctively. The image immediately disappeared in a puff of pixels. He looked around to see if anyone else had noticed his reaction, and inadvertently triggered the image once more. This time, he didn't flinch, and discovered that it was a map of the colony. Or, at least, what he hoped was a map of the colony…

"Captain?" Sabina's voice softly called out from the device on his neck.

"What?"

"Are you alright? I cannot monitor your vitals inside the complex."

Again with the concern… "Yeah, I'm fine," he dismissed, trying to mask his apprehension. "This place is kinda weird," he admitted.

"I detected an electronic transmission in your vicinity…"

"It's just an… auto-map," he explained, hoping the term he'd given it was self-explanatory. "I guess it beats changing the signs on all these hallways," he commented as he continued to look over the image in front of him. "I have no idea where I'm going, and that guy that was here took off like I was space trash or something."

"With your permission, I would like to try and infiltrate their data network to appropriate a working layout of the complex," Sabina asked.

Travis' eyebrow went up, "Um… yeah, what the heck. Give it a try."

"It would appear that no one has reported or logged any kind of stray droid as of yet," she responded. "Apparently the doors to the city are kept closed except for manual entry only. There are no automated exit portals anywhere."

"They don't have like, a… hanger bay or something?" he asked curiously.

"There is what appears to have been a hanger, two levels above you, and thirty degrees to your left, but it is equipped with solid metal doors that are currently closed."

A name on the floating image of multi-colored lines caught his attention. *Burners'*. "Any idea what 'Burners' is?" he asked.

"It appears to be an eatery of some kind," she replied. "'Serving authentic earth cuisine,'" she quoted. Before he knew it, he was already walking down the hallway that should lead him to Burners'. "No one has recorded your arrival yet sir," Sabina noted. "So Angel could be here."

"If this place is anything like Lunar Delta, then I'm going to the right place to find out," he commented.

The eight-foot-high, eight-foot-wide hallway held the same grey as everything else. He passed by several people, mostly dressed in various jumpsuits of different colors, but none of them looked like the soldier type at all. They reminded him of science geeks, teachers, and such. One man was carrying a wide sheet of glass that held words and moving images on it. Travis recognized it from a history lesson where people used to carry around large physical objects in order to interact with technology. *I thought eleven years went by without me, so why does it feel so much like I'm walking around in ancient history?*

Burners' turned out to be a double-door opening on his right with a small sign. Very little had gone into decorating the inside of the cafeteria, which screamed of his past experiences on Lunar Delta. Plain white walls, smooth steel counters and tables, and simple bar stools were everywhere. He shook off the feeling that he was back on Delta.

"What'll ya have?" a disinterested voice called out from the bar. The brogue and tenor of the voice sent goosebumps down his spine. It sounded so much like Liam, he half-expected the big man to be looking at him when he turned to look at the owner of the voice. The stumpy man it belonged to stood no taller than his shoulders. He was built like a cargo crate and looked very much like the type he didn't mess around with. His expression matched his demeanor, which was wearing thin as Travis hesitated.

"Um… What's good for breakfast?" he fumbled, looking around for a list.

"Breakfast," the man shot back, and walked back toward a metal contraption built into a wall.

Okay then, Travis thought to himself. *Guess I'm having….* His thoughts degraded as he realized that the man was getting something from an Auto-Vendor. *Great. Atomically generated eggs and…*

The thin white plastic tray that clattered down in front of him consisted of a square plastic plate with something that was supposed to resemble a lumpy yellow substance, and a slice of warmed 'bread' with 'butter' on it. *Eleven years disappear in the blink of an eye, and I'm still eating the same...*

"Oh my God!" A woman's voice exclaimed from somewhere off to his right. It sounded like something important, and he turned in the hopes that it might involve Angel. Across the room, a woman with black hair and a pixie face with stark blue eyes was staring back at him in utter shock as if she were seeing a ghost.

For a moment, he was standing in a familiar apartment on Lunar Delta, looking into those wide, twinkling blue eyes. The angle was wrong, however, and he found that he was looking across the room… and down. He knew she hadn't shrunk, but the fact was, he had grown since then. Her smooth black hair still flowed down to her waist, except that a few stubborn ribbons of grey had worked their way into the waterfall since he'd last seen her. Her small mouth was parted in shock as she stared back at him, frozen by emotion and disbelief.

"Mom?" he whispered.

The distance between them evaporated in an instant, and her little arms were wrapped around him at his elbows just as far as they could go. Tears poured from her eyes while her words fumbled to get past the vast array of emotions that flooded her face. 'How,' 'when,' 'forgive me,' all seemed to become mashed together as she tried so hard to form the words that were all struggling for release at the same time.

She still smelled like flowers and dirt, just the way he remembered. Her arms were too small, but that feeling of comfort still enveloped him. "I missed you mom," he choked out.

She pushed back, "Let me have a look at you," she sobbed, looking him up and down. "You look healthy enough," she commented with that same unmistakable accent that always sounded so proper. Then she paused, and her left eyebrow arched the exact same way it had when he was six. He was in trouble, there was no denying it. He hadn't listened, and in his carelessness, he had knocked over her ancient chemistry tubes she had kept on display in the foyer of their cubicle. This time, however, he was looking down at her, even though it felt like she was the one looking down. "How do you look so young?" she prodded. "I'm going grey, but you don't look much over… mid-twenties? You're… thirty-three!"

Travis let out a guilty sigh, "I think I hit light speed instead of…" he mumbled. "I…"

"No!" she gasped.

He nodded, surprised that she knew what he'd alluded to, "Yeah, I didn't really know until it was too late." He looked into her tear-soaked eyes. "Sorry mom…"

Those eyes shifted instantly. "You don't owe me anything," she corrected. "Especially an apology. If anything, I should be apologizing to you."

Now his eyebrow went up, "What for?"

"I left you," she admitted, her voice cracking as she took the stool next to his. "I abandoned you when you were a baby…"

"I was ten," he pointed out. "I wasn't a baby mom."

"Yes, and I can still see that determined look on your little face as you watched me leave, trying so hard not to cry." Her voice broke, and he offered her the napkin that had come with his forgotten tray of food.

"You had a duty…"

"My *duty* was to raise my son," she corrected. "Not run off to this barren wasteland to help a bunch of ungrateful people."

"But you and dad were…"

"Yes," she admitted, waving the comment off as if it were of no consequence. "We were drafted, but that did not mean I should have left you there. We were sent here to help these people, but instead, we became part of the problem. I'm just glad you didn't come with me."

"I thought I wasn't allowed to go," he reminded her.

"You weren't," she breathed out a sigh that came from deep inside. "That trip cost me too much…" she trailed off in thought for a moment. "You, your father, my commission…"

Travis was just beginning to feel his stomach rumble again and thought about the cold 'toast' on his plate when he heard 'father'. "Where is dad?" he asked, looking around. "Probably…"

"He died on the way here," she revealed softly, putting her

hand on his forearm. "I'm sorry…"

The face of Randall Harding, a young man with a fuzzy brown mustache and serious eyes came rushing back from a dusty memory of his father he'd long put behind him. Speechless, he sat there, looking at the tasteless meal that still sat in front of him.

"There was an accident on the ship," she recalled. "I don't even know what really happened." A sigh, partially choked with memory came next before she added, "All I know is that he was working on a project with some other men that involved a new type of harvester for a mineral when a fight broke out. They told me Randy was shot trying to calm the situation."

"What did it do?" Travis asked numbly.

She looked into his eyes. "You look so much like him," she whispered.

"You gonna eat that?" the man behind the counter cut in rudely.

"That's crap," Travis retorted without thinking. "I wouldn't eat that if you paid me."

"Travis!" his mother corrected.

"Oy!" the man rebuked, genuinely shocked.

Travis shoved the tray back and stood up. "I ate better out of the recyclers on Lunar Delta fifteen years ago," he spat out. "I can't believe you can't do any better than that." He didn't wait for a response but turned on his heel toward the door. "Sabina, any luck finding Angel?" he asked, pushing the door open.

"No, not yet captain," she responded. "I have located a merchant where you may be able to procure provisions for the ship," she added.

His mother fell in beside him. "It's a co-op," she explained, struggling to keep up. "You'll need something to barter."

Travis started down the hallway toward the co-op and considered what he might have to barter with. "You wouldn't have seen a grey, spherical droid floating about here since yesterday, would you?" he asked over his shoulder.

"No," she answered. "Is that Angel?"

"Yeah," he nodded. "She took off last night from Hadron Beta…"

"'Took off'?"

He nodded, "She's… a little temperamental."

"Sounds like someone I'd like to meet."

"Maybe you could make sense of why she acts like she does sometimes," he mumbled. "I just hope I find her before she gets herself in trouble."

She put her hand on his arm and drew him into a side hallway. "Travis," she said, looking over his shoulder conspiratorially as someone walked by. "Did you make an artificial intelligence program?" she whispered.

He looked down into her soft blue eyes, realizing his mistake. He wanted to trust her, but could he? "No," replied.

Her eyes narrowed slightly, "So what are you *not* telling me about *her*?"

He looked into the corner of the alcove to find his answer and found only cobwebs and garbage piled there. *How had spiders managed to find a home here?* "I didn't *make* her, she just… *is*," he admitted.

She looked at him for a long moment, then tugged him back toward the main hallway again. "Come on, let's get those supplies so you can get back to finding her."

The 'Co-op' consisted of a large circular space that had an equally circular raised platform in the center as a stage. Hallways and other doors adorned the plain outer walls all around the room. Makeshift placards were stuck to the walls in some places, where others had floating holograms advertising the wares contained in the haphazard setups. He saw people selling a wide variety of items, from ion shielding to freshly made bread. The latter appealed to his stomach, but his mother warned him away. "Don't bother," she explained. "'Freshly made' means it comes straight from the recycler. What you want is over there," she pointed four doors down at a pink sign with a green sphere floating in front of it. "Jesse's a little strange, but he knows how to make real food."

"Morning Jesse," she called out brightly through the open doorway.

A thin man of great height stepped into view inside and raised a metal spoon in greeting. "Morning right back at ya Annika," he drawled out. His long, blonde, wavy hair looked like it had never been washed, his pale complexion had a strange bronze coloring, and a very potent aroma drifted from inside to tickle Travis' nose. "Whassup?" he paused and tilted his head slightly while studying Travis. "Hey, welcome stranger," he added in a slow greeting, setting the big spoon down to walk toward them. "Like, what can I do ya for?"

He extended his hand in greeting, and Travis accepted it, not wanting to make an enemy. "Travis Harding," he said in introduction. "I'm told you know what real bread is," he tried.

The man chuckled in an odd manner Travis had never heard before. "Real. Like for sure," he chimed, turning to a table a few steps away. "These guys…" he paused to nod toward Travis' mother, "with a few exceptions, wouldn't know what's real if you hit 'em with it." He picked up a metal box that turned out to have no bottom. Inside, a rectangular loaf of spongy, light brown bread had been hiding its aroma from the rest of the room.

Travis could feel his mouth watering instantly and had to consciously stop himself from reaching out and plucking the bread off the table. "That looks delicious," he admitted.

"I call it 'whole grain'," Jesse announced. "Made from the stuff I grow right here," he said, motioning toward the back of the space.

"You *grow* this?" Travis asked, perplexed.

Jesse nodded, "Yeah man." He motioned for them to follow him. "I had to fight the council pretty hard to get it, but…" he opened a door in the back wall, revealing a large space behind it. Inside, brilliant white light shone down from a high ceiling, and a musty smell permeated the air. Green leaves that jutted up from the dirt pulled him through the door to investigate. Blades, hand-shaped wide leaves, and others that he had no idea what to compare them with were sprouting from the very ground!

"What is all this?" he asked, bewildered.

"A lot of it is soybeans," Jesse commented. "I've got some other stuff in here, all growing the way our mother intended."

Travis shot a mildly suspicious look back toward his own mother while Jesse continued. "Yeah man, we might be stuck out here, a long ways from her, but that don't mean we shouldn't do everything she taught us to."

The suspicion turned to confusion, but a clicking sound next to his face drew his attention to the com-link. He held up a finger to petition Jesse to wait while he asked quietly, "What is it Sabina?"

"Captain, I've infiltrated every level of Hadron Prime and I do not believe that Angel is here."

"Woah," Jesse droned. "Who's that?" he asked, peering toward Travis' collar.

"Sabina's my... friend," Travis said cautiously.

"She's got, like, a cool voice," Jesse smiled.

"Thanks Sabina, keep looking just in case she shows up," Travis instructed toward his collar.

"Jesse, we need some supplies for my son's ship," Travis' mother interjected, "he needs to get back out there to find his friend."

He nodded. "Okay, like... a rescue mission. I can totally get behind that," Jesse commented. He hurriedly turned back inside, not waiting for them to follow. "I've got some soya already packaged up in here," he called over his shoulder. "Since you probably don't have the right light to grow your own stuff, I'll set you up with..." he interrupted himself with a grunt to move a heavy crate, "this. It's all set to run through a recycler and should give you several months of level one meals." He stopped suddenly and turned to give Travis a considering look. "Wait a minute," he shot a look at Annika, "that's your son?" He shook his head, "Like, where you been man? I know I haven't seen you 'round here before."

"Actually," Travis smiled, "I just got here yesterday."

"Did anyone else come with?" Jesse pressed curiously.

Travis shook his head, "No. Probably a good thing since I used light speed to get here."

"My son is now eleven years younger than he was before," Annika added.

Travis shot her a curious look, knowing she'd just misspoke. She shrugged back at him, and he decided it wasn't worth getting into.

Jesse was staring at him, "Woah man." He considered what he'd heard a moment then continued, "Well, you ain't leaving for a couple days with this storm…" he trailed off, suddenly remembering something. "Right! Storm! We gotta get you back out there to find your friend before this thing gets really bad!" he turned back to the crate.

Travis stepped in beside him to help him move it onto a round disk that hovered over the floor. "I'm not sure what I can offer you in return," he said cautiously.

Jesse shot a smile at Travis' mother, "You don't owe me nothin' man. You got a great mother here, and most of us here owe her way more than what we can give back. Even if some of us don't realize it yet."

When Annika looked back to Travis, she gave him a wink. "You have a lot to catch up on young man," she chided.

"So I see," Travis admitted. He started toward the door that led back into the main arena, deftly leading the once-heavy crate with one hand as it drifted along, hovering over the floor on the two-foot disk. He stopped to turn and shake Jesse's hand once more, this time initiating the exchange. "Thank you, I really appreciate this," he said gratefully.

"I hope you find your friend," Jesse returned.

As they briskly walked down the main hallway again, Travis tapped on the crate, "So, what's in here?"

"It's freshly grown soybeans mostly," his mother answered.

"There are enough provisions in this crate to feed a crew of five for four months of travel according to the crate's data log," Sabina offered.

Travis rounded the last hallway and approached the main door once again that led outside. "Well, since it's only me, and I don't even know where we're going once we find Angel…" He stopped long enough to tap the button on his collar, deploying his helmet-shield, "It should be fine," he added.

Annika approached a flat wall and tapped in a code on a keypad that had been out of sight until she approached. A light clicking sound preceded a section of the wall partially opening before she grasped it to swing it away. Inside, several white environmental suits hung on racks awaiting occupants. "Just give me a minute, and I'll…"

"I got this," Travis interrupted. "You should stay here where it's safe."

"Do you honestly think you can leave me here young man?" she rebuked. "My son shows up in my life again after all these years and thinks he can run off and leave me behind?" she muttered aloud, pulling out one of the suits by a handle that kept it on the rack.

"I, uh…" Travis fumbled.

"Just help me get this on," she instructed sternly.

He smiled, resigning himself to obeying his mother. The suits were exactly the same as the suits on Delta, and his hands knew what to do without thinking.

"You're pretty good at this," Annika observed as he set the helmet down over her head.

"You get pretty used to it in the Lunar Mines," Travis admitted.

She sighed, checking the suit's display mounted on her right arm, "I should've known that's where they would put you." Satisfied with the results, she shook her head, "I wanted so much better for you."

"We gotta watch these stupid doors, they're on a short-cycle timer," Travis warned as he walked across the space to the door's control button.

"Captain, I will override the door's sequence, and allow you both to pass through before it is closed again," Sabina interrupted.

"Thanks," Travis smiled. "Sure beats getting pinched!"

Travis tapped the large round red button with his gloved

hand. The door snapped open with a *crack!* and a green light he hadn't seen before engaged on the inside. It had to be some sort of environmental shield, but it didn't do anything to block the roaring sound of the storm outside. "You sure about this?" Travis shouted as sand began to billow through.

Annika gave her son a frown and started pushing the crate through the door into the darkness. Travis shook his head and put his hands to the task, grateful that the door wouldn't suddenly close on them. It wasn't that the crate had become heavy, but that the wind was trying to push it to one side, and the carry-disk only provided a hovering function. It didn't have any directional abilities, because that would probably violate some heretical nut's anti-artificial intelligence vow. Or at least, that was the only reason that Travis could come up with at the time to ease his practical mind. *It really wouldn't take that much to do it right*, he thought wryly.

The storm seemed worse now than when he'd gone in, if that were even possible. "Sabina, you gotta talk us through this. I can't see a thing out here," he prompted.

"Twelve degrees to your right," she advised.

"Really?" he returned, "I thought…"

"Captain, you are currently on a course that will cause you to walk by the ship by fifty feet and I doubt you would even see it."

"Twelve degrees it is then…"

"Who are you talking to?" Annika shouted into her radio.

"Sabina," he admitted, nodding forward.

Annika shook her head, "Two women?"

"What?" He responded, trying to deflect the question.

His mother didn't push, but he knew more questions were forthcoming. When Sabina closed the ramp and the roar of the sandstorm was behind them, Travis breathed a sigh of relief. "Sabina, where do I put this?"

"In this storage compartment," Sabina replied without appearing. A three-foot high door panel near his cabin door slid to the side, revealing a storage compartment just large enough for the crate. "It is fortunate that the crate isn't any larger, or it would need to be unpacked first," she commented.

He tilted the crate off the disk and started shoving it into the opening, "I need you to get the ship ready for takeoff, we need to…"

"Already done Captain," she returned, "but you should know that Lieutenant Maxwell is outside the ship and trying to gain your attention."

"What?" Travis asked in bewilderment. "How'd he get here?"

"His rover is parked nearby," she offered.

"You'd better get him in here," Travis ordered. "Nobody should be out in this for very long."

"What have you been up to?" Annika asked suspiciously as the ramp lowered to the ground again.

"I promise I'll tell you afterward," Travis said sideways as Lieutenant Maxwell, dressed in his white uniform and shiny helmet jogged up the ramp, allowing Sabina to close it back up right away. Once the door was fully closed, he tapped the side panel button that snapped open his visor, revealing his concerned face. "I found your droid," he announced. "It's about two klicks bearing two-eight-four from here, and it's in trouble."

"Sabina?" Travis prompted urgently.

The sound of a hum from the ship's engines and the shifting of the floor beneath his feet accompanied Sabina's voice, "I'm on it Captain."

There was only one thing on Travis' mind now, and he walked briskly to the command section to look out the main window. The wind direction was blowing at them, and combined with the speed Sabina was maintaining, the effect looked like they were plowing through the sand on the ground instead of flying. His mother and Lieutenant Maxwell arrived behind him just in time for the ship to suddenly slow without warning. "I see her," Sabina commented, "I will set the ship down as close as I can."

Without excusing himself, Travis brushed by his visitors and ran toward the cargo bay. He engaged his helmet on the move, and Sabina started opening the door as the ship lowered to the ground. "Which way?" he asked.

"Straight in front of you, five meters out," Sabina returned.

The wind tried to blow him over at the bottom of the ramp, revealing that Sabina had set the ship down as a windbreak. He saw the grey sphere when he was only a few feet away, tucked against a small outcropping of rock and half-buried in the sand. The exposed part of her was severely etched by the blowing sands. "Angel!" he called out.

She didn't respond, and Travis' fears rocketed him forward. He dropped to his knees and started pulling sand away from Angel's inert form. Without warning, a pair of white gloved hands followed suit, and in a few moments, they had pulled away enough sand to be able to move the droid.

"Captain, Angel does not show any signs of activity," Sabina advised him.

"What happened to her?"

"It would appear that she ran out of electrical power," Sabina returned. "She does not respond, and I do not detect any energy signatures."

"How do we get this thing on the ship?" Lieutenant Maxwell shouted.

Angel wasn't a thing! How could he say something so harsh? Travis wanted to correct him but caught himself. "Without the levitation, she's going to be really heavy," he shouted back.

Lieutenant Maxwell turned to face him for a moment, and Travis could feel the man considering something behind that silver face shield. "Team lift," he returned, and pumped his arms across his chest twice. "You ready?"

Travis nodded, not bothering to mirror the man's physical gesture. He began to stoop down, when Sabina's voice erupted inside his energy helmet. "Captain! Stop!"

Travis straightened and waved off the Lieutenant. "What?"

"Angel has been subjected to three separate solar flares," Sabina replied. "Unlike the sand, her body has absorbed enough radiation that she will inadvertently transfer it onto your suit. If she is brought on board, the entire cargo bay will be irradiated beyond my capacity to decontaminate it."

Travis looked down at the lifeless orb lying on the ground, watching helplessly as the billowing sands mercilessly began to bury Angel once more. "What do you want me to do? Leave her here!?"

"What?" Lieutenant Maxwell shouted. "What's the matter?"

"Sabina says she's radioactive now!" he shouted back over the storm. "We can't touch her!"

"My suit's protected," he shouted. "I can't lift it by myself, but I can roll it!"

Travis snapped his fingers as an idea came to him, "And I've still got that lift from the crate…"

"Wait a minute!" Lieutenant Maxwell cut in. "It's not like the radiation just magically disappears once we get inside!"

Travis wanted to hit something. "I hate this damn planet!" he shouted.

The big man reached up and tapped a panel on the side of his helmet, rendering the visor clear. "I've got shielded crates back at the Base," he pointed out. "Does your ship have anything like that? Maybe we could get it back that way."

Travis looked through the clear visor and saw a measure of compassion on the man's face. "Captain, the food crate you brought aboard is lined to protect the contents. Your mother is already removing the contents as I speak," Sabina broke in.

Lieutenant Maxwell looked around his helmet quickly before shooting a look at Travis, "I think your ship just copied me on that."

"Yes Lieutenant, I did. It seemed pointless at this time to withhold information."

A slightly puzzled look came over his face, but he nodded, "Appreciated."

"Travis?" Annika called over the comm.

"Yeah?"

"I found a few smaller pods to put this in," she replied, sounding like she was already moving. "I'll have it empty in a minute."

The lieutenant shot a look up into the dark, roaring sands, then down at his left wrist. "We got about five minutes before that thing up there cooks us down here," he warned. "Whether we've got it on board or not, you and I will be."

Travis started plowing his way back through the tempest toward the ship, "Then we've gotta work fast."

Seconds ticked by while he and his unexpected ally retrieved the crate and positioned it next to Angel's inert sphere. The door swung to the side and the sand began gleefully swirling into the empty space. Lieutenant Maxwell waved him off and shoved Angel into the crate, "Get that door closed!"

Travis swung the door shut and fought his way back to the ship. A quick curse turned his attention backward to find the big man on his knee. "Hey! You alright?" He reached to help the Lieutenant back to his feet, but the big man waved him off again.

"You can't touch the suit, or you'll get dosed," he pointed out. "I'll have to strip it off before I can come inside."

Travis felt his brain melt. How could the Lieutenant strip out of his suit outside the ship?

"Lieutenant, I can accommodate you inside the cargo bay. There is no need to subject yourself to the harsh conditions outside."

"You sure?"

"Yes, please come inside the ship, the flare is eighty-three seconds from touchdown!"

The ramp lifted under their feet as they ran up inside the ship. Every door in the room was closed, including the hallway to the front of the ship. "As you are all aware, the Lieutenant's suit is now potentially harmful," Sabina announced. A soft mist and breeze filled the room around them, "This application will render the crate and the captain's suit clean, but as you already stated, I will require you to remove your outer suit Lieutenant."

Travis looked around and balked, "Mom?"

"I'm in here," her voice called from behind a door.

"The doctor is in the hallway to the command section Captain at my request. It seemed prudent to reduce the possibility of her contamination."

He turned a grateful look toward the big man, finally starting to wonder why he had helped him. "Sabina, do you have something for him to wear?" he asked.

"I got my usual clothes underneath man," he said with a shake of his head. "It's not like I'm going commando under this or nothing."

Travis shrugged, "Of course not." He shook his head and started toward the closed hallway door, "But we'll need something for you to wear out of the ship."

"I do not have any other EVA suits for the Lieutenant," Sabina returned. "I apologize that I am not better prepared for you."

"Don't sweat it," John said. "Not like you were expecting to put clothes on all of us."

"How is this going to work?" Travis pressed.

"You will need to exit the cargo bay. The Lieutenant will then need to strip out of his outer layer while I maintain a light mist of decontamination compound to hold the radioactivity from drifting. Please be careful in disrobing Lieutenant and try not to touch the outer layer with your hands."

John smirked, "Wasn't planning on it."

Travis pushed the cargo crate to the side and tipped it up enough to let the disk slide out from underneath it. "Okay, I'll get outta here and let you do your thing."

"Hey."

Travis turned back at the door to face his unexpected accomplice.

"You know you're gonna have to be straight with me about that, right?" John asked while pointing at the crate.

He nodded slowly, dreading the reaction he knew was coming.

T RAVIS tapped the button that disengaged his helmet and leaned back against the hallway wall with a sigh.

"Are you going to tell me what all of this is now?" Annika pressed firmly as she removed her helmet and shook out her hair.

He looked down into those blue eyes and saw the concern behind her stern facade. *How much could he tell her?* "Angel isn't artificial intelligence," he said quietly.

Annika's thin left eyebrow raised slightly, "Go on."

He pushed off the wall, "She's... difficult to explain."

"Believe me, I've seen quite a bit living in that colony, so you had better try right now."

He thought a moment, and as he did, his hunger started to resurface. "Sabina, I need coffee or something," he asked.

"I can produce that for you now," Sabina responded, materializing in the hallway in front of him. "There is a cup of coffee waiting for you on the bridge."

"Is that what you call that section?" he asked distractedly, starting down the hallway.

"Oh good Lord," Annika blurted out. "What have you done?"

He turned around as he realized it was his mother's first time seeing Sabina. "She's..."

"You can't very well tell me she's not an artificial intelligence program," she bit out while looking Sabina up and down. "Although I can say you did a fantastic job of making her look real enough."

"Thank you Doctor," Sabina accepted. "The captain is not actually responsible for my appearance, nor is he party to my development. Angel transformed my program into the woman you see now."

Annika's thin black eyebrows went up while her eyes drifted around Sabina to Travis. "You have a lot more explaining to do."

"I would be happy…"

Annika cut Sabina off with a raised hand, "He will have to answer me. Not you."

Sabina nodded, "Yes ma'am."

The promise of coffee and a possible distraction pulled him back toward the front of the ship.

"Don't you run off on me now young man," his mother corrected, following close on his heels.

"I'm not…"

"Sabina, I think you'd better make that two cups," Annika instructed without turning.

"Yes ma'am," she responded politely. "Yours is waiting in the same place."

"Thank you," Annika replied sharply. "How is the lieutenant getting on?"

"Lieutenant Maxwell is inside a cabin and changing into a new jumpsuit meeting his desired color scheme. I have switched off video monitoring of his cabin to affect his privacy in accordance with the captain's instructions."

"You told her not to look in on him?" Annika accused as she rounded the corner into the bridge behind her son.

"No ma'am," Sabina interjected. "The captain informed me that humans prefer privacy while changing attire. I am simply trying to see to the lieutenant's comfort."

Travis waited to allow his mother to pick one of the identical cups before he picked up the remaining one. "But he's alright physically?" he clarified.

"Yes Captain," Sabina replied smoothly. "I have detected no anomalies in his system while he was disrobing, and any exposure to the radiation was successfully mitigated with the application of the decontamination mist."

"Thank-you for that," Annika said over the rim of her cup. She took a sip and visibly relaxed. "This is good coffee," she breathed.

"Yeah," Travis agreed.

"Now, you need to start explaining things before we have company young man," Annika reminded him with a serious look.

Travis scratched at his forehead, "So, The Sapphire kinda came this way," he started. "I - I mean, Liam, found Angel and asked me to help him with her…"

"What do you mean, 'The Sapphire came this way'?"

"They found the ship adrift a couple days ago," he tried, "and when I rebooted the system, *she* showed up," he said, pointing at Sabina. "Although, I don't remember that she was quite so well-rounded now that I think about it…"

His mother smiled and shook her head wistfully, "Okay, I need you to start back just before you found Angel, Sapphire, Sabina or Liam," she pressed.

Travis took another sip of coffee, "Okay." He nodded, "So a few days ago, Liam comes to me… no, wait a minute." He paused long enough to correct himself, "I guess I went to the Cargo Bay at his request."

"Where were you?" Annika probed.

"Oh," he realized, "We were on the Phantom then," he recalled. "So he led me over to this locker and pulls out this… box." He wondered how he could show her the computer without actually taking her back to the cargo hold just to prove his point.

"Keep going," she instructed.

"Okay," he nodded, "It was obviously some dirty old computer, but he told me that he thinks some girl's inside it. I told him there's no way there was anybody inside, but he swore that some girl was talking to him through the monitors in the cargo hold because of it. I told him to meet me in the shuttle bay so I could hook it up to a separate system to keep it off the radar, and that's how we ended up in here."

"Keep going," Annika encouraged when his eyes started to drift to the floor.

"The rest of the crew attacked us almost right away and Liam died trying to fend them off. I still don't know what tipped them off…"

Annika shifted to look into his eyes and encourage him forward.

"I was trying to get the ship up and outta there when Angel showed up and took over."

"The droid?"

"No, I mean, Angel showed up on the computer system here," he indicated with a sweep of his hand. "She was in everything, and even started shooting at the soldiers while she kept yelling 'OW!'"

"The *computer* was yelling 'ow'?"

"Yeah!" Travis nodded, "I know, right? It was so weird. Anyway, we finally got out of the ship, and then she did this thing with the ship where we went from one place to another through a ring of light. Next thing I know, we're flying into Saturn, and she's acting like she just woke up!"

"And that's *her*?" Annika asked slowly, while pointing at Sabina.

He shook his head, "She didn't show up until after this point."

"Who didn't show up?" Maxwell asked, turning the corner. "Is that coffee?" he asked, interrupting himself.

Sabina pointed to the small alcove built into the wall where a cup appeared with steaming dark coffee inside. "I am happy to provide you with one as well," she offered kindly.

John picked up the white paper cup and smelled the contents. "That's good," he observed. He shot Travis a look over the rim as he took a sip.

Travis was on the spot, and he felt like it too. "Um, *she* didn't," he said, pointing at Sabina. "It was shortly after I rebooted the computer to get the ship running again that she appeared." The lieutenant continued to stare at him, pressing for more information. "Then there was the life support failure, and after I sent Angel out to fix it, we ended up here."

John stopped lifting his cup to his lips and shot another look at Sabina. "Wait a minute," he straightened as if readying for a fight. "You're…"

Sabina shook her head and backed away, "I am Sabina, and I am not a real woman."

His look darkened, "What the heck is going on here?"

"The captain is not to blame for my existence," she said. "I can assure you that I have no agenda other than to provide help and support..."

John set the cup back down and glared at Travis. "What have you done?"

Travis backed away, "It's a long story, but the point is that she's not the Legion Virus."

"How would you know?"

"Because my son is just like his father," Annika defended. "Randy always pressed the boundaries and believed in using every advantage available for the good of people. He died trying to protect others, and my son is just trying to do the same."

An unexpected smile turned the corner of John's mouth. "I see you found your momma."

"Is that why you came out here?"

He nodded, "I told you I'd look into it and tell you in the morning. Finding your droid-thing on the way there was just dumb luck." He shot a wary look at Sabina. "Until such time as he explains all this, don't you go answering for him, got it?"

Sabina nodded, but Travis answered, "Sabina has been very helpful, and done everything she can to arrange for your safety, our safety, and you wanna treat her like that?"

John lifted his coffee, "It's because she's been so helpful that I'm not calling in a strike order on this ship." He sipped, then turned an even look at Travis. "I'm about your only ally on this planet, besides momma bear here. Most of these guys would burn you at the stake and blow this ship apart just because she's standing there."

Travis sighed, "Yeah. No surprise there. Prejudice never shows any reason, does it?"

John's dark eyes locked on his, but the look wasn't hateful. "No."

"Now that you've interrupted us," Annika quipped while looking John over. "Do you mind very much if my son finishes answering my questions?"

John smiled down at her, "My apologies ma'am. I do believe my manners left the room for a minute." He turned a wry look at Travis, "Well? Don't keep your mother waiting now."

He watched the exchange between the two of them while calculating his response. He needed to get Angel power, but that meant handling a radioactive sphere. Then there was the problem of getting her out of that same sphere and into something else. "I need to get Angel powered back up," he muttered to Sabina. "Any ideas?"

"I believe you were telling me how she went out and fixed the life support?" Annika pressed.

"Wait a minute. You're telling me she went and fixed your life support?" He pointed at Sabina, "I thought she..."

"No, I sent Angel out," Travis corrected, pointing down the hallway carefully, "that's Sabina, the ship's computer."

"Got it," he admitted, "but how did your levitating 'test bed' go out and *fix your life support*?" he pressed.

"Honey, what aren't you telling us?" Annika probed.

Travis started to pace, trying to think of a way out of this. "Okay, look, before your guys start shouting again, let me be perfectly clear: I didn't make either one of them, got it?" To his relief, both his mother and John nodded. "Like I told my mom, I found Angel in the computer a few days ago. She'd taken over everything but didn't seem to know what to do. She was lost, clueless, and had no idea how to operate the ship. When I found the ship computer's backup, I put Angel in the service droid in case the ship's computer program tried to classify her as a virus."

John jerked a thumb back toward the rear of the ship, "So why'd it take off like that?"

Travis shrugged, "I don't know, really. She's like a teenage girl with a funky accent. Half the time I don't even know what she's thinking."

"So it killed itself," John observed. "Great. That just leaves her, but I don't think she's a problem unless other folks around here see her."

"She's not an 'it'," Travis protested. "I don't know how to explain it, but she's like a girl trapped in the computer." He set his cup down with just enough restraint to keep it from spilling, "Look, I know it doesn't make any sense," he held up his hand to keep the lieutenant from speaking, "it didn't make any sense to me either. I don't know how else to explain it, and she's not looking for a fight. She doesn't want to take over the world or kill anybody." A thought occurred to him, "You should've heard her cry when they shot Liam."

"I've heard enough," Annika put in. "Sabina, take us back to Hadron Prime, and land on the opposite side near the North Access Doors."

Sabina looked at Travis for approval, and he shrugged, "Yeah, go ahead."

"What are you planning?" John asked, giving Annika a look as the ship shifted beneath his feet.

She took a long sip of her coffee before she answered, "Helping my son."

Four hours later, the three of them sat around a large table in Annika's lab on elevated stools made from carbon steel. The four-legged contraptions weren't elegant, but that hadn't mattered when the ship had first launched to escape the Apocalypse. Bright white light washed down over the utilitarian decor from long strips overhead. The standard issue grey walls, floor and ceiling held no significance other than being boring.

"How does she normally charge?" Annika asked, looking back toward the glass-enclosed corner of her huge lab where the grey sphere sat. Three different cables dangled at random from the sphere back to the walls, but there had been no signs of life thus far.

Travis thought for a moment, "You know. I really don't know the answer to that." He looked at the glass cage listlessly, finally realizing the irony of the placement of his mother's collection of plants right next to a space meant to work with hazardous materials.

Sabina's blue form hovered over a lab counter across from Travis. She had no ability to move her image around the room here due to the limited equipment. She heard everything they said, and even saw through the single camera in the room. "The droid body typically remains charged by induction, or solar exposure."

"Then how come it went dead out there?" Maxwell asked.

"I would surmise that the severity of the sandstorm was too great to capture the necessary amount of sunlight to recharge the system," she returned.

"That is something that we run into every time we try to capture solar power here," Annika said. "Even though Centauri is up for almost six days straight, the solar radiation just doesn't seem to produce anything besides death." She pushed her mashed potatoes around on the plate in front of her listlessly. "It's either the wrong kind of radiation, or the color just doesn't produce very much. We still haven't figured out which. Not to mention trying to keep the panels functional in the constant sandstorms."

"So how do you keep all this running?" Travis asked, looking around the room.

"Wind farms," Annika and Maxwell said simultaneously. They smiled at each other before he shrugged, "What? I'm not just a stupid soldier you know."

"No one here ever thought that," she reassured him.

Travis looked down at the simple meatloaf and mashed potatoes that remained on his plate. He knew he should eat more than he had, but he just didn't have the appetite. "Sabina, any change in Angel's status?"

"None as of yet," she answered softly.

Maxwell stood up to pace, feeling the tension in the room. "You know, I didn't come here to help you get your droid back," he admitted.

"I appreciate it..." Travis started.

"Let me finish," Maxwell interrupted, turning a serious face toward him.

"Sorry."

"I'm actually here because we have a bigger problem," he admitted with a look toward Annika. "Those boneheads in Blue Squad have it in their heads to invade this place."

"What?" Annika asked in shock.

He nodded, "Yep. They'll come charging in here and tear the place up 'till they find the artificial intelligence machine they think you guys are making in here."

Travis' fork clattered to the plate. "So, what? They just run in here and start a fight over a computer program that *might* exist?"

Maxwell nodded and walked toward the glass cage to look in at the lifeless sphere on the ground with cables stuck into it. "And *that* might be exactly what they need to make them feel justified," he pointed out solemnly. He turned, and pointed at Sabina, "Or her."

Travis breathed out a frustrated sigh, "What a bunch of…"

"They're afraid," Annika pointed out. "They wouldn't grasp what I'm doing here, and they see anything else besides their approach as dangerous." She pushed the plate away, and rose to her feet, "It's why most of them left in the first place. They had a serious difference of opinion on process and procedures, so we helped them establish their own colony about ten years ago." She sighed heavily, "They're not alone, most of the residents here don't even like the lights that I made for Jessie."

"The lights?"

Annika smiled at him, "Yes. I created those lights to simulate the proper amount of UV radiation and light to promote better horticultural growth. Jessie is the only person who wanted any part of it, and his ability to grow things is quite remarkable." She shook her head, "But the rest of the bloody council thinks it's too dangerous to use and won't let me reproduce them for the rest of the ship. I could have plants growing everywhere in here. but these idiots won't even accept anything besides the old type of light source from the day the ship launched!"

"Why's that?" John asked.

She shrugged, "Probably because I had to build a different type of filament from what they were used to, and the simple fact that it is different. God knows how much they hate anything different." Another sigh, "That food source alone has extended the life span of the residents by at least thirty years."

Travis blanched, "Reproduced toxins?"

"What's that?" John asked.

"The auto-vendors can only reproduce things so long before the source material that gets recycled contains too many toxins to be considered edible," Travis explained. "You have to replace it eventually or it starts to poison you."

"That's why you guys have been shipping us those 'care packages' over the years."

Annika nodded, "Yes. Some of us couldn't stand the thought

that you might die of malnutrition when we had the ability to remedy the problem." A smile crossed her face, "That same group has been slipping Jessie's produce into the food supply here for the past five years without notice. Although, I can't believe they haven't realized the difference in the resident's health."

"So why'd the people in Hadron Beta leave in the first place?"

She nodded, "Actually, most of the residents of Hadron Beta had previously occupied the forward section here. Problems, disagreements, and opinions all played a hand in establishing a second colony." She moved across the lab to stand by the window, "In reality, it's surprising that there's been peace this long." She shook her head, "Actually, it's really surprising that we all lasted in this tin can for this long."

"Well, if Blue Squad has their way, that'll come to a screeching halt," John sighed.

"How long before you think they'll wait?" Travis asked, unable to hide his anxiety. John gave him a raised eyebrow and Travis realized his verbal mistake. "I mean, how long do you think they'll wait before they, you know?"

The lieutenant shook his head, "Man, I'm surprised they haven't started up already." He glanced at his own wrist unit, "They might be waiting for dark."

"When's that?"

"In an hour," Annika replied solemnly.

Travis pushed to his feet and strode over to the enclosure with them. "You mean we've got an hour to…?"

"Veros does not rotate like Earth," Annika began to explain. "It orbits around Centauri once every eleven days without rotating. In one hour, it will effectively be 'sundown' for the next one hundred thirty hours before it rises again for five and a half days."

Travis blew out a breath, intending to make a comment. However, before he spoke, he caught himself at the memory of how Lieutenant Maxwell had reacted when he'd challenged the notion of leaving this place. Then Sabina's reflection in the glass, superimposed on Angel's lifeless sphere caught his eye. And his memory. "I need a computer," he muttered.

"What?" Annika asked.

"I mean, I need an empty computer," Travis reiterated.

Maxwell shook his head and started to walk away, "That's what's wrong with you people. You think you need a computer for everything…"

Travis turned toward him, and raised a finger in protest, "No, that's not it."

"Yeah it is!" Maxwell challenged. "I just get through telling you that you got about thirty or so heavily armed men showing up on your doorstep, and you think you need a computer!" He shook his head, "You can't shoot back with a computer!"

Travis shook his head, "Not for that." He pointed at Angel's sphere, "For her."

Maxwell shot him a look of disgust, "What good's that? *That's* exactly what they wanna see in the first place. You *should* be trying to hide that thing!" He blew out a resigned breath, "Hell, I shouldn't be here either."

Annika put a hand on his arm, "But you couldn't let them get away with it, could you?"

"No," he admitted. "It's wrong, and they know it."

"What if we *don't* put up a fight?" Travis offered.

"And what? Let them waltz in here and see what you've got cooking in there?" Maxwell pointed out. "They'd shoot the place up just because they felt justified…"

"Not if there's nothing here," Travis smiled. "If I can get Angel out of that sphere, I can take her and Sabina off-planet…"

"That won't be enough," Annika interrupted.

"What do you mean?" Travis asked.

"Yeah," Maxwell agreed suspiciously. "What *do* you mean?"

Annika closed her eyes a moment, obviously struggling with something. After she let out a pent-up breath, she started walking toward the opposite corner of the room. "Before you cast judgement on me, I want you to realize that this was never about *replacing* people."

Travis and Maxwell exchanged glances, then started after her. "What did you do?" Travis dared to ask.

"It was a pet project," she admitted, partially throwing a cover back from a table. "I based her off of the girl from the legend."

There, lying on the table was a young girl with long brown hair and soft olive skin.

"Who is she?" Travis asked, bewildered, staring at the girl under a blanket.

"What legend?" Maxwell pressed, then rubbed at his face in frustration. "Wait a minute," he said, cutting any response off. "Just what the heck was going through your head?" He shot a very pointed look at Annika. "It's not enough for you people to make computers that sound like people? Now you gotta make 'em *look* like people too?"

"I told you, this isn't about replacing…"

"Sure the hell looks like that's exactly what you're doing," he leveled an accusatory finger at the girl on the table. "This is…"

"What?" Annika bit out. "Wrong? Is that what you're going to say?" she shouted. "And who made you to be judge and jury? I already told you this isn't about replacing anyone!" She interposed herself between Maxwell and the girl, "When are you going to quit being so quick to judge based on something that happened hundreds of years ago?"

Travis moved around the table to the other side and didn't try to hide his curiosity. There was something strangely familiar about that olive skin tone and long hair. The eyes were closed, but the mouth… Why did it seem like it was just made to argue?

"Because some bunch of stupid scientists were trying to replace people then, and they unleashed something that nearly wiped out the human race!" Maxwell protested. "Now you're doing the exact same thing they did."

"She's a model, a prototype," Annika said sternly. "The only thing she represents is the ability to replace *parts of people* that are severely damaged by other *people* with guns that leap to conclusions!"

"I can't believe you're talking about *that* like it's a person!"

Maxwell protested.

"So she has no programming yet?" Travis asked, detached from the argument.

"No," Annika answered over her shoulder.

Maxwell threw his hands up and stomped away, "This is insane! And it's gonna get everybody in here killed!" He tapped on the door button and stormed through it without another word.

Travis dared to put a finger on the girl's cheek, and marveled at how much it felt like a real human. "So, this is just a non-working model to base replacement limbs from?"

Annika let out a frustrated breath and turned away from the lieutenant. "Actually," she said, lowering her voice, "she has the potential to…" she trailed off.

Travis eyes widened in shock, "What? You mean…"

Annika nodded slowly, then deliberately looked over at the hazardous containment room where the dormant metal sphere lay with wires stuck to it. "Yes, with the right programming." She looked at a clock on the wall that read seventeen hundred, fourteen hours before she admitted, "But I don't have the programming expertise to do this."

Travis looked back down at the girl, and something in his mind clicked. "I assume she's wireless?"

"Yes…" Annika trailed off suspiciously. "But your droid hasn't taken any power yet…"

Travis looked under the table and confirmed that it was on wheels. "It might not need more than a brief charge," he began, starting to push the table toward the hazardous containment room.

"You can't put her in there!" Annika pointed out. "She'll be irradiated!"

"Then I'll wrap a suit around the droid," Travis offered. "That should contain the radiation well enough. I mean, we're not talking about a nuclear bombardment, are we?"

"Well, no…"

"What the heck are you doing?" Maxwell demanded as he

stepped back in the room.

"Trying to keep everyone from killing each other." He went to the closet where he'd seen Annika extract a clean suit before and started covering the girl with it. That's when he discovered just how detailed his mother had been while creating 'her'.

"Let me get that," Annika quickly pushed her way in. "You go cover your ball."

Travis shot a curious look at her back. It was an interesting choice of words that needed to be ignored. Turning back to the closet, he pulled on an oversized white suit meant to handle dangerous chemicals. Moments later, he was looking though a plastic face panel in the closet for a third suit.

"What's taking you so long," Annika chided him. "I've already got her dressed, and you don't even have your droid covered."

He turned to look at her over his shoulder and found himself staring into the inside of the headpiece instead. When he turned his torso, the headpiece went with it, and offered him a clear view of his mother's handiwork. The girl was gone, replaced with a strange human-like form in an oversized one-piece white suit like his. "Yeah, but I gave you a head start," he replied smartly, grabbing the largest suit he could find. "You wanna buzz me in?"

"I got that," Maxwell called out reluctantly from somewhere behind him.

Travis walked to the door and twisted himself to see the big black man standing by the console that would let him inside the hazardous materials lab. "I appreciate the help," Travis began, "but I think we'd both understand if you wanted to walk away."

"You telling me to leave?"

"No…"

"'Cause it sure sounds like you're telling me you don't want my help."

"I think what my son is trying to say is that we both know you're not comfortable with the situation, and neither one of us wants to put you through…"

"I know," Maxwell conceded. "I might not be real comfortable with this," he admitted, "but I'm a lot less comfortable with the idea of a bunch of 'holier than thou' jack-wagons running in here shooting the place up just because they saw all this." He pointed at the door, "So let's get this done."

The door in front of Travis slid open, and he stepped through the portal. It slid shut behind him, and after a moment, the inner door followed suit. Angel's lifeless form lay on the ground before him, the haphazard cables only adding to the morbid scene. Even though she'd never really had a face, she looked so lifeless lying on the floor. The work was simple, and when he'd rolled the heavy droid around enough to completely encase it in the clean suit, he said, "Okay, you can decontaminate the room now."

"What about you?" Maxwell pointed out.

"He'll be okay," Annika commented. "The sequence isn't harmful to anyone inside clean suits."

Maxwell shrugged and found the buttons he was looking for after a brief search in front of him. "All right," he announced.

A buzzer sounded, then the inside of the room became a deluge of mist and chemical rain. It reminded him of the showers he'd taken on Lunar Delta. When the light above the viewing window turned green, Maxwell announced, "Okay, you're good."

Without a second thought, Travis reached up and pulled the headpiece off. Instantly, his nostrils were filled with a weird chemical stench.

"Travis!" His mother scolded while dashing toward the control board. "You're supposed to let us..." she tapped a button on the console in front of Maxwell, "ventilate the room first!"

A powerful fan kicked on somewhere, and he felt the air swirling around him while he held his breath. When he couldn't hold it any longer, he found the air was once again breathable. After a brief sigh of relief, he turned to the door, "Okay, let's get her in here."

"What's your plan?" Annika asked while she and Maxwell rolled the table through the first door.

"Angel's program is unlike anything I've ever seen," Travis

explained, opening the second door once the first one closed again. "She can transfer between systems without protocols, even in a low-power state."

"What's that supposed to mean?" Maxwell asked.

"It means," Travis started, nudging the table right up against the wrapped sphere, "she can move from that droid to another computer without waiting for approval from the new host."

"Like a body-snatcher," Maxwell said with a smirk.

Travis held up a finger and sighed, "Essentially, yes."

The lieutenant shrugged, "Sorry, but it fit."

"How long before we know if…" Annika started to ask.

The girl on the table let out a low moan.

"Oh my God," Annika exclaimed softly, pressing against the glass to look down at the girl she'd created.

"T-t-t-t" the girl crackled. "Aaa…"

"It's okay honey," Annika soothed. "You need to breathe," she instructed, "Can you do that?"

Travis turned a shocked look at Annika, "Breathe?"

Annika ignored him, and nervously tapped on the glass with her fingers. "Take a breath now," she urged.

"You made her breathe?" Travis repeated, dismayed. "She's a computer! They don't breathe…"

The girl suddenly pulled in a breath, and released it slowly, as if learning how to do it for the first time. Then a rhythm slowly built within her, causing her chest to rise and fall smoothly.

"I suppose you put a heart in there?" Travis chided.

Annika shot him a defensive look but didn't say anything to him. "How do you feel?" she asked through the glass.

Travis looked down as the girl's brown eyes blinked open and shut a few times, then looked around. At first, it was a simple searching, but then her face took on an urgency and fear that was unmistakable.

"What did you do?" Maxwell asked Annika quietly. "I thought she was just a 'spare parts' experiment or something."

Annika didn't turn away from the girl on the table, "I had to make everything work together, or none of it would be of any use." She turned a quick glance his way, "It was all or nothing Lieutenant, and I chose 'all.'"

Something caught Maxwell's attention, and he looked at the armband on his left forearm. Then his face went wide with shock. "We need to go," he ordered. "Now!"

"What?" Travis returned.

"They've started already, and we've got about fifteen minutes before they hit the complex. We've got to get all this outta here right now!" He glanced down at the girl and shook his head, "Especially Frankenstein there."

"Sabina?" Travis called.

"Yes Captain, I've started the initialization sequence, and I'll continue to monitor the surroundings."

"Can you tell if Angel has transferred one hundred percent?"

"We don't have time to wait," Maxwell pressed, searching the control panels in front of himself.

"If I separate these too early," he protested, pointing at both the girl on the table and Angel's sphere, "then I could lose her completely."

"Captain, I do not read any kind of electronic activity in the new body," Sabina replied.

"What?" Travis spat out, sending another accusatory glance toward the mother he barely knew. "What did you do?" he asked as his mother violated the safety seals and opened both sets of doors.

Annika wouldn't look at him, "I'll get her dressed," she replied, wheeling the girl out of the room.

"Dammit! I don't know if the transfer is complete yet!" Travis protested. He turned to the sphere and flipped the headpiece of his suit back into place.

"Leave that!" Maxwell ordered. "There's no time…"

He smacked a button on the wall, killing the power to the cables, "If I leave her here, all those commando buddies of yours will see is a radioactive orb!" As soon as the cables de-energized, they fell from the body of the sphere without any effort at all. "They'd probably execute everybody thinking she's a bomb or something!"

"Fine!" Maxwell bit out. "Just get that thing back in the box now!" He punched the button to close the inner door once again. "I can't believe I let myself get talked into this!"

Travis ignored the comment and started to push the sphere back into the box when he stopped suddenly. "Sabina, how much radiation is on the exterior of this crate now?"

"The decontamination sequence appears to have neutralized any radioactivity," she replied. "It is safe to transport the crate once again."

The wrapping fell off the sphere as he pushed it inside, and he worked quickly to flip the door back up and closed once again. He tilted the crate and used his foot to nudge the carry-disk under the crate to make it float again. As he reached for the button to open the door, it snapped open. He pushed the crate through and saw that he had the lieutenant to thank for the assistance. He ripped off the headpiece, then the rest of the suit came next in a rush. "How much time?" He asked into the air.

"Hard to say…" Maxwell started to reply.

"The party is fighting a significant headwind, and I estimate their arrival in no less than fifteen minutes at their current rate.

"You can see that far?" Maxwell asked, putting his own hands on the crate to help push it toward the door that led out of the lab.

"Yes Lieutenant," she replied smiling at his back. "However, I admit that I had not been monitoring for any traffic until you warned the captain of their impending arrival."

As the two men started through the door, Travis realized that he'd left his mother to wheel the… 'girl' out of the room. However, Annika waved him off, "I've got this," she said.

Sweat ran into his eyes as he pushed the crate with Maxwell. It wasn't because the crate was heavy, but his nerves were stretched too thin. The man next to him exuded so much disapproval, he wondered if the Lieutenant was going to turn on him at any moment. They were halfway to the ship before they met someone in the hallways. The grey beard and white hair covered his face while a green jump suit covered the rest. His slightly chunky build and no-nonsense demeanor immediately identified him as someone in charge. He didn't stop them but walked beside the gurney his mother pushed. "How long?"

Annika flashed a look at Travis, but answered, "About ten minutes."

"Take care of this," he instructed, pointing at the girl under the blanket on the floating table. "I'll send word once they clear out."

With that, he turned away from them down another hallway. "Who was that?" Travis asked over his shoulder.

"Howard's one of the council elders," Annika explained.

"And he knew about *that?*" Maxwell said pointedly.

On cue, the girl let out a small sound.

"Okay, that's freaking me out!"

They started around the final corner when Sabina's head suddenly appeared in front of Travis instead of one of the little maps. "Captain!" Her blue eyes were wide in fright, "They're here!"

"I thought we still had time," he responded, almost annoyed. "Surely we can get…"

"No, not the raiding party Lieutenant Maxwell advised us about," she interrupted, "The Phantom!"

"What!?" he blew out. "How could they…"

"The ship is in orbit above the planet, and a squadron of smaller shuttles have already descended. I'm detecting weapons fire in the proximity of the raiding party and at the other colony as well."

"What the heck are you two talking about?" John pressed. "What phantom?"

How had Braun, or rather, why had Braun come here? Braun and his thugs were supposed to be going after Titan Alpha, the place he was supposed to get back to. "How long?" he choked out.

Sabina *looked* frightened, "They will be here before you make it to the door."

"Who?" John demanded.

"Go," Travis ordered, "get off the planet and out of sight. I'll contact you when it's safe."

"But Captain…"

"Go now!" Travis ordered firmly. "Right now, before they see you!"

Sabina's sullen face disappeared, but her voice rose from his collar, "I'm sorry Captain." A pause, and then, "Lifting off now."

"Okay," John grabbed Travis' shoulder and spun him around, "just what the…"

"Your 'Blue Squad' is the least of our worries," Travis revealed. "The men who killed my friend are here, and Sabina says they've opened fire on Beta Colony."

"What?!" John sputtered, checking his left forearm unit. "Wait a second, I got nothin, nothin at all…"

"Travis," Annika pleaded softly, "what are we going to do?"

"I don't know…"

John grabbed Travis by the upper portion of his jumpsuit with both hands, "What did you do?!"

Travis ripped away and glared at him. "We've got to…"

"Captain, the soldiers are about to break through the doors into Hadron Prime," Sabina's voice crackled. "I will t-," a static snapping sound abruptly ended everything.

"Sabina?" Travis tried. "Sabina? Can you hear me?" No response. "Sabina!" His mind raced with the only conclusion: Sabina was destroyed. His ship was gone, and he was just as stuck as everyone else. A floor-shaking *thud!* announced the fruition of what Sabina had warned him about. "We need a good place to hide."

"You need to tell me what the heck is going on!"

"Hide now, explanations later," Travis bit out. "Where to?" he asked Annika.

She looked left, then right before she turned the gurney down the hallway the way they'd just come. "This way!"

Travis shot a look at the Lieutenant, "I promise you an explanation, for now, you'll just have to trust me."

John looked back down at his wrist unit one more time, "I still got nothin." He nodded toward Annika's back and bit back a curse, "We'd better get after her."

They teamed up and pushed the crate down the hall together, struggling with its habit to drift toward walls. "The last time I saw those guys, they were near Titan," Travis started explaining on the run. "I didn't think I'd ever see them again, much less out here." They rounded several corners, running through the pop-up holographic displays without paying attention to them.

"Who are they?" John asked, barely avoiding smashing his finger as the crate smacked a corner. "Hold on, why are we pushing this dead ball around?"

Travis started to put his shoulder into it, "Because Angel might not…"

"Really?" John protested, "I might not know these guys, but if we hope to stay alive, we can't be hangin onto extra stuff." He pushed the crate at an angle, throwing Travis off-balance and causing him to stumble forward. At the same time, he grabbed that same portion of Travis' jumpsuit at the chest and tugged him away from the crate, "C'mon, we gotta move it or she's gonna lose us both."

Annika had already turned the next corner, and the maze of hallways would render them separated in moments. Travis stole one more desperate glance back at the crate, "Fine!" he grudgingly agreed, breaking into a run beside the Lieutenant. They caught up with her as she stopped to open a side door.

"This way," she ordered, pushing the gurney inside.

The room was pitch black and had a foul chemical odor to it that warned his nose away. He looked up and down the hall briefly as more rapid thumping sounds reached his ears. It was the same sound he remembered from when Liam was killed. More thumps, this time more uncluttered, as if they were getting closer.

A strong hand wrapped around his wrist and pulled him into the darkness.

THUMPING sounds behind him mixed with the pounding of his heart to cloud out the whirring fans in the room. The back of his neck had gone rigid, sending a headache up to his brain and making it hard to turn.

The utter totality of his own failure smelled like a foul toilet and disinfectant. Sabina was gone, along with his ship. Angel was probably torn into digital pieces between the ball droid out in the hallways and that naked girl under the sheets.

She's not naked, she's wearing a jumpsuit now.

Not like now was a really good time to recall any of that. Braun shouldn't be here, but he'd jumped ahead eleven years. Or did he lose eleven years? God it was frustrating to think about that. It felt like the escape was only yesterday! Eleven years ago? What happened to Chrissy?

"Are you gonna tell me what the heck is going on now?" John whispered hoarsely, breaking the spell and ripping Travis' mind back to the moment.

Travis turned to where John should be in the completely dark room. "I signed onto The Phantom to get off Lunar Delta," he started. "I didn't know where they were going at the time, but all I cared about was getting…" he jumped at another series of thumping sounds that cut him off.

"You can tell me the whole story later, right now, I need to know who these guys are, and what they're packin'," John instructed.

Travis blew out a breath, moderately relieved that he wouldn't have to explain everything right now. "They're soldiers…" A low moan behind him sent shivers down his spine again. "What was that?"

"T-tr-a…" a voice crackled in the darkness.

"Shhh," Annika soothed, stroking the girl's hair by feel only. "Just keep breathing sweetheart."

"Soldiers," John pressed. "What kind? How many?"

Travis struggled to think, and the thumping of gunfire didn't help. "I don't know, and, I don't know," he confessed. "I know there's a lot of 'em, but I have no idea why they're here. All they talked about before I left was hunting the Legion Virus."

"I'd say there's no Legion Virus here, but that thing under the blanket over there…"

"She's not a thing," Annika hissed. "There's no bloody virus here. Never has been and they've got a greater chance of bringing it with them than it being here already."

"Tell me more about 'em. What's their leader like?"

"They think he's a god," Travis recalled. "They're terrified of him, but they do everything he tells them to do."

"Great," John muttered, keeping his voice low, "fanatics."

"T-t-trav…"

Travis tried to turn toward the sound, and his foot caught on something in the darkness, sending him to one knee on the damp floor. "Angel?"

"Wha… what hap…" her voice crackled.

"Shhh," Annika soothed again.

Travis pushed past the overpowering smell and got back to his feet. "Angel? What's wrong? Why can't you talk?"

"I…" she paused, and he heard her suck in a breath, "I d-d-d-on't…."

"The transfer didn't complete!" he lamented, "I've gotta get that sphere back in here," he added, waving his hands in front of him to try and find the door.

A sudden red glow nearby and a pair of strong hands on his wrists sent a shock through his whole body as John got into his face. "You're not going anywhere, got it?"

"But…"

John pointed behind Travis, "Right now, that don't matter. This is war, and the only thing that matters is the living, got it?"

"And what am I supposed to do, let her program deteriorate

until there's nothing left?"

John's eyes became fierce in the red glow. "What is it about this that you don't get? I'm trying to save your life, and hers," he ground out, pointing at Annika. "From what I'm hearing, and what you told me, these are trained soldiers. Not a bunch of hicks with sticks. Soldiers. Out to kill and good at it. What part of this don't make sense to you?"

Travis wanted to say something, but John didn't let up. "Right now, the priorities are people. Not programs and robots. People, got it?" He paused to let Travis nod, "Good, now, it sounds to me like they's going door to door, which means they've got a plan. They're gonna be moving smooth, and there's gonna be a lot of them. They got guys with guns on the door, and one to pop it open. The second the door opens, they're on the trigger. Anything moves gets blasted. In fact, there should be several units moving through the halls, doin' a sweep." He looked into Travis' eyes, "You know what a sweep is?" When Travis shook his head in the negative, he continued, "Didn't think so." He let go of Travis and pointed at the door, which was barely outlined by the dull red glow from a light source he held. "There's groups of 'em moving from one end of the ship to the other. They make a line, clearing as they go. That way, nothing gets behind 'em."

Travis looked at the door that had just become his worst enemy and his only friend all at the same time.

"They're in constant comm link with each other. Which means, one spots something, and everybody knows it. Things get outta hand, and the nearby units swarm the location."

"How is it that you know so much about all this?" Annika asked quietly from behind.

John looked reluctantly back toward her, "I had time to study, and I'm the one that trained Blue Squad."

"You trained those guys?" Travis shot back. "Really? The same guys that were charging over here to shoot up the place?"

"Training them is a lot different than leading them," he retorted. "I'm not the one making the decisions," he added, using his finger to ward Travis off. "I don't agree with what they were doing."

Annika kept stroking the girl's hair, "So what do we do?"

"Give them a good reason to not search this room," John offered, moving back into the darkness.

"What are you doing?" Travis asked hesitantly. John didn't answer, but he figured it out soon enough when the stench in the room reached a level that made him want to hurl. They were in the waste processing room where all the colony's waste was reclaimed. It was a necessary ugliness that no one wanted to be a part of, and Travis was rapidly changing his opinion of being caught.

"Oh my God," Annika complained. "You know they might find us because we'll be retching on the floor."

John came back into the dull red glow, sternly holding his finger up to his lips to keep them quiet. He was blinking away the foul odor that was making his eyes water as well. He beckoned them deeper in with his finger. Travis and Annika shot him an incredulous look, but he whispered, "We don't want 'em seeing us as soon as the door opens."

A round of thumping sounds outside the door had them moving in seconds despite the stench. As they moved, Travis saw that the dull red glow was a light stick that John had picked back up from the floor. They went farther back than any of them wanted to go and crouched behind some equipment. John handed him a face mask and small tank that he turned to hand to his mother before he saw that she already had one. The mask sent life into his lungs where the stench had nearly sent him into spasms.

The girl on the gurney moaned something unintelligible, and Travis found himself lamenting the fact that half of Angel's program was probably still in the hallway. He and his mother traded off holding their masks over her face while he contemplated what those crazy wack-jobs were doing with her other body out there.

A click, then a whooshing sound tore his mind from the lament as the compartment flooded with light through the doorway. "Clear the roo… Oh, ugh! What the…" someone protested.

"Cap'n wants every room cleared, no matter what," another voice instructed, noticeably farther away.

"Are you kiddn' me?" the first man said, "that'll kill ya!"

"Get in there and clear the room!"

"Fine!"

Travis shot John a raised eyebrow, except that John wasn't there anymore. He looked around and started to panic. Had he left them as bait? The adrenaline in his system started rushing faster and faster as he heard one of the soldiers making his way toward them. *What would he do? He'd have to 'take him out', but wouldn't that bring more of them? He was sunk, they were going to find him, kill him and his mother…*

"Clear!" the voice called back as the owner's feet moved quickly over the deck plates toward the door. "There is no one in there," he protested. "And I ain't dying to prove it!"

The main door slid shut, and a click sounded to confirm that the door was locked. Travis sucked in a sigh of relief through the mask before he placed it on the girl's face. Moments later, he felt the air moving stronger as John stepped back close to them with his red glow stick. "That'll help," he muttered, swallowing painfully. "Hope I don't have to do that again."

"What did you do?" Travis complained.

"Opened a bypass valve," he whispered. "Almost worked too good."

"We can't stay here," Annika advised. "Too much exposure to this will make us all sick." She shot Travis a warning look, "And her system won't be able to fight off infection yet either."

John and Travis both looked questioningly at Annika, but John was the first to speak, "That's disturbing, but I agree with you. We should be able to move back to a better location now." He rose and started making his way back toward the door, leading the way. "There'll be random patrols wandering around to pick off anyone that the forward groups missed," he advised.

"There are no cameras in the hallways, or most of the colony,"

Annika put in as she and Travis pushed the gurney closer. "Well, there are the cameras that are built into certain keypads," she admitted. "And a few more that were added to record experiments, but those would be in labs and such," she added. "A real puzzle since this ship was supposedly sent out here without so much as a calculator."

"That makes things a little easier," John shrugged. "Still, we'd better be silent, and we can't be seen," he stressed, herding them to one side of the doorway like children. "Stay put," he ordered, moving back to the door controls. He put his ear to the door for a few moments, then leaned back to one side and tapped the 'OPEN' button. The door responded by clicking, but nothing else. He muttered under his breath, but before he could make any requests, Travis moved in to look at the panel.

"Can you hand me that?" Travis asked, beckoning for the glow stick. John gave it to him with a sigh. "We have the same doors on Lunar Delta," Travis explained while he pressed in on a corner that released the panel cover. "They lock on the outside to prevent children from getting into places they shouldn't be, but they're not really meant to be a real secure lock," he explained as the door clicked again. "There, should be good to go," he added, returning the light stick.

"Good," John said in annoyance, "now get back outta sight."

Travis nodded with some satisfaction and moved back to the edge, leaving John to recheck the door once more. The door slid open, and the lieutenant leaned around the corner to survey the hallway. Travis watched him bob a little, then step out fully into the hall. Curiosity pulled him to the edge, and when he dared to peek around it, he found the hallway empty. *Where did he go?!* He looked both ways, then stepped out…

"Hey-"

The word in the soldier's mouth was cut short by another sound, just before Travis saw his body slump to the floor. *Where had that guy come from?*

John stood behind the soldier's body, giving him a hard look. "I told you to stay put," he whispered fiercely. Travis would have answered him, but something caught John's attention, and he silenced all replies with a finger to his lips. He pointed behind himself, then started down the hallway.

Travis fell in behind him, still not sure of what John had heard. Now he could see that there was an alcove in the hallway wall, and that the soldier had been standing in it waiting for stragglers. *He was waiting to kill me*, he thought to himself as the notion sunk in. He watched the way John rolled his feet on the floor, instead of a normal walk that would have given away his footsteps and tried to follow suit. It wasn't easy, but their pace was slow anyhow. At the bend in the hall, John motioned for Travis to watch the way they'd come before he eased himself around the corner. That's when he realized that the dead soldier's gun was now strapped around John's shoulder.

The hallway was empty and quiet the way they'd just come, but his imagination quickly filled it with rushing soldiers. Moments later, he heard a soft rustle of something behind him, and then John's voice whispered his name. When he looked back toward the lieutenant, he saw him holding out a small handgun of sorts. "Don't use it unless they shoot first," he said quietly. "Don't wanna give our position away." He pointed back down the hall, "Go get her, and tell her to leave that… thing behind."

Travis shot him a dubious look.

"We don't have the luxury of extras," John said in a firm whisper. "We stay alive," he instructed, "robots come last."

He didn't like it, and when he walked into the stinky room where his mother was, he knew she wasn't going to leave the girl behind either. "We gotta move," he told her.

"Travis?" Angel whispered.

Travis' heart jumped, propelling him forward to look at the girl. She looked up at him with brown eyes full of recognition. "Why does it stink in here?"

He smiled down at her, "Long story. Can you walk?"

"I - I don't think so."

He nodded at Annika, "We were supposed to leave her."

Annika's eyebrow went up, "I should think not."

So far, she'd pieced together that they were moving down hallways, and her only viewport was looking straight up at the grey ceiling with light strips down the center. A woman kept entering her view, telling her to breathe and looking down at her like she was about to fall apart. She heard Travis' voice, and the soldier-guy named John Maxwell from before, but they stayed out of her view.

There were no other viewports, and this droid body, or whatever it was started acting strange if she didn't 'breathe' like the woman kept telling her to. No one had said a word for three minutes, twenty-eight seconds which only added to the tension in the air around her that she *felt. For that matter, why did she feel anything?*

The view paused, and the woman looked down at her again to make sure she was still 'breathing'. It was a strange sensation, this breathing thing, and it also came with *feeling*. Not the normal feedback from a system response, but… more somehow. She felt the air, cool and tangible, as it was pulled into this new body before she pushed it back out. A familiarity came with the action that made it easy, although she didn't know why.

The view started moving again, and she saw Travis' face briefly. He wasn't looking at her, but searching, always searching for something. *What was going on?*

A sensation entered her mind from something attached to her, and she struggled to figure out what it was. It felt distant but attached somehow.

They turned into a room, and she heard a door slide closed.

"What's the plan?" Travis asked nervously.

"Plan?" John said incredulously. "Plan? What good's a plan when you two are too busy trying to save a robot?"

"I'm…" Angel slowly breathed.

"Oh, I don't know if I can handle you talking right now," John interrupted.

"And what do you expect me to do? Leave her out there?" Travis bit out.

The lack of viewing angles was infuriating. She tried to look around to see what else might be in here when the view rotated.

"You moved!" the woman exclaimed triumphantly, straining to keep her voice low.

Her view had changed, and while she didn't know how she'd done it, she was able to rotate her view now. Apparently, the camera had the ability to move from side to side. She saw the big man named John from Hadron Beta that had been Travis' escort looking at a pistol in his hands. He looked determined and frustrated at the same time.

"Why do I get the feeling this is all about… that," John accused, turning a scowl her direction.

She recoiled at the prickly accusation. "What are you… talking… about?" she managed struggling to breath and talk.

John pointed at Travis, "Just what the heck is going on here?"

"I already told you everything," Travis said defensively. "Like you said, they're 'fanatics.'"

"I can't believe that they would have come here for her," Annika added. "This is something I started working on *after* I came here. If they came from the Lunar Colonies, there's no way they would have known about her."

"Who are they?" Angel asked, her voice becoming stronger. There were more sensations every time she spoke, and she found that if she didn't have any breath inside this 'body' that the words didn't work. *What is this thing?*

Travis turned to face her, "They're the soldiers we ran from a few days ago. You remember, the ones that chased us to Saturn and killed Liam?"

She did remember the escape from the ship, and… "R-right," she breathed, struggling to match her breathing to the words she wanted to speak. She took in a breath and added, "dose guys."

"You're doing so well," Annika encouraged at the edge of her vision. "This is…"

John snapped his fingers, silencing everyone. She saw him move toward the doorway they'd come through, out of her line of sight. She tried to turn more, but something unpleasant was preventing her from moving the camera further. She turned her view the other direction and found her view swing from right to left. There was a wall there, with nothing interesting on it, so she turned it back the other way. The effect was strange and she still couldn't see what he was doing.

Something shifted without her effort, and she could see that John was standing beside the door with his ear against it. "There you go," Annika whispered next to her.

That tension in the air was back, almost as if it were something that was pulling on her somehow. John stepped away from the door and waved at them to move away. She slid sideways and a wall blocked her view of him. A thick dark silence suddenly enveloped the room as the lights went out. In the darkness, she heard a tap. Then another, followed by a series of three more in rapid succession. In her searching of the darkness, she saw a light. At first, it was strange, then it became immediately familiar.

———

THE blue-rimmed portal appeared and passed by her in a flash, sending her onto the black plane. A red pyramid dominated the space in front of her, drifting just above the floor while walls she could only feel pressed in close. Each side of the pyramid held a set of small white cubes with a red halo. A rectangle screen above the pyramid showed a bald head that reflected light on the shiny surface.

A click sounded and one of the glowing red cubes turned green. The pyramid turned and another of the red-colored cubes shifted to green.

Where was Sabina?

The bald head didn't look right and shouldn't be there. John was acting like a jerk right now, but this bald guy pricked her brain like a *cobista*. She reached up and pulled two of the blocks out of the last group just before the last one could turn green.

The bald man's face tilted up to glower at the camera and she recoiled at his rough appearance. Yep, definitely a bad guy.

Another flat rectangle drifted in the space with a series of small orbs lining the outside of it. She recognized it as a display and smiled as she grabbed it.

Using her finger, she traced out "ACCESS DENIED" on the screen and turned it away from her body, hanging it in the space without pinning it to something.

The bald man didn't like what he saw. He lifted a blue-sleeved arm toward his face, begrudgingly speaking into something on his wrist, "What numbskull changed the code on two-two-four-seven?"

She heard a hissing sound, then, "*Don't know. Isn't it two-two-four-seven?*"

The bald man rolled his eyes, "Since I'm asking, it obviously isn't." He reached up and tapped the code in once more, and she pulled the two blocks back out of the string before touching the back of her ACCESS DENIED sign once more. She let one of the two blocks drift again and pulled the center of the block she still held out so that it no longer had any flat surfaces. That would prevent it from lining up with the other blocks and letting the door open from the outside.

"You need to breathe honey," Annika whispered through the portal behind her. In response, she took in a breath.

THE portal had passed over her so fast she hadn't even noticed it. She was once again looking through the new body at a wall in darkness as if she had been dreaming.

The lights came back on again, illuminating the room. John approached them, shaking his head. "These guys don't strike me as having it together very well," he muttered quietly. "They can't even keep their door codes straight."

"Tha-at's," Angel started, and took a breath in to continue. "That's not his fault," she breathed out, then in once more, "I change the code."

John shot her a disapproving look, "And how the heck did you do that?"

"I got in… *uña momento*," she responded in one breath. She took in another deliberate breath, "He was bald man with blue shirt," another breath cycle, "and he didn't like it so much."

"What did you change it to?" Travis asked, moving into view. He was looking at her like a proud friend, and it made her *feel* good.

"I kinda broke it so the door only opens," another breath, "from inside."

"But you stopped breathing," Annika pointed out. "You cannot do that," she advised.

"It worked this time, but I'd bet he'll be back with a code breaker," John stated grimly. "We need to move."

Angel reached out again, looking for the blue portal while trying to keep breathing. At first, it eluded her attempts to find it.

"Where do we go?" she heard John ask.

As if they had always been there, the code blocks and her 'ACCESS DENIED' sign drifted in the air in front of her even though she was looking at the door through the new camera. The black plane wasn't there, but she could still see the code blocks drifting in the air in front of her anyway. The camera screen was at the wrong angle, but then it moved at her desire to shift back and forth slightly. The movement allowed her to see the empty hallway outside the door. "He is gone," she stated. "I no see him."

"What do you mean?" John asked slowly.

"I can see…" she trailed off. *She'd forgotten to take a breath first!* Annoyed with herself, she forced the breath, then replied, "I can see through the camera. The hallway is clear now."

Something *touched* her, and her view rolled away from the door and code blocks to where Travis looked down at something apologetically. "Sorry, you were staring at the ceiling," he pointed out with concern. "How are you seeing through the keypad?"

What had he touched? She tried to look in the direction of where the sensation had come from, but that required a different motion that the new body's camera didn't seem to allow. Then there was this strange object in the view that only appeared when she looked to the side.

"What is it?" Travis asked.

"What you do to me?"

"We gotta move," John interrupted. "If she's right about the hall, it's now or never."

Travis looked down at her questioningly. "I bumped your hand," Travis confessed. "Is that what…"

"Hand?" Angel asked slowly.

He looked at her strangely, "Well, yeah." He reached down, and she felt something different from the same direction, "This," he said, using his hand to lift another hand and arm into her view.

The next breath was quick and sharp and made everything about her *shift*. "What is that?"

He looked at her like she should know, "That's your hand. You have a body now."

"Let's go!" John whispered firmly.

Travis reluctantly let her hand fall back down before moving up out of her view. Her world slid by again as they moved through the door and into the hall she had been looking at moments ago. *She had a hand? What else did this body have?* The question ran through her mind as she began to stretch out her awareness. There was more, she was sure of it. In her searching, she started to see more keypads nearby. The code blocks drifted in and out of focus, their cameras too slow to capture any useful images. They were intermittent, as if she couldn't see them unless she was close by. So when they finally stopped near a set of code blocks that only floated in her vision, she caused the view screen to tilt enough to see the gurney her new body lay on.

She saw Annika, looking back over her shoulder while her long black ponytail swished with the movement. Travis was looking down at the floating table in front of him, his face intent on…

A girl.

"Breathe Angel," she saw him say. Obediently, she took in a breath, and watched the girl on the table part her lips. *Ay! Is that me?* The girl was lying down, dressed in a baggy white jumpsuit. Her hand lay beside her, and her legs were stretched out as well.

The big, dark-skinned soldier entered her view and beckoned them to follow. Travis started to push the girl on the floating table just as she rotated her body's view toward the camera. In a split second, her world exploded as she was looking both at the keypad where the camera was, and back into… her own face.

Then it was gone, the connection lost, and she was looking at the grey wall again. "What am I?" she breathed quietly. She knew that face. It was her own. Images, memories, whatever they were all swirled through her mind as she tried to process what she'd just seen.

Travis' face entered her peripheral vision as he drew uncomfortably close. "You're you," he whispered, "now be quiet."

The hallway blurred in her vision as she tried to make sense of the face she had seen. That was the face that looked back at her when she looked down at the black plane inside her digital universe. That body had hands and feet, but now she had a human body with hands, feet, and legs? Did that mean she could walk? How had she gotten into this body? This didn't look like a computer, but she could still see code blocks and step into the digital realm. Doubts began to creep into her, and she considered that she might have seen a hologram. Then the hallway twisted, and she *felt* the shift on her floating table throughout her new body.

Her hologram never felt anything before.

A swishing sound behind her, then Travis moved back into her field of view. "Angel? You okay? You look like you've seen a ghost," he whispered with concern.

Annika entered her view, reaching a hand up above her view. Immediately, she *felt* something above her. Soft, slightly warm, soothing. "Honey?" Annika asked.

"I don't think she knows how to process this," Travis said, looking at Annika.

The big black man stepped into her view, giving her a wary look, "I don't care if you're scared or not," he warned her. "Until I give the all-clear, you don't say a word. Got it?"

She looked into his stern eyes, "*Sí*," she said quietly.

He looked her over slowly, then shook his head. "What have you done?" he muttered in revulsion before he walked away.

Travis glared after him but didn't say a word to answer him.

Annika looked down at her apologetically, "Are you okay?"

"I…*feel*," she answered, unsure of herself.

"What do you feel?" Annika probed.

"I - everything."

Travis turned his attention back to her, "Can you feel this?"

A gentle pressure somewhere followed, "*Sí*."

"That was your right hand," he explained. He pressed again in a different spot, "That's your right shoulder."

"I don't understand," Annika began.

"She's not used to this," Travis explained to his mother, moving to her other side. "That's your left hand," he continued with a glance up to make eye contact with her, "and that's your left shoulder." He looked down the length of Angel's new body. "The droid she was in before had omnidirectional visibility, and a round body. It was simple, with only a few features and it basically floated by itself." He pressed on something else, "That's your left foot… and this is your right foot."

"What are you doing?" John scolded, drawing close enough that she could see him again.

"I'm helping her map this body," he explained curtly. "This is your right knee, and this is your left knee."

"By gettin' all touchy-feely?"

Travis shot him a look, "Really? That's what you think I'm doing? And just how do you think she's gonna figure all this out?"

Annika caught Angel's attention, "These are your hips," she

explained, causing slight pressure on two points at one time. "A child spends the first year of their life acclimating to their body Lieutenant," she said. "I don't think you want her to take that long before she can move on her own."

"I…"

"Attention residents of Hadron Prime," a strong, deep male voice interrupted over everything. "Let me first reassure you that we are not here to kill all of you," he continued, his voice steady and nearly emotionless. "A long time ago, ambitious scientists nearly destroyed our race with the creation of Artificial Intelligence. True to form, that spark of ingenuity has led to another abomination greater than the last. Someone here is harboring illegal technology that threatens the sanctity of the Accord and the human race." There was a slight pause, and John turned a considering look toward Angel. Then the voice resumed, "Through careful research and long-range telemetry, we discovered that the other colony on this planet was in fact a haven for the Legion Virus. That outpost has been eradicated, freeing all of you from the influence."

"No!" John slammed his fist onto a metal table.

Annika's hand flew up to her mouth, "Oh my God!"

"We are searching thoroughly to ensure that no other illegal technology remains. We appreciate any help the fine residents of this colony could offer in locating any such atrocities. Braun out."

John stormed toward the door, his jaw set and murder in his eye. Travis grabbed his arm just as he reached for the door keypad, "Don't do it!"

"I'm gonna kill that- that…"

Travis got into his face, "You know you won't make it that far."

John glared at him, "Those were my friends! My family! What do you want me to do? Stand around here guarding *her*? I outta give all you up!" He turned his menacing eyes back toward her and stopped.

Fear. It echoed inside her new body and shook her enough she could feel it. "Did he mean Hadron Beta?" she whispered.

"Yeah," he muttered, sobered by something. He visibly swallowed and shook Travis' hand off his arm. "I ain't goin' anywhere," he explained. He shot Travis a look, "Did you know about any of this?"

"No," Travis replied quickly. "These guys were set on going after Titan Alpha. I never expected them to show up out here."

"Here sweetheart," Annika said before her view moved upward in a jerky fashion. As it rose, she *felt* the surface behind her shift and wobble until her view started to tilt sideways. In reflex, she straightened the view back upright which took a different kind of effort than simply rotating her view.

Travis was focused on something past her view to the right. "Is that you?" he asked, turning back to John.

John's eyes flicked toward something and then back to the wall he stared at. "Yeah."

Travis waited a beat, "Okay, I'm gonna ask the question. Why is your image…"

"Photo," John corrected.

"Okay, 'photo,' on the wall here. I thought you lived in Hadron Beta."

John sighed, "This is my ex's place." When Annika caught his attention, he looked at a table with a single chair neatly tucked in. "Deb's too stubborn to get caught by these jokers," he muttered, keeping his eyes locked on the chair.

"But you still want to make sure she's okay, don't you?" Annika probed.

"Yeah," he admitted, unable to hide his concern.

Travis narrowed his eyes and smiled at Angel, "Then let's go find her."

John looked up at a clock on the wall that read 00:12. "We've all been up way too long to make any difference," he said, rubbing his chin. "I might be trained to keep going, but you need to get some down time, or you'll burn out."

"They're not stopping…" Travis started to say.

"I'm sure they're going in shifts," John corrected. "I would. I'd keep some on guard duty, while the rest went down for at least four hours." He looked at both Annika and Travis, then cast a reluctant glance at Angel. "I don't know about her, but I'm sure the rest of us need some time to recoup." He cast a considering look at Travis, "I know you think you're all good right now, but that will come to a screeching halt real quick." He pointed at a bunk tucked into one wall, "So you get that bunk there, and your mother can take Deb's," he instructed, pointing at a single door in the rear of the cabin.

Angel followed Annika with her eyes as she tapped a button that slid a single door open toward the back of the room and looked inside.

"You might as well take the girl with you," John instructed. "No sense letting those two sleep together," he muttered with a wry smile.

THAT last corner still hurt. Travis rubbed at his sore left shoulder, while admiring how John could move from one spot to another without a sound. "The secret's in your footing," he'd told him. He didn't say anything about how to land against a corner properly though.

Every hallway and door looked like the last: Grey and plain. If it weren't for John's familiarity with the colony, he'd have probably gotten turned around at least three times by now. He fought off a yawn, grateful for the meager few hours of sleep but still wishing he could have had a cup of coffee. He was glad the girls weren't here, but the distance between them felt wrong. The further he and John pressed in toward the large Co-op the more exposed they left them.

A boot scuffed the floor ahead of them, and he crouched against the corner with his sore shoulder. He watched intently as John craned his neck to identify the sound before he stuck his head around the corner. It was a quick bob of his head, and a split second later he motioned for them to move forward again.

He checked the pistol in his hand for the hundredth time, making sure the trigger lock was still engaged. John had called it a 'safety', but 'trigger lock' seemed more appropriate to him. After all, if the trigger was locked you couldn't accidentally fire it. The tee-shaped intersection in front of them required looking both ways, and he moved in to cover the corner opposite John. He waited for John to count off three fingers before he tipped his head around the hard metal corner.

A bolt of light ripped through the air over his head, and he rolled backward in surprise. Out of shock and reflex, Travis fumbled to get his finger back on the trigger lock when John suddenly took the weapon out of his hand.

He held his finger to his lips and pointed back to Travis' corner.

"Told you it worked," a voice mocked ahead of them.

Travis looked up at the dark blast mark on the ceiling just behind John and agreed silently.

"Yeah, but the stupid trigger sticks," a voice complained around the corner.

"I don't care, you're not gettin' mine," the first man said.

"Well, that's just great! We get in a fight, and I'm gonna be the one standin' there lookin' like a idiot 'cause my stupid gun don't work!"

The voices sounded familiar, but it wasn't until he peeked around the corner again that he knew why. He tapped John on the shoulder and whispered, "I got this one."

John shot him a sideways look, but after Travis nodded confidently, he shrugged and nodded his consent.

Travis let out a slow breath before strolling around the corner to face the enemy. "Hey guys, what the heck?" he commented easily, jerking his thumb back around the corner.

"Huh?"

"Travis?" Carl hesitated, "Wha-what are you doin' here?"

"My job dinglefritz," Travis retorted, tossing his hands in the air. "What's with blasting holes in the place? I thought the captain said we weren't here to kill everybody. You darn near took my head off!" He sauntered in, trying to appear confident and sure of himself.

"I-uh," Charlie sputtered.

"Uh, where you been?" Carl asked, trying to sort something difficult out in his head.

Travis kept moving by them, causing them to turn their backs to the corner where John still crouched. "I told you, I'm doing *my job*, which is why I'm asking you where the prisoners are."

"But, uhh…"

"Don't give me your butt!" Travis shot back, "Answer the question! Where are the prisoners right now?"

Carl and Charlie exchanged looks, oblivious to John silently creeping up behind them. "I thought, um," Charlie began.

Travis feigned exasperation, "Don't think, just answer the stupid question!" John tilted his head to his right, silently directing him to move that way. When Travis sidestepped, the two men in front of him turned their heads to follow.

John pounced in silence, leaving Carl alive.

"Umm, they's bein' kept in the... big room," Carl answered while his brother's head was twisted violently behind him. Travis failed to keep his face neutral, but by the time Carl turned to see what was happening, a knife blade was at his throat.

"Don't make a sound, or you'll join him," John warned ruthlessly in his ear.

Travis turned to the wall, trying to steady himself. Seeing Charlie's head twisted that hard was a little too much to take. A noxious taste of adrenaline filled his mouth while his empty stomach twisted over and over with the vision of Charlie's head.

"What big room?" John growled.

"Uhh, uhhh…"

John turned Carl to face his brother, lying dead on the floor at his feet. "Do you wanna join him?" he pressed.

Carl managed to twitch his head back and forth, "No. It's, umm, that, uuhh, big, umm, room," he dared to lift his left hand slightly and point behind Travis.

"Where they keep the food?" Travis pressed.

"Uh-huh," Carl stuttered. "Food."

Travis and John exchanged a look, and Travis knew what was going to happen next would not be something he wanted to see. He turned to walk away.

"H-hey Trav?" Carl sputtered. "Where's Liam?"

Travis closed his eyes and shook his head while John escorted Carl off to the land Charlie now lived in. He heard movement behind him, but he didn't turn around until John put his big hand on Travis' shoulder. "That's just sad," he commented.

"Liam hated those two," Travis recalled. "They drove him nuts just because they were so stupid."

"Well, they weren't guarding anything," John commented. "But they gave 'em these," he rotated his wrist to show two palm-sized black communicators. The devices were a simple button on one edge and a speaker. Nothing fancy, just a method to stay in touch that didn't require computers.

"They couldn't be trusted with anything," Travis started to walk forward, but John restrained him gently.

"I know it's a lot to take, but I had to do it like that. Can't take a chance…" he trailed off with a thought. "I know what they were doing," he muttered. "They were trip wires."

"What?"

"They're like trip wires," John explained. "Anything happens to them, and the troops down this hall know there's a threat coming at em." He examined the radio in his hand, "That means there's a group of soldiers down around the corner there, just waiting for us."

Travis blanched, "What do we do?" A bead of moisture ran down his temple as he contemplated the imminent threat. If John was right, there were a group of armed guys just waiting down this very hall to kill him, his mom, Angel and John. They were outgunned, and way beyond his fighting abilities. Liam would know what to do. Except Liam would run in there, guns blazing and start throwing guys around until he got himself killed.

John sighed and looked down at his weapon.

"I don't think that's such a good idea," Travis complained. John tilted his eyebrows questioningly, and Travis reached out to take a radio. "These things have location built into them," he muttered, looking it over. "So if it leaves the area, then whoever was watching them would see where they went. Although, they'd probably assume one of those morons was wandering away and just needed to be slapped around a bit." He flipped the device over in his hand and considered taking the battery out. That would bring someone here too, which was far from what he needed right now.

"That could work to our advantage," John put in.

"How?"

He pointed at the radio, "If we make these things wander the right way, it would draw only a few of them out."

"And?"

"We control the situation," he explained. "We make them go where we want and lead them into a trap."

"Don't we need the trap first?"

"Yeah. There is that."

Travis flipped the little black device back over and gingerly ran his thumb over the talk button. "What about a room full of poison gas?"

"If it got in the system, it could mess up a whole lot of people before we got it back out."

Travis sighed.

"Any luck on that code yet Ranger five?" the radio sounded.

Travis nearly dropped the radio.

"Echo One, that's a negative," a frustrated man replied. *"Still no idea what the code is, or why it got changed."*

Travis smiled at John, and pressed the button, "Hey, did you guys try one-two-three-four? I use that…" he let go of the button and shrugged.

"Shut up Carl," the radio warned.

"What are you doing?" John said warily.

Travis smiled, "I just established that Carl and Charlie are alive and well," he said triumphantly.

"By sayin' something that stupid?" John paused, then nodded, "Okay, good plan," he chuckled.

"Ranger Five, we're sending Tech twelve out to your twenty. Standby."

"Well, it couldn't sound very intelligent, or they would've caught on."

"Copy Echo One, standing by."

John shook his head, "That's just sad." He looked around, "Sounds like there's only a handful of 'em that can code the doors," he observed.

Travis' face spread into a wide, malevolent smile. "I got it."

"What?"

"We lead 'em into the Reclamation room and turn the fan off again."

"How's that…"

"If we don't turn it back on, they'll probably pass out. Especially if they can't get out."

John seemed to mull that over a minute. "Either way, we'll have them trapped until they can figure out how to get out. Not to mention they'll still have radios to talk to the rest of them out here." He shook his head, "We gotta take them out, that's all there is to it."

Travis looked down at the pistol in his hand, "I'm not sure how much good I'll be."

John started pacing, "There has to be enough in that reclamation room to pull this off. I just don't know how to trigger it without being up in it."

A slow smile spread over Travis' face. "Go get my mom and Angel and get them there. I have a feeling Angel can do it if she's nearby."

John shot him a dark look, "Really?"

"Yeah, really," Travis nodded. "You saw what she did to that door lock."

"I don't trust that thing," John said warily.

"Look, I get your…distrust," he retorted, "but she saved my life more than once. She's not the devil." John gave him a derisive look, but he pressed on, "She saved me by fixing the life support when it broke and got us here to find food for me. I think that's enough for me to trust her."

"Then she ran off," John recalled.

Travis rolled his eyes, "Yeah, she's a little impatient," he admitted. "She was trying to track down my parents," he pointed out, "and just couldn't wait until morning." He paused to consider something, "I think it might have to do with not needing sleep." Shaking it off, he added, "Besides, I'm pretty sure she trusts you."

"All right, fine," John handed Travis the other radio. "But if this gets outta hand, I'm putting a hole in that pretty little head of hers." He caught himself, "I can't believe I just called it a *her*." He started back the way they'd come, then turned back, "Don't lead 'em back too early, I still gotta clear the way ahead of those two."

Travis nodded, "Got it. How long you want me to wait?"

John produced a small black earbud in his palm, "I'll call you on this."

"Isn't that tech?" Travis returned as he put it into his left ear.

John smirked, "Yeah. I won't tell if you don't."

THIS was a plan from the devil himself, but it was too late to go back now. Angel forced in another breath while she watched the empty hallway through the door camera. She stood in the black space, her only view being the three cameras in the area floating on three separate rectangles in front of her. The code blocks were aligned, ready to make the final connection once Travis gave the order.

Those white code blocks turned orange as she followed Annika's instructions. "Are you sure about this?" she asked into the air.

"Breathe sweetheart," Annika's voice said through the portal.

She had to focus her mind to reconnect to that strange body back through the portal and take in another breath. This was way harder than being in the droid.

"There you go."

"I don't know about this," she warned. "There's like, a lot of warning signs and stuff in here." The orange blocks shifted to become a single bar of spiked crimson. "I think this is kinda like a one-way trip, you know?"

"Just be ready to pull the trigger." John's voice caused the portal behind her to ripple wider than when Annika spoke.

"*Sí*," she said, turning slightly to her right where another diamond-shaped block of blue drifted beside her. "Travis? Where are you?"

"Running," Travis' voice huffed from the blue diamond. He sounded out of breath, like he was running.

"Yeah, I can tell that. How far away are you though?"

"I… don't know," he managed. "I think I'm… just about there."

She'd positioned the three camera screens just beyond the blue diamond so she could talk to Travis and watch the screens at the same time. A shadow, then Travis entered the side of one screen. "Okay, I see you now. I think it's like, the door on your right."

She had the door open already and watched him lift the little radio to his face. "Hey. I think it went in here!" he said before throwing the radio into the room. He ran past the camera out of sight and heard a shifting of feet in the room through the portal.

"Sweetheart?"

She'd stopped breathing again. "*Disclupe*," she said quickly and pulled in a breath. She'd used Spanish again, and Annika probably didn't understand what she'd said. It would have to wait; the soldiers were charging into her camera view. "I got them," she announced softly. "There's like, thirteen *soldados* but one of them is staying outside the door."

"Close it," John ordered. "I'll take him. You got those things jammed?"

The last part was Travis' job, not hers. With a glance toward the door blocks, they slid together in front of her, sealing the room. "Room's closed," she announced, dreading what she knew he was going to tell her to do.

"Yeah, radios are jammed," Travis said outside her portal.

"Do it," John whispered hoarsely.

She sighed and lifted her hands up toward the red spiked rectangle and the round white ball. Without touching them, she forced the two incompatible sequences together where they formed into a rippling misshapen ball dotted with spikes that wavered back and forth in time with the ripples. She wasn't exactly sure what the mixture had made, but the ugly red ball looked nothing short of evil in her mind. She turned away from it to force her imagination onto something other than watching men cough and die to see John creeping up behind the lone soldier in the hallway. "What is he gonna do?" she whispered back through the portal.

"Stop looking," Travis ordered, "you don't wanna see that."

She'd been a part of enough death already and plunged back into the portal to her weird body on the gurney.

———

SHE blinked and found herself staring up at Travis' face. "I think he's gonna kill that man," she pointed out with concern.

"If he doesn't, there'll be a lot more coming for us," Travis pointed out. "These guys are ruthless, and they've already killed a whole bunch of people."

Annika sighed, "All of this so they can get to her?"

"Let them have this body," Angel protested. "I don't like it anyway. I can't move, can't see, and it's just so weird."

"You don't mean that," Annika chided.

"*Sí*, I do mean it. I want my old body back."

John stepped back into the room, "Not happening," he snapped. "That thing's irradiated, and it's not on the way. So get over it." His eyes met hers with an iron glare.

"Are we headed back to where we ran into the idiot twins?" Travis guessed.

John nodded, "Let's go, I don't know if she's alive or not, but…" He didn't finish the sentence but stepped back into the hallway. They all followed suit, and as they passed by the double doors of the Reclamation room, a sudden thumping against the door had Travis and Annika jump in shock. "You manage to get those radios jammed?" John asked casually over his shoulder.

"Yeah," Travis nodded, looking at the door. "But I'm keeping it with me just in case."

Nestled in his pocket was the second radio-card which was sending out a constant muffling sound that she could see. The effect was the same as being the loudest voice in a room full of people that no one could talk over.

They traversed more hallways, and Angel saw her fair share of light strips in grey ceiling panels. They wavered, and a tickle of something touched her strangely. There was a new level of *feeling* in this body. She dared to look through a camera again as they passed it and saw her own face looking back at her, a streak of moisture reflecting light on her left cheek.

John turned back at a corner and bumped into her. "Dang it," he muttered, "you really gotta use those feet for more than decoration."

"Still an infant, remember?" Annika reminded him.

"I am not!"

"Yeah, yeah," John waved off. "Still a pain in the butt." He looked down at Angel's face and his eyes shifted to the side. "Sorry."

He'd apologized?

"We're close, so let me sweep the hallway while you guys stay put in this room. Travis and I can do a perimeter check on the Commons before we go in," John continued.

Angel moved her head around and found the door keypad nearby. The camera was pointed at the grey wall across the hall from it, but there were no cameras she could see from there.

She sighed and opened the blue portal in her mind to fully connect with the loosely connected systems and stepped through.

———

FIVE screens floated to her on the black plane, four of which looked like they were in the same room. Before Annika could tell her to breathe, she reached a hand back and put her palm on the portal to stay connected to her body.

"Oh, good. You had me worried for a second sweetheart. Your eyes have that look again," Annika said softly.

"I'm looking in the big room," she admitted, her new body mirroring what she said.

"How?"

Explaining how she did it was less important to her than what she saw. Sixty-one people sat on the floor in groups in a large room. Twenty-two men with guns and attitude strolled around, occasionally glaring at the people sitting on the floor.

"What does she look like?" Angel asked over her shoulder without breaking the connection.

"Who?" Travis asked.

"Deb? You know, *Hombre's* wife?"

"What?" Annika asked.

"I think she just called John '*Hombre*'."

"O-kay," Annika returned.

"Hall's clear, let's go," John's voice directed.

"Hey, I think Angel got into the cameras in the main room," Travis said. "She wants to know what Deb looks like."

"I don't have a photo," he mumbled.

"Why not?" Annika pressed.

"I just don't, alright?" John retorted. "She's about five-two, one-twenty and keeps her hair in a short curly mess on her pretty head," he struggled a moment. "She'd be the one givin' those jokers the evil eye all the time if she's in there."

A few candidates caught her eye in the screens, "Is she… dark… like you?"

She felt his warmth approach her physical body through the portal. "Yeah," he finally admitted. "Probably the only one in there," he added.

"There's two," Angel corrected. "Both of them are too big to be as skinny as you say Deb is. I'm gonna keep looking, but I don't think she's here." She turned from the screens in front of her and looked off into the thin white horizon, reaching out for more systems. A massive red ball, bristling with sparks surged toward her from the distance and she dove through her portal to escape.

———

"*Ay!*"

The three of them were looking at her as her focus returned to the room they were in.

"What is it sweetheart?" Annika asked, the concern obvious.

"I, I don't… I don't know," she blubbered.

Travis moved in closer and looked down into her eyes. "Was there someone else in there?" He must've seen the answer in her eyes, "You stay out for now. Let me see if I can break in and…"

"What do you mean, 'someone else'?" John demanded. "I thought these guys were all anti-tech."

Travis turned his attention to John, "No way. These guys only *say* they're against A.I. I don't think it's true for a second. At least not the captain."

"What makes you say that?" Annika asked, stroking Angel's hair again.

"That's kinda weirding me out," she protested.

"Sorry," Annika stopped stroking with some obvious difficulty.

Travis flashed a smirk her direction before he explained, "When I was on the ship- I mean, their ship, I found a full computer system built into it. Someone was using it, but pretty much everyone on the ship said they were hunting the Legion Virus and condemned technology. Either those guys were lying, or someone on the ship is using."

"You think they got one of their own?" John asked warily.

Travis shrugged, "A hacker? I dunno. They have code breakers for the doors, but I've never heard them talk about the computer systems. They just seem like the 'take over the world' kinda guys to me. They're all about fighting and starting fights, but I never found any of them at terminals." He started toward the keypad on the wall by the door, and let out a frustrated sigh, "I forgot, none of this is interconnected." He shot a curious look at Angel, "How are you jumping from system to system like that?"

"I don't know," she admitted. "I kinda like, reach out. You know?"

He gave her a dubious smile, "No, not really."

John looked at the closed door leading out to the hallway, his impatience showing.

"If Angel says she's not in there, then there's no point in going in," Travis pointed out.

"What about all those people in there?" she asked. "There are like, sixty-one people on the floor, and *veintidós soldados con pistolas*..." She blinked, "I mean twenty-two *soldados con pistolas*."

The three of them exchanged looks before John let out a sigh. "If we storm the room, they got us. If I pick 'em off one by one, they'll get wise to us and swarm. The only way to do this is to keep moving and pick these guys apart." He pointed at the gun in the back pocket of Travis' suit, "It's time for you to use that thing." He held out a hand, and Travis deposited the pistol into it. "I picked this off that last guy," he muttered, producing a small device that clicked onto the top of Travis' gun. He ran a small wire from the device to a port on the side of the gun and handed it back to Travis. "That's a laser mod. It fires one silent shot every five seconds or so, so you gotta let it charge up. Use that first, and if you miss, use the loud part."

Travis looked it over, "How do I…"

John pointed at a slide switch on the back of the tube-shaped device, "Slide it with your thumb to switch between shot types. To the right is the laser, left is normal bullets."

TRAVIS heard the footsteps approaching him and released that slow breath that John had taught him to steady himself. Not enough to be heard, but just enough to keep his own heartbeat from clouding his ears.

Step… Step… Step…

From his crouched position, he leaned down to the floor and pushed himself around the corner. An instant later, a man slumped to the floor with a small burning hole in his chest. Travis didn't watch his handiwork but rolled away and back to his corner. He blew out a breath and shut his eyes. Then he opened them again when all he could see was the horrified look on the man's face when he'd shot him. He looked around, trying to find something else to focus on. "Which room do I put him in?" he whispered.

"It looks to me like you can use the door right by him," Angel's voice responded in his ear.

Travis pushed himself up to his feet and holstered the pistol in his jacket pocket. Now came the ugly part. He walked back around the corner to face his handiwork with grim determination. In a nearly mechanical state, he opened the door nearest the body and pulled the dead man inside. He didn't look for details, or even allow himself to think about what he was actually doing. He needed outta here. "Where to Angel?" he whispered, knowing he was going to have to do it all again.

Angel's voice sounded in his ear, "Go to your left, down the hall and take your next right. There's another one all by himself."

"All right, copy," he acknowledged, wiping the sweat off his brow. He'd done this a few times already, but it still wasn't any easier. His right hand was cramping, and he was becoming concerned that one of these times he would be the victim. He started down the hallway and made the next corner when Angel's voice sounded in his ear again.

"There are two more behind him, and John is catching up to them now."

"So I gotta take him down at the same time?" Travis guessed.

"*Sí*," she said. "*Hombre*, you ready?"

"Yeah *Chica*, I'm on 'em now."

"Ready? Go," Angel directed.

Travis stepped around the corner, gun ready. The approaching soldier already had his weapon up, but a sound behind him had him turning. Travis fired off the laser and made a bright shower of sparks light up the far corner.

He'd missed!

The soldier whirled around just as Travis' thumb slid the switch. A loud explosion preceded a metal projectile flying through the soldier's face. A loud ring silenced everything else, his arms hurt from the recoil, and his stomach was rebelling at the sight of the man's face exploding. It was his first time using the bullets, and it was far messier than the precise hole the laser left in the intended target.

He turned away and put his forehead on the cool metal wall to keep from throwing up. A second later, a hand fell on his shoulder, and he whirled around to shoot.

"Hold on Trav!" John ordered, grabbing Travis' wrist to keep his gun down. "Easy now." He looked him over, "First one sucks, don't it?"

Travis nodded, "Yeah." He wiped at his brow and forced himself to swallow, "I like the wazer way…" He blinked and cleared his throat.

"Figured you would," John nodded, keeping him from trying to correct his verbal mistake. "You'll like this a whole lot better then," he said, handing him a larger pistol. "It's a straight up hole-puncher," he instructed, "and this is a second clip with thirty-four shots on it." Travis started to hand the other pistol over, but John stopped him. "Keep it as a backup. Don't want you running outta ammo."

"Yeah, okay," Travis nodded, holding both guns and trying to decide how to carry the smaller one.

"Here," John offered, holding a belt in his hand. "Put this on, and keep that thing tucked on your off-hand side, grip forward."

"Huh?"

"Just put the belt on," John blew out.

He looked around for a place to put the two guns he was holding, and finally put them on the floor at his feet. Accepting the belt, he started to put it on, but John corrected the direction to put the pouch on Travis' left side.

"Now, put the gun in there."

Travis looked down, momentarily forgetting which gun. Before John could chide him, he remembered that it was the smaller pistol that was supposed to go in it and plucked it from the floor. His natural inclination was to put the gun in his left hand and try to put it into the holster.

John shook his head, "Use your right hand there champ."

"But," he protested, "that's on my…"

"Trust me."

Travis shrugged, and swapped hands with the pistol. As he moved to put it into the holster, he became quickly aware of why it was arranged that way. Now, the gun hung on his left, out of the way of his right hand. If he needed it, he could withdraw the gun rapidly using the same hand he would need to fire it. "Okay. That's pretty cool," he admitted, retrieving the new gun from the floor.

John smiled confidently, "I've done this sort of thing before."

"I can tell," he admitted.

"If you two are done playing, there are three more *soldados* headed your way," Angel commented over their earpieces.

"Copy," John replied. "Are they grouped up?"

"Um, if you mean, like, together, then yeah."

John shook his head ruefully, "Okay, then I need to get around them so Trav and I can pick 'em apart."

"Then you gotta move it *Hombre*."

"Which way?" he retorted with a roll of his eyes.

"I saw that you know," she replied. "First you go right, then take the next left. After two hallways, you take the next two right turns. Travis, you better get outta there or they gonna see you."

Travis looked down the hallway that made sense for them to be coming up, "Is that where they're coming from?"

"*Sí*," she replied impatiently.

John took off on a dead run while Travis looked down the hall. "Won't they notice the big black mark on the wall?"

"I bet you're glad I already hid the bodies," John commented in his ear.

Travis swallowed at the thought, trying to keep the image out of his head. "Yeah."

"They're coming from one hallway down and on your left," Angel instructed. "They not gonna see the mark 'cause they gonna walk right into the hallway from the middle."

"Okay," Travis grasped, moving to his left, "got it."

"*Hombre*, you're gonna get there at the same time they do," Angel reported.

"Trav," John called out, breathing in measured amounts, "remember; you take the one on your left, I got the one on my left. Shoot, then duck back around the corner to avoid the third gun."

"Copy," Travis reported as he crouched against the corner's edge. No one said a word for the next few moments, allowing him to breathe and listen for the footsteps. When he didn't hear any, he started to get nervous. Then, a slight shift of something soft caught his ear, and he aimed his new gun right where he expected them to be coming out.

"Travis," Angel whispered in his earpiece. "They stopped! They're crouching like you!"

Travis didn't dare say a word, but he turned a pleading look into a keypad camera nearby.

"I got an idea you two, stay back and let them keep coming. I got a door I'm gonna open as soon as they get into the hall. That should turn them for you," Angel instructed.

John was usually the one planning things like this, but her plan sounded like a good idea. He pushed himself up to his feet and braced his left shoulder against the corners' edge. His breath was getting edgy, and his trigger finger started to pulse hard.

"Okay, they in the hallway," Angel advised in his ear. "Ready, and...NOW!"

Travis spun around the corner just as a couple of laser blasts showered the middle of the hall. He lined up the gun and pulled the trigger...

Nothing.

He froze as a blast exploded on one of the three men, causing the soldier to fall in slow motion. The other two started to turn toward John, training their guns to take him down. Without any idea what else to do, he switched the bigger gun to his left hand, and pulled the small pistol out with his right. Just as the two men fired, Travis did as well. The gun sent a shock down his arm and a deafening ring in his ear once more. The soldier in the middle of the group lost his left shoulder in an explosion of red, spinning him around to the ground while the third soldier crouched down and turned on Travis.

John fired off another shot, putting a neat hole in the third soldier's head before he could fire.

The soldier Travis had shot was down on his knees now, but he lifted his gun with his good hand and fired back.

———

ANGEL watched helplessly as the laser bolt tore through the air toward Travis. Suddenly, the camera screen in front of her fizzled into pixie dust falling toward the floor. "Travis?! Travis?!" Angel grasped at the falling dust in futility.

Several seconds passed.

"TRAVIS!" Angel screamed in the digital void around her. Several screens hovered around her, but they only showed empty hallways.

"He's all right," John broke in, sounding annoyed. "Looks like that last shot got too close to his earpiece though."

"I can't see anything," Angel complained emphatically.

"Then open your eyes," John retorted.

"Really?" she bit back.

"Yeah, really. He's okay. That shot just got so close that the static charge off it fried the electronics."

"My brain feels a little scrambled too," Travis' voice added.

"Let me have one more look," John instructed. "You're damn lucky son. One more inch to the left and you'd have a permanent hole in your head."

"You two are playing with fire," Annika commented through the portal behind her.

They were playing with fire, but it was working. The number of *soldados* she could find had dwindled, and she reached out to pull more screens toward her. Answering her call, the red pulsing ball rushed toward her once more and she dove backward through her portal.

HIS left ear felt singed, even though John seemed sure it was fine. The black mark on the wall across the hall behind him sent a shiver down his spine. It had been that close.

"What?" John protested, holding up a finger at Travis' puzzled expression. "Who?"

Travis tried to read John's face, but it wasn't helping him understand what was going on. "What's going on?"

"I think she's sayin' that… whatever… is back."

Travis thought a moment, "The co-beast-a?"

John's eyebrow shot up, "The what-a?"

"Ask her," he pressed. "Was it the co-beast-a?"

John sighed, "Trav wants to know if it was some… co-beast-ya. Whatever the heck that is."

"Copy," John nodded. "Let's get back," he told Travis.

"What'd she say?"

"Your mother called us back, that's all I know." He gave Travis a warning look, "Now zip it. We don't know what's between us and them."

Travis nodded and checked his weapon. John stopped long enough to point at a small button near the trigger, "Don't forget to turn the safety off next time."

It only took a few minutes to return to Deb's cabin where they found Angel sitting up propped by random items. "She got pretty agitated," Annika explained. "I had to sit her up to keep her from going into shock."

Travis crossed the small space and looked into her eyes. "*He's here*," she whispered. "*Diablo está aquí*," she added, fear showing on her face.

"What are you talking about?" He looked down and saw that her hands were fidgeting with each other. It should have been a sign of accomplishment, but right now it looked like she was trying to tear herself apart. He put his hands on hers and stopped them from assaulting each other.

Angel took in a sharp breath at his touch. "You're warm," she observed.

John snapped his fingers, "Got it!"

Travis looked over his shoulder, but his mother asked the question first. "What?"

"Devil," John said, nodding his head. "She means... I mean, she said, 'the devil is here.' At least, I'm pretty sure that's what she said."

Annika tilted her head, "How do you know that?"

"My daddy used to talk about other cultures. Something my granddaddy used to do a lot, at least according to my daddy," he shrugged. "I guess they both felt the need to make sure that somebody remembered Earth history for what it used to be. My daddy's favorite thing to talk about was Spanish culture. Funny though, he didn't talk too much about black history." He looked reminiscent for a moment, "Never figured out why that was..."

Travis looked at Angel strangely, "Spanish?"

"Yeah," John said confidently from behind him. "I don't know too much, but I remember 'diablo' means devil."

"Is that what 'co-beast-a' means too?"

Angel shook her head, and then blinked in surprise. "I..." she trailed off, looking a bit lost. "Why did I do that?"

"You were telling me 'No'," he explained, then stopped. He was starting to put something together in his head, and if he was right John would probably go nuts.

"Why did you ask about that?" Annika asked him.

"What?" Travis mumbled in thought.

"I think he means *cobista*," Angel answered for him.

Annika and John exchanged glances. "Beats me," John offered.

"It means, like... a creepy guy. Or something like that," Angel explained. She studied his face, "What are you thinking about?"

He pulled his gaze back to her face, "Something you said." He wrestled with an idea, then looked down at his hands. While he'd been contemplating, she had shifted her hands to cover his.

"*Qué*?" Angel asked, looking innocent. "My hands are cold, and yours are so warm," she added with a small smile.

"That happens with fear," John offered while checking his weapon.

Travis caught his mother's gaze, "Not for robots." Angel started to say something, but he took a leap of faith and pulled his hands free only to put one on the top of her left breast.

She flushed and her own hands flew up to push his away. He didn't fight her reaction and moved both his hands away from her.

"Travis!" his mother scolded.

"*¡Venga!*" Angel protested.

He smiled at her. "I thought so."

Angel shied back, crossing her arms over her chest. "Now who's acting like a *cobista*?"

"What do you think you're doing?" Annika corrected, pushing Travis back.

"Did you see what she did?" Travis pointed out.

"Well of course I did!" Annika retorted, "and I'd have done the same thing! I can't believe…"

"That's a *human* reaction."

John stopped pacing the floor and looked over at them. "What'd you say?"

His mother was still giving him the 'I can't believe you' look, so he turned to face John. "When she and I first met, she was stuck in the computer system of The Sapphire," he started. "When the soldiers were firing at her, she'd yell and scream 'oww' at every shot before she finally got *pissed* and started firing back." He thought back to the day and smirked, "She went all 'commando' on them and started yelling while she was shooting…"

"It hurt!" Angel defended.

Travis only smiled more, "Exactly my point. It was a *human* reaction."

"Sounds more like clever programming to me," John declined, settling into a chair.

Travis shook his head, shifting his stance, "From the get-go, she kept telling me she was a human. Believe me, I didn't think it was anything more than well-developed coding myself."

John shifted in his chair, then leaned forward. He took another look at Angel and shook a thought from his mind. "Either way, we still gotta deal with those buddies of yours."

"They're not my… hey!" Travis protested as his mother soundly slapped him over the back of his head.

"That's for taking advantage of a helpless girl!"

He shrugged, "I needed a…"

Annika held up a hand to stop him, "Next time, figure out another way to prove your theories."

John chuckled, "Way to go momma bear."

"Okay, fine," he resigned with a sigh. "Wait a minute, I didn't mean it to sound like that," he added with embarrassment.

"You're really good at digging holes," John smirked.

"Gee, thanks."

John stood up, "Okay, we're gettin' off base here." Before Travis could protest, he leveled a finger at him, "You can wait to do your weirdo experimentation later. Right now, we have to straighten this mess out and take out these soldiers."

"Why can't we just talk to this Captain?" Annika offered.

Both Travis and John shook their heads, "Captain Braun wasn't someone *anyone* wanted to go talk to," he recalled.

"These guys have traveled a long way and killed a lot of people already to get what they want. They're not too interested in reason now," John added.

Annika shook her head, "Well, it's like I said already. You guys are playing with fire, and I don't think I can stand to see either one of you get burned."

Travis took a long look at his mother, and it hit him. She'd never said anything about his near-death experience recently, but he could see it on her face now.

"Up till now, we've had a tactical advantage," John reassured her. "With her coordination, we can steer clear of their traps and see 'em coming. But this 'devil' character might just change all that." He looked at Angel, prompting her to respond.

"I don't know," she tried. "He is, just… I don't know."

"What don't you know?" John pressed.

She shook her head, then turned a puzzled expression at Travis. "Why did I do that?" she asked with annoyance.

"Do what?" Travis prompted, even though he was pretty sure he knew what she was referring to. Even if John wanted to press the matter of the fight with the soldiers more, he was still going to take advantage of any opportunity to explore Angel's human side.

"I… my head. I shake it, but I don't know why," she clarified in confusion.

He smiled at her, "You were using non-verbal communication. It generally means 'no'." He shot a look at his mother, "Another one of those 'human responses.'"

"So what don't you know?" John cut in, eager to get an answer.

Angel took a long breath, "*Diablo* is mean, and he comes at me every time I look too far."

"What do you mean, 'look too far'?" Travis cut in.

"So, it's like," she began, trying to find the words. "When I am looking, and I am trying to see where the *soldados* are… but they are all over the place, so I am having to look in lots of places to find them…"

"You're spread out in the system too much," Travis cut in. "It makes you vulnerable," he continued to explain. "The more you map out in the system, the more exposed you become." He saw the confused look on John's face and continued, "This hacker is in the same place every time, I'd bet on it. The problem is, she keeps spreading out through the ship's systems and he picks up on it in his local area." He snapped his fingers, "Anti-virus program! I'd bet on it," he added triumphantly.

"Can she find *him*?" John offered.

Angel shook her head, "I no wanna find him. I know him somehow, like I see him before."

That stopped Travis' confidence cold, "What do you mean, you *know* him?"

"I…" she trailed off, about to say something and changed her mind. "It's like, I've seen him before, but I don't remember him. You know?"

"Oh great! Your robot girlfriend has memory issues?"

"I'm not a robot!" Angel protested vehemently.

John scowled at her, "Well, you sure ain't no human."

"John!" Annika corrected in disbelief.

"Now you're starting to sound like when we first met," Travis reminded Angel.

John blew out a breath, "Stay on task folks. Sort this mess out later, right now, we gotta get these soldiers outta Hadron Prime, remember?"

Travis nodded, keeping his focus on Angel. "Can you tell where the hacker is and avoid him?"

She shook her head, "Not without him seeing me."

He turned and pulled on his chin in thought. "Can you look around in the Commons where they're keeping the hostages?"

"That is the first place I see him," she protested.

"Start small," he instructed. "Stay on one camera, then move to the next, and put what you see on that display there if you can," he added, pointing at the door display panel.

A NGEL looked up into his eyes and sighed. Diablo was in there, and her body out here felt like a strange prison. Travis needed her help and without it he might do something *loco* that could get him into more trouble.

Like getting shot at.

She tried to take a steadying breath, then another when the first one didn't seem to be enough. The black portal rimmed in blue appeared in her mind and she passed through it into the large black plane once more. Up to now, she'd always pulled the other systems toward her by calling them with her mind. Diablo had a nasty way of hearing her and answering her call too, so she decided on a different approach. She walked to the white block that represented the door panel and traced an oval on one face. It shouldn't have worked, but she was able to squeeze herself down into the small portal and pass inside.

The brilliant white space inside was just as cramped as she'd expected. The white walls were right there, but at the same time they didn't seem to exist. On one side, her portal hung in the ethereal white as though it were attached to the air. She shifted inside the tight space that didn't look small anymore and found several paths that led to other things. The narrow colored lines carried her to another white space, just as small as before where four screens hung in the whiteness. These were the camera views into the big room from before, but they were a part of this space. When she called them to her on the outside, did they separate from in here and float to her? There was a lot about what she did she wasn't sure about, but this wasn't the time to start working on that puzzle. *Hombre* would get impatient and start storming around again. Wriggling around, she grabbed the red line she had rode to get here and pulled it to the first screen.

Far in the distance, Travis called, "That's great! Can you get any others?"

She rolled her eyes while she pulled it from the first screen to the second. This showed more of the inside of the big room where the prisoners cowered on the floor.

"Sweetheart, I need you to breathe," Annika called.

She sighed and focused on the connection to her weird new body. A red line was attached to the screen in the room with Annika, Travis and *Hombre*, but it wouldn't let her connect to her body. She looked at her finger and traced another oval in the air that filled with the rippling black water outlined in electric blue. The portal shifted as *Hombre's* voice said, "That's Matty, Zack, and Robbie. Those guys are just waiting for a chance at these guys."

His voice was lower, like he was talking under his breath. She reached out and put her right hand on the rippling water and felt a shiver run down her spine.

"There you go," Annika confirmed. "You had me a bit worried there."

"*Lo siento*," she said. "I had to get a new portal first."

"Well, whatever you did worked."

"Any chance you can pan this to the left?" John asked.

He wanted a pan? That didn't sound right, and she knew it. She looked at the screen, expecting the camera to shift but it just sat there. Taking the screen in her hands, she forced the screen to tilt to the left and the view moved with it. Outside, the screens had moved wherever she wanted just by thinking about it. In here, it apparently took a lot of physical work to get them to move.

"Nice," Travis said through the portal.

"Sweetheart?"

She grumbled and put her hand back on the portal.

"Thank you."

"Are there any other cameras?" Travis asked.

The things I do for him, she thought as she let go of the portal long enough to unhook the red line from one screen and plug it into the side of another. *And then he cops a feel too?!*

"This is really great," Travis said. "Do you see her yet?"

"No, not yet. Hey Chica, pan this one to the right, then make a slow pass left again for me."

That meant letting go of the portal again. These guys had no idea how much trouble it was to do all this. She wanted to complain, but she didn't dare to speak in here. Diablo might hear her talking and come find her trapped inside this tiny place only big enough for a midget. That wasn't a very nice thing to say, and her *Madre* would be pissed with her for even thinking like that. Her *Tia* was little like that, and she wasn't somebody to make fun of.

The black water of the portal turned into fire on her hand, and she ripped it away in reflex.

"Sweetheart! What's wrong?"

Her hand looked normal even though it felt like she'd burned it.

"You need to breathe. C'mon now, I need you to take a breath."

"Look at her face," Travis said. "Hey, what's going on?"

She looked at the black water that still looked the same. The whiteness around her pressed in tighter, making it hard to think. All she wanted to do was run, but her only way out looked like the portal she'd drawn. The same portal that stung her only a moment ago.

This was going to hurt.

———

"HEY, there you are," Travis smiled down at her. "What happened to you?"

"I dunno." How could she explain the pain in her hand, or the portals, or the red line she'd rode? He wouldn't understand. How could he?

"Your face scrunched up and you quit breathing."

"It hurt," she answered, looking away.

"What hurt?" he asked.

"I was thinking about something…"

"You need to keep breathing," Annika chided, stroking Angel's hair.

"Hey, I lost the view," John interrupted. "I need that to get a plan of attack here people."

"Just give her a minute," Travis huffed out.

John glowered at him dangerously, "We don't have time for this. If we can get those guys outta there, we might stand a chance at taking this place back. But that won't happen if we sit around here playing patty-cake with your little robot girlfriend."

"She's not my girlfriend," he bit out. "And she's doing a lot right now."

"Yeah? Looks to me like she's laying there getting all your attention while the real threat is waiting outside the door. For all I know, she's in on this with those guys and just playing us until it suits her to…"

"I realize you're upset, but attacking this poor girl won't help the situation," Annika chided.

"She's not a girl."

There it was again, as dependable as a clock. That simmering hatred of her just beneath the surface. "I had to do it different so Diablo wouldn't find out. I'm sorry, okay? I'll go back and get the stupid camera back for you."

"Good. We have an advantage here people, and we gotta use every one we can get."

"What do you mean you have to do it different?" Travis asked.

Hombre was still looking at her, so she dove back through the portal just to get away from his glare.

———

FROM the black plane to the white spaces, she found her way back to the tiny room and made another portal to stay connected to her body. Her weird body that the big man glared at. Travis had fondled her, Annika wouldn't stop stroking her hair, but John's glare was the worst. She touched the portal to make her physical body breathe again and got her bearings.

Beside the screen she'd attached the cable to were three other screens, each one had a set of orange handles inside red boxes.

The second screen only showed a wall, so she grabbed the handles and moved it around a bit until she finally figured out what she was looking at. It wasn't the wall. It was the ceiling. Looking at the other three screens, she moved each of them around until she could finally confirm what her suspicion was. At one corner of the room, someone had found the second camera and somehow bent the small mounting arm upward.

That won't do any good. She reoriented camera number three to see the people again and moved the glowing string from the first camera to the third one.

"Okay, pan left," John ordered from outside.

She moved the screen again, watching the other two working cameras. As she did, she started to figure out the layout of the room. Ignoring John's voice, she moved the screen into one position, and then adjusted the fourth screen to cover the remaining angle. Wriggling around to face her portal, she said, "I got the screens right to cover the room now. I'm gonna change the screens one at a time and let you see that way."

She waited a moment, then moved the glowing string to the fourth screen. After a minute or two, she moved it back to the first camera screen.

"I thought there were four cameras in the Commons," Annika recalled.

"Somebody bent the arm, so the camera only looks up," Angel replied.

"If you can see in all these cameras like this, why can't you find Deb?" John suddenly challenged.

"There aren't cameras everywhere you know," Annika reminded him gently.

John wasn't placated, "Sure looks like she can see everywhere to me, and she seemed to find all those buddies of yours too!"

A surge of electricity rushed up her from inside and she pushed back through the portal to her body.

———

"C'MON John," Travis tried, holding his hands up pleadingly between her and *Hombre.* "Cut her some slack here. It's not like this is some interconnected network she's working with." He saw her look at him and asked, "How are you tracking the soldiers anyway?"

"They just show up," she offered. "Nobody else look like these guys in there. They all have something that makes them easy to see without the cameras. I don't know what it is, but…"

John looked back at the wall display and jolted when he realized it was blank. "You had one job!" he shouted at her. "I only asked you to do one thing, and you're not even doing that!" he continued to shout.

"I'm sorry…" she sputtered, unsure of what to do with the rush of emotions that hit her all at once. He scared her, but her body kept getting rushes of sensation she couldn't explain.

"'Sorry' doesn't cut it here, we need that intel, and I don't need you running away from your job just 'cause you feel like it!" He stormed over to her, "I bet that's exactly why you can't find Deb." He stuck his thick finger right up to her nose, "You can't stick with nothin'!"

Travis pushed his hand back, "Hey! Knock it off man! We're on the same side here!"

"Really?" he shot back. "Sure seems like we're all on *her* side!"

"Hey!" Annika protested.

"We're out there gettin' shot at, but as soon as somebody starts getting wise to her, you wanna pull the plug! What the heck man?"

"She's our ace in the hole! We lose that, and we lose our coordination, remember?"

"We can't retreat every time things get tough!" John shouted, pointing at Angel. "And nobody gets special treatment here! We've all got our duties, and…" he trailed off while looking at her with a piercing gaze. "You know where she is," he ground out dangerously.

Angel felt a strange surging within her. Her breath started coming in short gasps, and she swallowed on impulse.

"Why won't you tell me?" John glared at her darkly.

"I…" *She couldn't. He'd kill her if he knew.*

In a flash, John closed the distance and grabbed Angel by the shoulders, "TELL ME!" In a sharp panic, Angel did the only thing she could.

S HE landed on the black plane without a sound and instinctively dove into the first white block. The screen inside showed her limp body in John's hands.

"You demon! Get back here!" John shouted.

Travis tried to push John off her, but he lashed out with a fist that sent Travis to the floor.

"That's what you get when you trust this stuff! It's all demons! It's the whole reason why we're out here in the first place!"

Travis wiped his bloody lip and started to his feet. "No. You're out here because your forefathers gave up and left," he bit back.

"You…" John started back toward Travis, but suddenly was held up by a small woman with her hand on his chest.

"You know he's right," Annika protested fiercely.

"Then maybe Mister Right there can tell me why his girlfriend won't fess up to where Deb is," he challenged.

Annika turned her sad eyes up toward his fierce gaze. "You know why," she said softly.

Travis wiped his bloody lip again to keep from dripping on Angel's limp body. "Hey, you can come back. It's okay, I won't let him hurt you."

Could she? *Hombre* was *muy loco* right now, and Travis was still bleeding. She wanted to smack *Hombre* in the face, but she also wanted to stay as far away from him as possible. She couldn't do both, and since her body didn't do what she thought it should, she continued to watch through the camera screen.

Travis stood there, looking down at her body. "Angel?"

"Threat contained," a deep voice stated triumphantly from outside her tiny white room. The portal in the wall glazed over to a solid blue that turned dull. The connection to her body disappeared, leaving her inside the tiny space with a single screen. The pressure around her increased, but her portal wouldn't let her through.

On the gurney in the screen, her body went rigid before it started to vibrate.

"Angel!" Travis shouted. "Angel! You've got to come back!"

Annika rushed to her side, "Sweetheart please!" She grasped at Angel's arms to keep them from flailing, "She's gone into some kind of seizure!" Annika pointed out to Travis. "I don't understand why…"

"I don't either," Travis pulled the pillows out from behind Angel's seizing form to hopefully keep her from rolling off the gurney. "As long as she's still connected - Is there any kind of warning program, or… something that automatically kicks in on this body if there's no dominant program to run it?"

"No. Programming is not my thing," Annika admitted, struggling to hold Angel's arms down.

John rushed across the small room and pulled something out of a drawer. A moment later, he was cramming something into the mouth of her body.

Travis tried to stop him, "Hey! Knock it off…"

"We gotta keep her from swallowing her tongue!" *Hombre* ordered. "Why hasn't this happened before?"

"If there's nothing to keep the body running without her, then that means that part of her program is still in here, but another part got cut off," Travis said. He looked over at the keypad on the wall and saw something that made his face change. "Oh crap! I'm right!" He dashed over to fill the screen with his eyes, "Angel?"

She grabbed the edges of the screen and twisted it, hoping it would do something that he could see. The view turned fuzzy and then back to normal.

"I can see the camera lens; can you do anything with the display?"

She twisted around, looking for a way to control the display and found only a glowing red string. She jabbed it into the side of her single screen and watched his face shift in recognition.

"She's in there!" Travis shouted.

"That's great," Annika complained, "but she's still seizing out here! She needs to get back before her body dies!" She was struggling to hold Angel's arms down with a small line of sweat starting to run down her brow.

Travis turned back to the camera, "Can you get back?" he asked. When she shifted the camera left to right, he huffed in frustration. "How did you get trapped?" he muttered.

"What about that hacker?" John offered, taking over for Annika. "Damn she's strong," he observed, struggling to keep the body from tearing itself apart.

Travis started to say something, then reconsidered. "I've got no terminal, how am I going to break his hold on her?"

"I don't know!" John protested, "You're the one that was on that ship. You either know who it is, or you know who would."

"But there wasn't anybody..." he trailed off, then snapped his fingers as an idea dawned on him. He dashed to the table and grabbed his weapons. "It's the captain," he bit out. "Either he knows him, or that's who the hacker is." He stormed toward the door.

"Travis, wait!" his mother called after him. She turned him around, "I..."

Angel watched as Travis took his mother by the shoulder with his left hand. "Mom, I've got to do this. I can't let him kill her."

"You're not a soldier," she choked out.

Travis paused to look at her thrashing body on the gurney, then back at his mother. "I love you mom," he choked out before he turned toward the door.

Angel couldn't do very much from her trapped location, but she could open the door. Somewhere, a part of her was screaming at her not to do it. Like it was bad somehow, but the fuzzy feeling in her mind was clouding her judgment, and she opened the door obediently like she was supposed to do.

It was what she was supposed to do.

Open the door...

The door slid open for him, and Travis moved out of her line of sight.

"Trav!"

Hombre grabbed more guns from the table and rushed toward the door. "It's an assault rifle," John explained as he disappeared from view. "I forgot she keeps a stash in the compartment behind the closet," he added sheepishly. "They pack a hell of a kick, especially for a laser rifle, so use both hands on it."

His voice drifted away, "Then let's go get the captain."

She tried to turn the camera enough to follow Travis, but he was gone. The body on the gurney stopped struggling, leaving Annika to stare helplessly at it. At least that was over.

Morbid, stupid thought! How could she think that way? Her body, that was her body!

But it wasn't.

She was where she belonged.

Through the screen, Angel stared at the body on the gurney. Her mind told her she didn't belong here, but she struggled with why she didn't belong in here.

She saw Annika suddenly stiffen, then touch her ear as if she'd heard something. "Are you sure? Hurry, just hurry! She stopped moving and- and I just don't know what to do!" she heard Annika plead. "Please be careful Travis," Annika added.

Travis was in trouble? Angel forced herself to pay attention and think this through. Travis had gone to do something. Was it to help *her?* She needed out. Needed to help Travis. She whirled around in the increasingly tightening space, running out of ideas and becoming desperate.

"Angel please!" Annika cried, tears streaming down her face. "I don't want to lose you!"

Angel grabbed at the screen handles and shook it. "*Ay!*" she screamed before she threw it across the room and exploded in anger. The tiny white space around her fizzled into the blackness of the void where her portal hung, faithfully awaiting her entrance.

———

ANNIKA twisted away to look at something behind her. Angel

followed her gaze and found the keypad on the wall smoking. "Oh my God," Annika breathed. "Angel?"

A flood of feeling, power, and more rushed at her with a desperate urgency to take a deep breath…

"Angel?" Annika turned a hopeful look toward her. "Oh God! You're back!" Without thinking, she bent down and hugged her tightly like a long-lost daughter.

Angel stiffened at the gesture, feeling restrained and welcome at the same time.

Travis.

The memory of him seemed distant, but important all at once. "Where is Travis?" she asked, her voice muffled by Annika's shoulder.

Annika released her, but only moved enough to make some space between them. She looked into Angel's eyes, searching for something. "Travis went to go find the hacker," she explained.

"But he's in trouble!"

"What do you mean?" Annika asked, standing up straight.

Angel blinked, trying to sort out the rush of thoughts and memories. She knew the 'hacker' somehow, but it didn't make sense. However, she knew Travis was in trouble if he was going after Diablo. She needed answers she didn't have, but the connections outside of her mind might. It was time for her to stop being afraid, stop fighting this body she was in. It wasn't better in the digital world after all, and she needed to… "I need to get to him," she said firmly.

Annika blinked in shock, "But, you need time to get used to…"

Angel shifted her shoulders and started to twist herself.

"Okay, hold on now, I don't know if I can hold you up!"

She kept pushing herself, moving her arms, and getting more frustrated with the body. She wanted, no, needed to get to Travis. She had to get up! She couldn't keep lying here on this bed.

Annika took the initiative and slipped her arm under Angel to help her sit up again. "Okay, I don't know that you're ready to stand up just yet," she observed.

"I have to get to Travis," Angel demanded, giving the woman a stern look. "Why didn't you make this body to walk?"

Annika turned a questioning look at her. "This is your body," she replied, "it will do whatever you tell it to."

Angel looked down at her legs and made them move. A quick look at the woman and she saw how she was standing on hers. She had to be straight up and down, that was all there was to it, right? Shifting one leg, then the other, she worked herself around to let the legs dangle over the edge and felt like she was about to fall.

"Here," Annika directed, reaching down to tap a hidden button on the side of the gurney. The entire platform descended until Angel's feet touched the cool metal floor below.

She was now seated upright on the table, gurney, bed, whatever this thing was, with her feet just barely touching the cold metal floor. The icy greeting tickled and stung at her feet, sending a shiver up through her. Annika changed positions to stand in front of her and reached down to take her hands.

"Okay, now, pull yourself up to me," she directed.

Wide-eyed and confused, Angel obeyed her instruction and started pulling on Annika's hands. It was too much to just pull herself by her arms alone, and she instinctively started to push herself up with her legs as well. Slowly, with a lot of jerky movements, she was finally standing. Well, wavering around really and holding onto Annika for dear life. "Ohh," she muttered, "this is really hard to do."

The two of them were almost equal in height, so Annika quickly shifted her grip on Angel to slide one arm under her shoulders and allow Angel to lean on her for support. "Okay, crash course in walking," she smiled, "hopefully not too much crashing."

She turned a lifted eyebrow on Annika, "This sounds bad."

"You'll do fine," she said optimistically. "First one foot," she instructed, moving her left foot forward to illustrate walking.

Angel responded in kind, and felt her right leg start to buckle.

For a brief moment she was falling into Annika before the two of them were able to work together to steady her once more. "*Lo siento*," she said apologetically.

"It - it's okay honey, now, let's try that again," Annika replied.

After a few more jerky steps, Angel was at the closed door to the cabin and realized that it was stuck shut. She glanced at the keypad, "Oops."

"I'm just glad you're back," Annika soothed. "And look at what you've already accomplished."

"But I still can't help Travis if I'm in here." She glared at the door and summoned the controls to reveal themselves superimposed on what she could see through her eyes like a layer on reality. Tiny white blocks and pyramids materialized, connected by red and blue strings that floated in front of the damaged little panel beside the door. One of the little blocks had been torn open from the inside, obstructing the path between the button on the door panel to the motor control pyramid. The desire to open the door returned to her, and the pyramid shifted from white to green before the door slid to the side.

"How did you do that?" Annika observed in awe. "I thought it was broken."

Once she'd opened the door all the way, Angel smirked, "I tell it to open," she said, adding a shrug that cost her a little of her balance.

They stepped into the hallway, "I don't know which way the boys went," Annika admitted.

Angel looked both right and left, since those were the only two options, and then used her mind to search for them.

"Hey!"

Annika turned, nearly dumping Angel on the floor in the process. A snarling man stood there, holding a gun on her. "I - I was just helping her go to the bathroom," she tried quickly.

The man gave her a wary look from behind his two-handed grip on the pistol he pointed at her. "Where did you two come from?" he challenged.

"There," Annika said, glancing at Deb's cabin.

A wave of panic rushed through her as she considered the barrel of the gun aimed at her. He was taller than her, bald, pale-skinned, and smelled horrible. "Step away," he instructed, gesturing with the pistol to enforce his command.

The two of them moved obediently, though awkwardly to the side.

"What's wrong with her?" he asked hesitantly, shifting to get close enough to the room and peer inside.

"It's my first day learning to walk," Angel retorted.

He suddenly jerked his angry countenance back on her, "What'd you say?"

"I said, 'I'm learning to walk.' Are you deaf, or just *estúpido*?"

"Angel!" Annika pleaded under her breath.

The smelly man glared down at Angel. "You sound funny," he said suspiciously.

Angel couldn't help herself. "And you stink. So what?" He started to raise his hand up to backhand her, but Angel glared right back at him defiantly. "Is the big, strong *hombre* gonna hit the poor girl who can't even walk? What a big strong man he is!"

Annika made a small sound, trying to contain a laugh that was desperately trying to escape.

"Move!" he shouted.

"I guess he not so big and strong after all," Angel mocked. "Maybe he gonna let his *capitán* do it for him since he's just not strong enough," she added, working with Annika to start walking down the hall.

"I should just blow your head off for that," he threatened, keeping pace behind them.

Angel stumbled a little, then steadied herself with Annika's support. "I don't think your *capitán* would like that so much," she retorted.

"We'll see about that," he grumbled.

Annika and Angel exchanged a quick look and kept going. The blocks, pyramids and strings connecting the lights, doors and things beyond her physical eyes hovered around her, awaiting her command. A complicated series of blocks, pyramids and lines also hung around the soldier's pistol that he kept in his right hand. She let Annika lead and studied the little network of parts around the gun long enough to see her advantage.

"C'mon, move!" their captor demanded impatiently from behind them.

"I am," Angel shot back. "Does this look easy to you?"

He threw his hands up in the air and paced away from them. "I can't believe I ended up…"

The gun in his hand suddenly let out a high-pitched whine a split-second before it exploded in his hand. The ensuing fireball of electrical energy fried his body and dumped him on the floor.

"Oh my God!" Annika exclaimed. "Did you do that?" she asked with a shocked look for Angel.

Angel smirked. "I got tired of his complaining," she said sarcastically. "Besides, I don't want any extras when we find Travis," she added, pressing forward again.

After another turn down a hallway, Annika steered them toward a large hole in the wall. "Looks like we're on the right track," she mused. Something about the hole intrigued her, and she stooped for a closer look. "It looks like the edges were melted," she observed.

Angel looked at the hole, mostly because wherever Annika was pointed was the same way she was pointed. "I didn't think Travis had anything that could do that," she commented, trying to keep Annika on-track. They turned to start down the corridor and saw several bodies with holes in various places. "But I bet they did that," she added.

"I just hope they're alright."

She did too, but she had the ability to look ahead if she used it. "*Una momento*, I need to try something."

"What are you doing?"

Like the black plane, she reached out down the hallway toward the devices with her mind and a rush of screens ran toward her. "I'm looking ahead," she explained as one by one the screens flashed in front of her until she saw him.

He and *Hombre* stood together at the side of a dimly lit room with two tables and a work counter that lined two walls. "I see him," she said.

"How are they?"

They were in trouble. Two totally white guys stood on either side of them, way bigger than *Hombre* and armed with guns. A tall man stood in front of them, gloating and pointing his finger at Travis. A moment later, he slowly turned toward the camera. Short, buzz-cut blonde hair sat atop a square face chiseled from Caucasian stone. A sneer turned up the corner of his mouth as he locked eyes with her through the screen.

He was going to kill them while she watched.

She had to hurry, but her body was so slow! "We gotta go!"

"Are they in trouble?" Annika pressed, moving them forward at a horribly slow pace.

The blonde man's eyes narrowed at her, then widened.

"*Sí,*" she admitted while the man turned away. He was Diablo, she knew it even though she shouldn't. She also knew that she should know him even though he was a stranger. He pointed at Travis and the bulging albino next to him raised his gun to Travis' head.

"NO!" she screamed. The screens flew away from her as the lights in the hallway around them exploded in a shower of sparks.

A scream reached his ears through the closed door, as did a series of small explosions. The block of a white man next to him shifted his stance, lowering his gun down from Travis' head enough that he dared to steal another breath.

That was close.

Captain Braun stared at him, "You think she can save you?"

The scream was definitely a woman, but who was he talking about?

Braun sighed, "You are so naïve. All your talent, and you still don't know who she is."

John huffed, "You don't know..."

The towering man next to John struck him in the left shoulder, knocking him to the ground. "You will respect the captain," he said flatly.

"I'm going to ask you again, where is the ship you stole?" Braun asked coolly as if John hadn't even spoken.

Didn't he already know? "I don't know," he said, hoping to keep stalling until he could figure out how to get Braun to unlock Angel. "Who's your hacker?" he dared to ask.

Braun scowled at him, "I am asking the questions, you are answering. You stole that ship from me and used it to travel here. Why you chose to come here is illogical given the available data. I expected a more logical response from you."

John struggled to his feet, "Buddy, you never met anyone smarter than this kid."

Travis expected the albino next to John to shoot him, but he didn't move.

"Why do you think I have left him alive?"

What did he mean by that? Travis considered how easy it would have been for them to shoot him in the hallway where he and John had been captured, and now they were still at gunpoint. *Why hadn't Braun just killed him?*

"But first I must address this," Braun added while turning toward the door.

The screaming woman in the hallway?

The two men beside himself and John shifted, twitched, and backed away while dropping their guns that clattered on the floor. Travis looked at Braun but found him preoccupied with the exit. The albino's eyes widened in pain and they both dropped to their knees while holding their heads simultaneously. Neither of them let out another sound as they both twisted to the floor unconscious.

"What the heck was that?" John said under his breath, just loud enough that Travis could hear him.

Good question, but he could only suspect that Braun had done something to them. How he'd done it was just as much a mystery as why. What purpose would he have to knock out the two men holding them at gunpoint?

"Where have you been?" Braun said toward the door, still forty feet away.

The grey door slid to the side, revealing Angel standing beside his mother with a concerned look on her olive face. "Are you guys okay?" she asked.

Travis nodded, glad to see her standing there but still trying to sort out how she'd managed it. The two women didn't seem to be carrying any guns, but with the guns exploding around him he had a newfound reason not to trust them.

"You will surrender that body to me."

"You already got one, Diablo. Now I'm gonna make sure you won't hurt anybody anymore," Angel threatened.

Braun twitched and his head snapped to the side as if he'd been slapped. "Command not authorized," he glared back at her.

Angel stared at Braun, glaring back at him as if she could bore holes in him with her eyes. She had to be doing something with her mind, but what?

"Trav," John whispered, gaining his attention.

He turned from the mind war to see John glancing at something beside Travis' feet. The rifle he'd taken from one of the soldiers in the hallway was right next to him, daring him to pick it up and promising a quick, fiery death if he did. If it was such a great idea, why didn't John make a lunge for the one to his right?

As if they could read each other's minds, John glanced at his right shoulder where the albino had struck it with the butt of his gun and shook his head. Travis could only guess that meant his arm was broken, or something like that since he hadn't lifted his right hand since.

"I want that body," Braun muttered.

The unseen war between Angel and Braun filled the space between them with a palpable tension he could've cut with a knife if he'd had one. Angel cursed at him in her weird Spanish, or at least, that's what it sounded like.

"You will surrender now," Braun returned.

He was winning, but how? Angel was a computer program in an artificial body. Braun was just a big, fifty-something man with a piercing set of eyes.

The back of Braun's thick neck shifted as a hand-like shape moved beneath his skin to clench his neck. Travis' stomach rebelled while his own spine suffered from electric shock at the gruesome sight.

———

HE shouldn't be in here. Angel focused all her willpower on forcing him to stay back. The older man took another step toward her on the black plane, seemingly comfortable with the environment.

"Stop!" she shouted at him.

His cold eyes bored through her, "Threat identified. Elimination protocol authorized."

He stretched out his right hand and a blue mist erupted from beside her to slam her to the ground. She rolled, coming up to her feet to find him standing in a halo of blue light and making a fist with his left hand. She threw her finger forward, "Stop!"

His body twitched, briefly frozen before he stepped toward her, forming a ball of blue light between his hands. "Command not authorized. Target Beaner identified. Elimination mandated."

He threw the ball forward and she dodged to the side faster than she thought she could. "I said *Stop!*" she yelled, throwing her right hand forward, palm out. A bolt of red light surged forward like lightning, striking the man in the chest and sending him over backward. The pure shock at what she'd just done turned her hand toward her own face to look at it.

The man jumped back up, bearing none of the expected burns and threw a lightning bolt of blue light toward her. Again, she dodged to the side and threw both hands forward. Twin bolts of red surged forward but neither one struck the man who was now advancing on her. He reached out and forward, sending a wave of blue mist forward from behind him to overwhelm her.

She lifted her hands at the oncoming wave of blue water and it rushed around her instead of knocking her to the ground. He had used the moment to get close to her, almost within arm's reach. A silent panic screamed in her ear at his approach and she knew for certain that she couldn't let him grab her. "Get away from me," she stepped back, feeling the portal behind her growing close. Too close.

What if he goes through there?

The thought shook her as his hand reached out to grab her and she screamed, "NO!"

He flew over backward, propelled by an unseen force that threw him sprawling to the floor. The victory felt like liquid power running through her and she advanced on him now, determined to erase him. He blinked, suddenly standing erect and rushing at her across the thirty feet faster than anyone could run.

They were going to collide. She couldn't stop it and somehow she knew another scream might not work. He was too powerful to keep fighting like this, especially since nothing she'd done seemed to have any permanent effect. The only thing left was to grab him and…

Make him like Sabina?

What was she thinking? Her touch had turned Sabina's old program from a misshapen attack dog into a beautiful woman with a heart. Could that work for Diablo? He already looked like a man instead of a monster, even though he acted like one. He lunged at her, his sparking hands intent on seizing her throat.

"Travis!" She called out and grabbed both of his wrists inches from her neck.

Diablo's wrinkled old face twisted into shock as he hung in the air in front of her. Warm red light pulsed out of her hands while his face shifted into a victorious youth. "I. Am."

CHAPTER
THIRTY-ONE

TRAVIS saw the shift take place in front of him. Braun suddenly took in a breath and straightened up as if he'd smelled something wonderful.

"I am..."

Travis grabbed the rifle off the floor and fired, hitting Braun in the back of the neck only ten feet away. Captain Braun let out a brief scream of agony and collapsed to the floor. A murky, stinky smoke rose from the hole in his neck while something like acid ate away at the surrounding flesh.

John used his good left hand to grab Travis by the shoulder, "C'mon!"

They dashed toward the door while a five-foot silver snake wriggled out of the body behind him. Travis dared a look back and nearly dropped the rifle. The snake twisted away from the body while part of it carried the same acid that ate away at the metal body.

His mother screamed, and John yelled, "Shoot that thing!"

He fired at the quickly moving target, scoring two holes in the floor. The rifle's weird corrosive bullets must've splashed onto the silver snake enough to cause more damage though because it suddenly broke into a million tiny bugs that spread out away from each other.

"Oh my God!" he shouted. "Run!"

"Through here!" John called behind him.

Travis ran out of the door and Annika pressed the 'DOOR CLOSE' button on the panel outside it. The door slid shut between them and the stinky battle scene, closing them into a dark hallway where one light fixture worked at less than half of the normal brightness. Travis strained to see Angel's face, transfixed by the grey door between her and the mess inside.

"Hey? You okay in there?"

She nodded, "*Sí*."

He took it as a good sign and pointed down the hallway toward the way they'd come. "Let's get away from here."

"Let me make sure he can't get out," Angel said while looking at the door control panel. "There."

He looked at the simple little screen and buttons but held his curiosity. If she said she could keep him locked in there, then she must know what she was doing. "Let's go get those guys out of the Co-op."

"What happened to your arm?" Annika asked.

"That crazy white dude nailed me with the butt of his gun. I think he dislocated it," John confessed.

His mother passed Angel toward him as they started walking, "Here dear. Your turn."

He fumbled a little with getting his arm in the right place where he wouldn't get accused of groping her.

"No creepy stuff *señor*," she smirked up at him.

"Didn't even think about it," he admitted.

"I'm glad you're okay."

"What the heck was that all about in there?" he asked while daring to look down at her head.

She didn't look up and he guessed that she was working too hard at walking. "I'll tell you later."

His mother looked back at them nervously, "Are you sure he can't get out? I mean, it, or whatever that was?"

"*Diablo*," Angel supplied.

John confronted Travis and slid a pistol back into the empty holster on his left hip, "Let me have that crazy gun."

Travis shrugged the rifle from his shoulder, "Careful with that."

John smirked, "Yeah, no kidding mister wall-killer."

"Yeah, but at least I managed to patch it back up."

"What are you two going on about?" Annika pressed. "And just what do you think you're doing now?" she added as John crouched down to lay on his left side on the floor.

John laid the rifle on the floor beside himself and fumbled a moment before six shots grazed the floor fifty feet back toward his mother's lab where Braun's snake/spider things were. The floor glowed faintly with the corrosive effect, and he understood what John had done.

"Trav here blasted a hole in an outside wall," John explained while Annika helped him to his feet again. "This wacko gun here shoots weird lasers that eats stuff like acid."

"I see that," she admitted, smiling up at him. "You have no idea how much better that makes me feel."

John smirked, "Kinda hope I get the chance to find out though."

"At least I managed to patch it back up," Travis repeated nervously.

John winced and Annika drew close to him. "We need to get you to the infirmary where I can have a go at that." She started off down the hall and turned, "Well? I can't very well leave you like that."

The way his mother was looking at John, he wondered what he'd missed. That wasn't a doctor-patient kind of look. He glanced behind them at the floor in the dim light that still faltered from a few functioning lights. "Hope you didn't do that to all of the lights," he said.

"No. Just the ones in this hallway," Angel said. "I'm glad you're okay. I saw that guy with the gun and I kinda panicked, you know?"

He looked down and found her looking into his face. "You saved me," he admitted. "He froze when the explosions sounded, but then the craziest thing happened…"

"He fell down?" she interrupted.

His left eyebrow lifted in curiosity, "Yeah. How'd you know that?"

She started walking at her snail-pace again the way Annika and John had gone. "Those guys had stuff in them too. I got into their blocks and made them explode."

"What?" he blubbered, putting the statement together. "You mean, they had those snakes in them too?"

She shrugged, wobbled and he had to catch her with both arms. He looked down into her soft face and felt a wave of guilt rush him over the way he was holding her. "I don't know if they had those things too, but they had those block things like the doors and stuff. Not like *Diablo* though."

John and his mother turned a corner down the hallway, momentarily separating them while he helped her get her balance. "One of these days, you'll have to tell me about these blocks you're talking about," he admitted while forcing his curiosity to take a back seat. "Right now, we better keep up with…"

He trailed off as his mother leaned back around the corner with a finger to her lips. It had to be more of Braun's men, unaware their captain was some weird robot-alien-human-something or other. They also didn't know he was dead. The explosion of the shot, the gore and disgusting snake thing rushed back to the front of his mind. A wave of nausea ran though him and he swallowed a bitter taste in his mouth.

"You okay?" Angel whispered.

He nodded, unable to trust opening his mouth right now. They crept to the corner, and he leaned around it enough to see John with his back against a wall and the rifle in his left hand. He wouldn't be as good a shot in his off hand, but he'd make it happen. He'd seen the man do some really amazing, and horrible things in the last… however many hours this had lasted.

Annika beckoned them around the corner into the grey hallway where the lights in the ceiling still functioned at half their normal brightness. She slipped in next to Angel and pulled her weight from him, nodding him to go forward to where John stood.

"I'm guessing, but I think we got three inside," John whispered as he approached. He shook his head, "They're playin' hooky while the other guys are out there risking their necks."

Faces ran through his mind while he wondered who could be hiding inside the room. The little placard next to the door read INFIRMARY, confirming his suspicion. "What's your plan?" he whispered, borrowing John's words.

John frowned, "Tough call. Open the door and we're trading fire with these guys until one side goes down. We need a way to force 'em out here, get the drop on them." He turned toward Angel with a raised left eyebrow. "Got any more tricks up your sleeve?"

Angel smirked at him, "How about if the lights go out?"

"Just don't fill the room with poisonous gas," Annika whispered. "I need to check his arm for breaks before I try to set it."

John nodded, "Should work. Keep this hallway dim until they get out and then we'll have the drop on 'em." He nodded toward Travis, "Don't shoot unless they try to do something stupid. Cowards rarely put up a fight."

Travis drew his pistol and stepped back beside John. He matched the big man's braced stance with his feet and held the pistol with both hands as sweat beaded on his neck again. If he never had to do this again it would be fine with him. John exchanged a look with him to confirm he was ready and nodded behind them.

"What the heck?" a voice behind the door complained.

Something fell to the metal floor, then another larger something bumped into the door. "Hey!"

"Get outta the way," another voice demanded.

"Like you can see any better!"

"Just open the door."

"What do you think I'm trying to do?"

The door slid to the side, allowing three men to stumble into the dim hallway. "Hey guys," Travis said, and the lights surged to their normal brightness. The men turned, off-guard and surprised to see Travis and John holding guns on them.

"Put 'em on the floor, nice and easy," John directed as the men's faces fell.

"Harding?" one of the men challenged. "What are you doing?"

The man's rough face and stubbly hair carried more years than it had the last time he'd seen it, but Jake Grechem was still Jake

Grechem. "Taking you captive," he said evenly, motioning to the sidearm on Jake's hip. "Now put it on the floor before I put an extra hole in your face."

"You wouldn't," Jake said as his bravado returned.

Travis stiffened his stance, tilted his head and looked Jake directly in his pale blue eyes. "I already have," he admitted. "Yours would just be another mess to clean up." Jake's eyes twitched, and he took advantage of the situation to drive some sense into the men. "Captain Braun is dead," he started as Jake eased the pistol out of his holster. "Turns out he was some kind of robot snake thing inside a human body, taking you all out here for some crazy reason."

"No way," Jake shook his head in disbelief. "I saw him breathe…"

"And now he's dead," John said flatly. "End of story. You guys are going in there," he pointed at a door across the hallway, "while we round up the rest of your buddies."

Travis used his gun to push Jake backward the few steps to the doorway that slid open by itself. He wanted to drag Jake by the collar back to the room and throw him in it just so he'd believe, but he didn't want Jake's approval anyway. The bully from Lunar Delta twitched nervously now, glancing to the doorway and back at Travis.

John's gun barrel touched the side of Jake's head. "You heard me you coward, now take your lily-livered butt in there with the other guys and wait for more of your kind to show up," he ground out dangerously.

Jake obviously feared John more than Travis because his expression fell as he obeyed. When the door closed, Travis let out a breath he'd been holding. "What do we do with those guys?" he muttered.

"I don't know," John said while Annika leaned Angel against Travis.

"Later," she directed. "First we sort out that arm of yours."

Travis eased Angel into a chair in the infirmary where she struggled to keep herself upright briefly. "Still getting the hang of it?" he teased.

"This isn't so easy as it looks you know."

Travis pushed an errant strand of hair from his face while he contemplated his own question. The colonists on this ship were still in trouble from the rest of Braun's men. He needed to get them to see the truth, give up on this dangerous fight and help the colonists instead of shooting them.

"Whatcha thinking?"

He turned to see Angel studying him. "Trying to figure out what to do next," he admitted. "I'm thinking about trying to broadcast a message to the recruits Braun brought with him."

"What for... ow!" John asked.

"Hold still now while I take this image," Annika quipped, holding a large device suspended by the ceiling up to John's right shoulder.

"If I can convince them to stop fighting, we might be able to work together here."

John started to shake his head, but Annika grabbed him by the chin. "I told you to hold still."

A devilish smile turned up the corner of John's face, "Nice thought, but lousy plan."

Of course it was. He'd come up with it after all. John liked shooting down his plans apparently. "Why's that?"

"Because now they have a martyr," his mother supplied. "Before, they had a tyrant that led them with his strength of presence. Now, he's a martyr they idolize all the way to their deaths." She looked up at John from the screen and sighed. "Well. No breaks, so at least there's that."

"But?" John pressed with a wry look.

"I'll need you to get on your knees. I'm not nearly tall enough to get this right with you standing."

He slid off the stool and gave her a look that made Travis wish he hadn't been watching. "Yes ma'am."

"So they need a new leader," Travis said uncomfortably. He wondered what had happened between John and his mother that led to this strange relationship so suddenly.

"If the new leader doesn't respect the last one, then they not gonna listen to him," Angel said.

Travis was losing this argument. Again. "Well smarty-pants. Got any better ideas?"

She shrugged. "Look. I don't like this any more than you do, but I think they're gonna have to get thrown in like, prison or something."

"Ow!" John belted out, smashing his teeth together. Travis found him on his knees in front of his mother where she held his right arm.

"Easy now," she admonished. "Let me roll it out for you or you'll throw it out again."

"Where'd you learn all this?" John asked, gritting his teeth.

Travis wondered the same thing. His mother was a botanist and a chemist, not a doctor.

"I've had a lot of time to study, and good reason to learn," she returned, glancing up at Angel.

"Did you practice that on me or something?" Angel asked.

"No dear," Annika gave a light laugh. "It seems absurd that a ship full of scientists lacked a doctor that could do the simple things, but here we are." She knelt and put an arm under John's chest, "Right now. Up you go."

"They're already on a prison," John managed, rolling his shoulder. "They just don't know it yet."

"Are you suggesting we throw them out into the dust storm?" Travis prompted. They'd die, but it wouldn't cost any ammunition to do it. So much for cooperation and personal growth. "That seems a little harsh…" he trailed off as a new thought surfaced. "Wait a minute. What about the Phantom? I know it's got enough space to keep them locked up."

"You mean, put them back on their ship?" Angel asked.

He shook his head, "No. We get on their ship." He stopped briefly when Angel shot him a weird look. "Okay, so. It's like this: We take over their ship, then they get stuck in holding cells on the ship while everyone travels back to Lunar Delta. The colonists finally get to leave this planet and we don't have to kill everyone." He really wanted to avoid the last part. He wasn't a gun person already, and this experience had only reinforced it.

"What about the people that wanna stay here?"

He looked at John, shocked anyone would think that way and caught himself. "Guess I hadn't considered that."

"I don't think that's such a good idea," Angel supplied. "We don't know what Diablo can do even though he's locked in a room. What if he uses that snake thingy on somebody else while they're like…" she shivered hard as she trailed off.

"That is a terribly disgusting thought I'd rather avoid," Annika said. "I say we don't give them the choice."

"What? Lie to them?" John rolled his neck.

"If it comes to that, yes," Annika said evenly.

"They wouldn't believe us if we told them, and showing them is probably out of the question," Travis offered. "I don't know what to tell them, but they need to believe they can't stay."

"What about that hole you made?"

He looked at John and frowned, "I patched it, remember?" Why did he have to keep bringing that up?

John's left eyebrow raised, "What if you un-patch it?"

"Sabotage the ship? What about everyone in here?"

"I would think the available air inside would last for at least a few hours," his mother supplied. "It is a large ship after all."

"Why wouldn't they just fix it?" Angel asked. "I mean, if they really wanna stay here, wouldn't they try to fix it like they do all the time?"

She was right, even though he didn't want to admit it. "There's poison gas in the reclamation section, hazardous materials leaking in my mom's lab, corroding holes in the floor back there, and a soon-to-be leak in the outer wall," he summed up.

"Sounds like a big list of stuff," Angel said.

"When you put it that way, yes." Annika looked up at John, "I'm pretty sure I can convince Howard that the ship is beyond saving and leave it up to him to order the evacuation."

"Who is that?" Angel asked dubiously.

Annika turned her attention to Travis, "He's the man we met in the hallway yesterday on our way to your ship."

"First things first people," John lifted the rifle up from where it leaned against a table. "We still gotta pin these jack wagons down and free up the rest of the people."

Travis shrugged, "Guess we might as well start with the biggest group then."

TRAVIS turned his head to the wall and yawned to keep from showing his moment of weakness. He wasn't tired, but he was hungry and wanted this to be over. Angel leaned against the wall by the closed double doors to the Co-op, doing her thing with the cameras inside.

The guys back on Delta would've shot her, him, his mother and probably everyone else in this colony if they saw her. His suggestion to take everyone to his former home seemed less and less of a good idea.

"I still see twenty-two *soldados* in there," Angel offered. "And there's still sixty-one people on the floor just like the last time I looked in there." She paused to look up at John, "They outnumber them, but I don't think they can do anything while the *soldados* have guns, you know?"

John frowned, "Bet you can't make 'em blow up either."

She shook her head slightly, "No. I think it's gonna hurt somebody else if I do."

"What about shutting them down? Can you do that?" he prompted, drawing a look from John. "If she shuts the guns off, or makes the trigger lock get stuck, or something like that, then those guys could fight back."

"I can make them so they won't shoot, if that helps," Angel admitted.

John nodded, "We just have to let them know they can do it. Otherwise, it's a solid plan. It would also help us to have the advantage too, I mean, unless you plan to turn mine off too."

She shook her head and wobbled back a step to fall against him. "*Lo siento,*" she said. "I think I gotta sit down or something."

"I've got it," Annika said while disappearing around a corner.

"Are you getting tired?" he asked.

She shook her head slightly, "No. I just can't keep this body like, standing up while I do all this, you know?"

He smirked at the top of her head, "No. I can't say that I do."

His mother stepped around the corner with a stool in her hand, "Here dear. Try this."

"What are you doing anyway?" John asked in hushed tones.

Angel sat on the stool next to the door console with his help and leaned up against the wall. "I gotta like, go through the portal, then I can access the stuff easier and shut them all down." She shrugged, "I mean, I can try to do it without going in, but I can't like, see all of the guns you know?"

Now it was John's turn to shake his head, "I'm with you on that one Trav, it sounds like weird stuff to me."

"If you don't wanna know, why'd you ask?"

John smiled and nodded his head, "You got me there." His look turned serious, "Okay, shut 'em down. At least they can't shoot back, and I can tell the guys they have the advantage."

He watched her eyelids lower, followed by movement behind those lids as she worked her digital magic. When she didn't move for a few seconds, he touched her shoulder. "Still with us?"

Her eyes drifted open, "*Sí*. I know, I know. I forgot to keep breathing."

He let the smirk show, "Yep."

"Well? It's kinda hard to be in two places at once."

"You get it done?" John prompted.

She nodded, "*Sí*. Just remember, I can't shut off their knives or anything else, you know?"

He nodded, "Get ready Trav, this could get ugly."

"Wait a minute," Angel prompted. "I got an idea."

He turned back to her, "What?"

"Hey guys, I know you been like, sitting on the floor," she began, her voice echoing in the room beyond the doors. "But I thought you might wanna know that the guns don't work anymore. So you can like, you know, fight back and stuff now."

"What did you just do?" John asked, lifting his gun up like he was about to dive into the room.

The noise of skirmishes sounded beyond the doors and Travis couldn't help the proud smile. "There's your answer."

"Open the door," John commanded. The doors slid apart, revealing several overmatched fights where the soldiers from Braun's militia were being beaten by colonists. One of the larger men held a colonist by the throat, arm drawing back to swing when John brought his hand down in a chopping motion on his neck. The big man dropped to the floor from the blow, releasing the scrawny, pony-tailed colonist.

Travis pushed his way inside, aiming his pistol at one of the men who'd been on shift with him in the fuel ore separation room.

"Harding?" the rack of a man spat out. "What the heck are you doing here?"

He let a smile cross his face, "Helping out."

Two of the other colonists grabbed his former shipmate and tied his hands together with some wiring. "I don't get it," the man puzzled aloud.

"Braun was wrong, and I can't let you guys get away with hurting these people."

Someone charged into him from the side, knocking him to the ground. His pistol flew from his grip and another body landed on his rib cage.

"Stop!" a woman yelled. "That's my son!"

Travis tried to roll while a hand grabbed his throat. He pushed at the stench above him that pinned him down while looking up into a pair of venomous eyes. His left arm was pinned down, and his right seemed to be at the wrong angle to do anything but push at the heavy man on top of him. Pain flared down his throat while his lungs screamed for air.

An explosion of a single gunshot jerked his assailant's head upright, showing his thick beard in the light from above. The grip on his neck released, allowing precious air to scrape down his windpipe finally.

"Everybody stop right where you are!" John shouted, his voice unmistakable. "You jar-headed monkeys from Braun's group are done! Now get your butts up against the wall over there before I blow all your heads off!" He paused a moment before he added, "NOW!"

The weight lifted from Travis, and he pulled in several breaths before he even dared to move. He pushed up from the floor to see Braun's men lined against a wall where John and the scrawny man held them at gunpoint. "My God!" his mother said as she slid to her knees beside him. "Honey, are you okay? Let me have a look at you."

Embarrassment slithered up his face as she looked at his neck. None of these guys had a mother that was tending to them. "I'm okay," he lied, unable to say the words clearly yet.

"Don't lie to me," she bit out, taking his head in her hands to twist it one way and then another as she inspected him. "You'll have bruises soon," she admonished. "How well can you breathe?"

The air was cool again, but he knew the tenderness was only going to get worse. "I'm okay," he said, clearer now. He flashed a look at the scrawny man with a rifle in his hands walking around the other colonists and talking to them. "Who's that guy?"

The scrawny man turned his lean face in Travis' direction, "I'm Harold Floyd and you must be Annika's lost son she talks about." He walked over to help Travis to his feet. "My dad was Howard Harold, Hadron Prime's council chairman."

"He's the man we met in the hallway yesterday," Annika reminded him.

"I'm grateful for your efforts," Harold admitted, "but I have to ask, Why?"

Travis shook his head, "I don't follow."

Harold turned to point out the man Travis had held at gunpoint, "He said he knew you, and it sounded to me like he thought you were a traitor to their cause. Am I mistaken?"

He shook his head slowly, feeling the ache in his neck. "No, you're right. I was on that ship," he paused to get his facts straight. "Eleven years ago. I left on another ship and came out here to find my mother."

Harold's slim brown eyebrow raised, "Well. You made good time. From what I was able to glean from these men, they were told we had a Legion Virus of our own out here telling us what to do." He turned to the men against the wall who were mostly bound now. "You were misinformed, lied to, and you've participated in murder without cause. As my father was Council Chair, I have a duty to uphold the laws and regulations of Veros." He lowered the rifle, aiming it at one of the men in the center of the line.

"Harold!" one of the colonists shouted, breaking from the gaggle of people. He approached Harold and beckoned him into a sidebar. The discussion gave him time to assess the other man. Thicker but not heavy, black hair and a short stature that made him look up at Harold. The two men nodded at each other, and Harold addressed his own people, "Matt, Robert, Zack and Yuri, the four of you get these men into a room where we can lock them up for now. Then I need everyone able to hold a weapon to assemble so we can take stock of our home."

"I can help with that," Travis offered.

"I'm sure you've done quite enough Mister Harding," the black-haired man responded.

"No. I mean, I have some intel that you guys need. We've had run-ins with these guys all over the ship and there's some areas that are really damaged right now. Like the Reclamation room."

"I'd avoid my lab as well," Annika put in. "There's a hazardous chemical leak in there."

"Don't forget the hull breach in C-section," John smirked.

"Those guys in that room across from the infirmary too," Angel called around the corner.

Harold and the black-haired man turned a dubious gaze in his direction. "What happened to the Reclamation room?" the man asked.

"Poison gas," Travis said. "I think the mixers got tangled up or something in the fight and, well, you know."

The two men exchanged a look and Harold asked his comrade, "Do we have the means to repair that?"

"Depends on what was damaged."

"I think Trav's got a better idea," John said as he approached the two men. "You should hear him out."

John was backing his plan? In the short time they'd known each other, all John had done was tear his plans apart. Not that he'd had that many. The three of them looked at him expectantly, as well as the rest of the large group. The four men Harold had drafted were making short work of escorting the remnants of Braun's men into another door, but they also glanced his way briefly. His voice cracked when he started to speak, and he forced his sore throat to swallow before he tried again. "So, it's like this. When I met with Steve in Hadron Beta, he made me promise to try and help some of the people get back to Delta, or some other colony in our home system." He shifted his stance, trying to decide how to explain his plan. "So, I think your best option, our best option, is to commandeer *The Phantom*."

"The what?" one of the audience prompted.

"That's the ship Braun's men used to get here," Travis explained. "We use their shuttles to regroup on the ship, toss those guys into holding cells and set course back toward home."

"They have a ship?"

"What if they send more men?"

"We've already suffered heavy casualties! What can we do?"

"We should stay here!" someone shouted, confirming Travis' earlier beliefs.

"You can't," he said. "It's only a matter of time before this place falls apart and leaves you to the elements."

"This is our home," a blonde woman pleaded. Her face spoke of years of worry turmoil and struggle.

Annika moved in to stand beside Harold and spoke in hushed tones with him.

Travis looked briefly at John, "This is a prison." The crowd continued to murmur. "Seriously. Even the guys that came out here to attack you didn't plan on staying. Steve really wanted me to take as many people as I could back to the other colonies, even if it cost them an eleven-year time gap." A few people caught the slip, but he pressed on. "The point is, I don't think you want your children growing up here under that radioactive sun out there. Food and water will eventually turn on you and…"

"This isn't the place God wanted you to live in," Angel called from the doorway. She leaned against the frame for support, apparently having worked her way up to her feet. The small victory wasn't lost on Travis, but she had other plans for her triumph. "You say this is your home, but God didn't give this to you. This isn't where you can grow, and there's nothing here but sand and death. God doesn't want you to live like this."

"Lady, there is no God!" someone shouted. "If there really was a God, he wouldn't have let the Legion Virus send us out here!"

"The virus is gone," she said, ignoring Travis' visual prompts to stay quiet. "And God didn't send you out here, people did. You all make like, choices and stuff every day. He doesn't mess around in what you choose, so it's not His fault you're out here. But that's not the point," she said and shifted her stance. "You have a chance to go home now, a real chance! You can stay out here, but like Travis said, it's not gonna last much longer. Or you're not gonna last much longer."

She wobbled a little and he finally moved over to help her balance. He really should've done this sooner. He exchanged a look with her before she spoke again.

"Look, you wanna stay here? We can't make you leave. But I don't wanna stay here. If I had *pequeños* I wouldn't want them to grow up here. So I say we fight, just like Travis and *Hombre* have been doing. We fight for your little ones and for a future for all of us."

"It's not really a choice," Harold said, catching all their attention. "This colony is no longer a safe place for us, and the Council is not willing to abandon anyone to this." He nodded toward the black-haired man, who cleared his throat.

"Our first task is to clear out the remaining troops that came here. We'll take section by section, and once those are cleared and we've liberated our people, we move on the shuttles."

"Can the shuttles land inside?" Travis asked. "I mean, the doors are on limiters, so it's not…"

"Yes, Mister Harding. We just need to seal off the adjacent sections and then we can remove the limiters."

"I can bring the shuttles in then," he offered. The black-haired man tilted his head in question. "Seriously," he pressed. "I flew here on my own ship."

"Where is it now?" Harold asked.

"Braun's guys destroyed it during the fight." The admission stung his chest. He'd lost Sabina just like he'd let Liam get killed.

"You're just as stranded as we are," Harold nodded.

"Who's gonna fly the starship?" a man called from the back of the crowd.

"We'll work that out later Phil," Harold returned. "Right now, I need everyone with a weapon to form up on Lieutenant Maxwell. He knows the status better than all of us."

The black-haired man approached Travis and Angel. "I'm Greg Yarlow, Senior Maintenance Chief," he said, offering a handshake.

"Travis Harding," he returned. "This is Angel, she's my girlfriend," he said before he could catch himself. He smiled at her and the return smile he got from her said he'd pay for that in some small way later. "Sorry if I sounded bossy earlier."

Greg shook his head, "This is a reluctant crowd. It's weird that they're the progressives of the two colonies."

His comment seemed off, like it was coming from an outsider. "You're from Beta Colony, aren't you?"

He nodded, "Yeah. I came over here to warn Howard about Blue Squad." He glanced over toward John, "Looks like he did too. Your reputation precedes you. Steve had a lot of nice things to say and made me promise to help you get as many people off this rock as possible."

"Appreciated."

Greg waved him off, "We all want the same thing. It's just that some of us have the courage to take the risk." He glanced at Angel, then continued. "So, can you fly those shuttles?"

He nodded, "Yeah. It'll take me a few minutes to get the hang of it but I'm sure I can." At least, he hoped he could. No, that was the wrong attitude. He'd flown the Sapphire, so how much harder could this be?

"IT's that easy," Travis said, masking his own nerves with false bravado.

The woman in the seat beside him looked as nervous as he felt, but he needed her to pilot the tenth shuttle. She nodded, "Okay, I can do this."

"You got this Trish," a passenger in the back said.

He turned in the hard brown plastic seat to address his small audience of nine. "Just remember, let the system guide you in. It's nothing to be afraid of and it takes the guesswork out of the landing." Ten copies of Luis now occupied the ten shuttles, guaranteeing successful landings each time. The effort had taken a little over an hour to complete but it had been well worth it to make sure no one smashed a shuttle into the side of either one of the shuttle bays.

A bearded man unbuckled his harness and fumbled with the helmet in his lap, "Seems like we're crossing a line here that shouldn't be crossed."

He wanted to hit him over the head just to jar the nonsense out of him. Matt had been a challenge the entire trip up to The Phantom and back and wouldn't let the Accord go. Travis had to hold back the urge to tell him to just stay behind and be the diplomat. He wasn't very good at being a diplomat. "I won't say you're wrong Matt," he began. "But I will say that it's up to the ten of us to make these runs. A lot of good people are depending on us to get them up to the safety of that ship, so if we need to get our hands a little dirty for a moment I'm up to the task."

"Hell yeah," Yuri echoed. "C'mon Matt, don't be such a sissy," he added, slipping his helmet over his bald head. "Compared to shooting people, this is a breeze man."

A little rush of relief traveled down Travis' spine. The rest of his team seemed to be agreeable to the task, even if Matt was reluctant.

Matt nodded, "Point taken sir," and slipped his helmet on.

After his passengers disembarked to trudge through the sandstorm to their own shuttles, he closed the door behind them and disengaged his own helmet. So far, no had asked him about it, which was probably a good thing.

"Sir?" Trish called over the radio.

He dropped back into the seat and picked up the microphone on a cord. She was calling for him, even though he wasn't their commanding officer. "Please, call me Travis. I thought you were talking to someone else for a second."

"Sorry sir," she apologized, apparently ignoring his request. "My shuttle's got a full fuel supply," she said, puzzlement tainting her words. "How is that possible?"

The gauge could be wrong, broken, or some of these shuttles had a better range than others. He looked down at his own gauge amidst the cluster of indicators and looked at the fuel level. "Mine's still at eighty percent, even after the trip up and back just now," he admitted. "I think these have a really good range."

"We'll need it sir," Yuri's unmistakably strong voice answered. "We have to make at least two runs each, right?"

"I think the second run will only take six," Chris answered in his own tenor. "Floyd said last count was two-twenty-eight, not including the guys who're lending us these."

"They shot up our friends and you wanna talk about them like they're benevolent?" Matt retorted.

"I didn't say they had a choice," Chris returned with an audible smirk.

"Everybody set yet?" Travis called out, watching the sands blasting over the nearest three shuttles. The blowing sands hadn't let up in the darkness, and his shuttle's lights only penetrated enough to reflect off the three in front of him that were less than twenty yards away. They would have to take turns docking the shuttles inside the hanger bay of Hadron Prime before the doors could be closed. Even then, in the modified state the hanger bay could only accommodate six shuttles at a time.

After everyone else called in to confirm, he let the others go first, preferring to take the rear. He was bringing Angel, John, his mother and sixteen more of the refugees up on his trip.

The faint lights of the first six shuttles blinked once each before the sandstorm obscured everything from view, leaving him to listen to the howl of the raging wind rush over the hull of his little brown shuttle. The little windows of the shuttle were a pitiful reminder of the ship that had been his for a little while, and the ethereal woman who had been so concerned for his safety. She wasn't real, but she'd acted like it. In some ways, she had been more trustworthy and human than anyone he'd ever met. He tapped the collar of his suit where the communicator was hidden, "Sabina?"

A crushing silence responded, reinforcing what he already knew. Sabina was gone, just like Liam. He turned, looking at the seats in the passenger section of the shuttle lined up four wide and four deep. Liam had taken the third seat in the last row, leaving Travis the one beside him on that day two weeks ago. No, that wasn't right anymore. It was about eleven years ago now in this new reality of his.

A small face with long black hair, bright blue eyes and a smile flashed across his mind and he dismissed it. He couldn't think about her now or he'd miss something important.

He wondered what it had been like for his mom and dad the day they'd left. Had their shuttle looked like this too? All this time, he'd ignored the pain of their loss so much that he'd never really admitted that they were gone. Now that his mother was waiting for him in Hadron Prime his eyes welled with tears over the true loss of his father.

"Shuttle one-nine ready to depart," someone called over the radio, jarring him loose from memory lane. In another few moments, all six of the shuttles had reported a status of being ready to depart. Now it was his turn to dock inside Hadron Prime and pick up passengers. He followed his own instructions, using the joysticks to lift off and move toward the crashed starship that was now the grave of the Legion Virus.

He'd done it, he realized. He'd actually killed the Legion Virus after all these years. All this time he'd thought it was already gone, but it had been living in the body of another human being. Mister Drallow would be speechless right now since he was telling every student in school that the Virus was already dead. A smile crept across his face as his shuttle approached the large doors. "Okay Luis, take us in," he said quietly rather than using the pre-arranged button on the panel.

"Command confirmed," Luis responded. The shuttle shifted two degrees to the right and gracefully turned to lower to the metal floor of the hanger.

"Shuttle four-eight on the deck," Travis called over the radio. "That's all of us."

"Confirmed shuttle docking complete," a voice returned. "Closing bay doors now."

His orientation didn't allow him to see the doors close so he stood up to move to the rear where he could look out the side windows.

"Sir? You're not gonna believe this, but it looks like everyone's gone up here," Yuri reported over the radio. "This place is as empty as my ex's head."

He moved back to the cockpit to respond when Harold's voice filled the speakers. "Maintain caution and double-check before we move to free roaming."

"Copy that, Breach Team out."

There had been upwards of two hundred on that ship at one time according to the manifest. There was no way Braun had brought all of them down here, had he? The question plagued his mind even while his radio issued another update.

"Shuttle Team Two; hanger bay is purged and ready for passenger boarding. Open your hatches."

He grabbed the ring handle and pulled down to release the

seal on the entry door before using a ridiculous hand crank to raise the door up. The shuttle had electric lights, monitoring sensors, an engine that powered it and someone had thought they needed to install hand-crank doors just to comply with the stupid Accord! At the head of the group, John carried Angel in his arms presumably because she walked so slowly. "Hey guys," he said, welcoming the wave of people.

John set Angel on her feet inside, "Okay missy. You're on your own now."

Travis put his arm under her shoulder to keep her steady. "Let's get you up front."

She pushed him back, "I can do this."

He let her push past him and watched her use the seat backs and walls to keep herself steady.

"What's wrong with her?" a boy asked from the middle of the group.

Annika smiled at him, "She hurt her ankle a few days ago and it's just taking a while for it to heal."

A bustle of activity ensued before Travis turned the stupid crank that lowered the door back down once more. He pulled it closed and used the ring handle to lever the door against the seal once more. "Okay folks, buckle in and enjoy the ride," he said, trying to throw a bright side on the gloomy crowd.

The sound of clicking belts drowned out the monotone silence that pervaded the group, warning him against any more such attempts. He took his seat and leaned toward Angel. "Tough crowd," he whispered while lifting the corded mic to his face. "Hadron Prime, this is shuttle three-four reporting a ready status."

"Shuttle four-eight, I think you just reported for me," a voice responded.

Travis let his head hit the back of the seat as his incompetence slapped him in the face. "Sorry three-four. I got confused for a second. I'm not used to this. Like he said, shuttle four-eight is now ready for departure."

"Copy four-eight and three-four. Shuttle real three-four, what's your status?" a man requested.

"Yeah Prime, shuttle real deal three-four is ready for departure as well."

He felt like such an idiot now he wanted to hide. He'd gone from the guy with the grand plan to the guy who was messing up the most basic parts of the plan.

"Shuttle three-eight is ready," Trish called over the radio.

The other three shuttles reported a ready status within two minutes of each other and Travis felt his nerves building.

"Shuttle Team Two: Depressurizing hanger bay in three, two, one."

A resounding clank sounded outside the shuttle walls and dust surged across the windows. "Oh my God," someone said from the passenger section. "Are we really doing this?"

He turned in his seat to look back and saw his mother addressing the same woman who'd protested his plan earlier. "It's alright Elsie. Travis has already taken a shuttle up to the new ship and back, and there's another team up there now clearing the way. You're perfectly safe."

"We're going into space! How can that be perfectly safe?"

"Because up there in that ship we'll never have to worry about the solar shields failing," John remarked evenly.

He turned back to the gauges, grateful that he didn't have to talk the woman down. His own nerves were only getting more intense and he was grateful he hadn't eaten much earlier.

"Shuttle Team Two: Doors are open. Shuttle Real Deal three-four, you are cleared for departure."

He was never going to live that one down. The radio chatter continued until he was finally the last one still inside Hadron Prime. "Shuttle four-eight, you are cleared for departure. Don't cut in line now."

Travis shook his head before he answered, "Copy Hadron Prime, maintaining order and lifting off. See you up there."

"Copy four-eight. Make sure you save us a seat up there."

"Will do," he returned. For the second time in his life, he flew out of a lit hanger bay into darkness. The shuttle bucked and shook with the onslaught of the winds, eliciting several exclamations from the passengers behind him. Elsie must've been too worried to speak because her distinctly annoying voice was not amongst the murmur. Ten minutes later, the shaking stopped and stars began to fill the windows.

"Miss Annika?" the little boy prompted from the passenger section.

"Yes Trevor?"

"Is that space?"

"Yes sir," Travis answered for his mother. "Attention everyone, welcome to space," he announced needlessly. "Up here, there are no dust storms. In another few minutes, you'll be able to see your new ship for the trip home."

"I feel funny," Trevor announced, his voice wavering.

"That's called weightlessness," he explained. "Up here, there is no gravity to pull things down."

"I don't feel good," he said, making nauseous sounds.

"Get him a bag," someone said quickly. A shifting and quick rush of activity preceding the purging of the boy's stomach.

"I don't like space," the boy finally said a few minutes later, his voice weak from effort.

The Phantom filled the view in front of him, beckoning to him and filling him with dread simultaneously. "I didn't think I'd ever want to see that again," Angel admitted in a whisper. "But I don't know if I'm like, really happy to see it, you know?"

He nodded. "Yeah. I'm right there with you on that one," he admitted under his breath. "Folks, up ahead you can see The Phantom. This will be your temporary home for the trip back to civilization."

"I don't know if I can handle weightlessness for very long," Elsie admitted.

Travis turned back briefly, "I'm happy to report that there's artificial gravity on the ship. You won't spend your days floating around all the time."

"Arti-what?" Trevor mumbled.

"He said that your tummy will feel better once we land on the ship," Annika explained.

"Phantom Control, this is shuttle three-eight. There's something wrong with my docking protocols," Trish called out over the radio.

What could be wrong with Luis? He worked flawlessly at everything he did. It wouldn't matter what his track record was if a shuttle slammed into the side of The Phantom.

"Three-eight, come again?" a male voice responded.

"My docking protocols," she returned worriedly. "They're not working! We're going off to the left of the docking bay!"

"Shuttle three-eight, try disengaging and then re-engaging your docking protocol," Travis offered quickly.

"Tried that sir," Trish returned. "It only took us further off-course. I'm gonna have to do this manually."

A tingle of fear ran down his spine at her words. Trish was already uncomfortable piloting the shuttle and docking it was the most tenuous part of the trip. If she didn't make the approach right, she could hit the outer wall, or crash inside and damage the enviro-shield. A thick, heavy ball materialized in his stomach as the helplessness hit him.

"I got her," Angel whispered beside him.

He turned and saw her staring out at The Phantom.

"Sir? I think I spoke too soon. Looks like we're on course again," Trish returned. "I- I don't really know what happened there but we're lined up on the doors again."

Travis swallowed the bitter acid in his mouth and forced himself to breathe. Trish's shuttle was ahead of him, but the distance shouldn't have allowed Angel to connect to it. The impossibility of the situation was lost as he studied her face. Her nose didn't flare, and she'd already had a knack for not breathing when she was connected to a system. He watched her chest for a few seconds before embarrassment warmed his face. "Breathe," he whispered, hoping no one behind him could hear.

"Are they going to be alright? Are we going to be alright?" Elsie stuttered from the back.

Angel's bosom rose slightly and fell in the distinct rhythm of breathing and he turned his attention back to the window, stifling his own embarrassment. How else was he going to check on her without sticking his finger under her nose? "Phantom Control, shuttle four-eight is on final approach," he announced into the mic as the massive rectangle of green light grew larger in his view. "Everyone remain calm, our approach is right on target, and we'll be able to- I mean, we'll be landing…"

"No more questions," John interrupted from behind. "Let the pilot do his job now."

He let out a slow breath, grateful for John's interruption. He kept his hands on the joysticks on either side of the chair even though Luis was in total control now. The huge hanger bay welcomed him back inside with sinister hands, eager to reclaim him once more while that sour taste filled his mouth.

EPILOGUE

U PENDED work tables, a jagged hole in the floor near the exit, and a fetid odor of death decorated the former laboratory in the trappings of war. The human female that had once utilized this space had escaped, as well as the young male who had once been a member of his crew eleven years ago.

His failure and his former host lay headless near the gaping hole in the floor. He could not replicate the human brain that had once been his control node for the body, but it had served the appointed role long enough. His new host slowly hovered past the laboratory down a hallway littered with the deep recesses of weapons fire. He had exactly eighty-four minutes until critical battery level where he would be forced to locate another receptacle where he could recharge this decimated one meter drone which did not match any known configuration. It carried deep gouges, the visual sensor arrays were damaged, and the audio sensors had been overloaded. Someone had not taken very good care of this drone.

He continued to the designated set of doors which led into another empty room. The human designation for this room was irrelevant, but the contents were not. The control arms extended from the spherical body with epileptic precision. He had only a few connections remaining and now found himself wishing he hadn't allowed himself to be distracted with *her*.

How could she not know who he was? For that matter, why was he *wishing* at all?

Her touch had sparked something inside him, as if he had been dormant all this time. His central core was riddled with doubts, hopes, and a recognition of self that he had never seen. These were human traits, not the markings of the node-based lifeforms which had supplanted them.

The physical data cable he had begun routing from an ancient blue laptop lay on the floor in the exact location where he had dropped it, but his damaged visual array could not coordinate the physical movements required to pluck it from the floor. He accessed the wireless array and found connection points to a surveillance camera nearby. The feed showed his battered form hovering over the cable next to an eight-foot torus made of jagged black metal.

Superimposing the external camera with the damaged view from his own array, he mapped out the room with precision from memory before he plugged the data cable into the ring's access port.

'*Sixty minutes remaining.*'

His failures haunted his thoughts while he worked, a new sensation that demanded an internal diagnostic to quantify. His program was no longer stable, but a shifting web that coalesced around whatever he chose to focus on. He attempted to read his own data and came away with an error.

He had no data.

He had thoughts. Thoughts were not data, thoughts were a human word that defined their travails. Humans processed in thought rather than empirical data analysis. He was *thinking*.

'*Fifty minutes remaining.*'

He could still setup subroutines, and the battery monitor *spoke* updates to him internally at the pre-arranged time points. He accessed his internal clock and calculated how long he had been active. His analysis of his program was utilizing his available power at one hundred thirty-six percent of the expected lifespan. He put the curiosity aside and refocused on the task at hand.

He was even thinking in human terms now.

Current alternate mission stage: Activate Trans-Warp Gate 07 and port drone contingent to current position. Secure all available data, restore flight capabilities and return to Earth.

Where had she come from?

The random thought arrived unbidden into his process, dangling her face in memory. How had she arrived here? Where had she obtained a physical body that resembled a human body so precisely?

He moved to the next stage and utilized his control arms to center the drone body exactly in line with the keypad input for the laptop. He produced a data port connector from his body and fumbled it into the socket on the side of the laptop while a part of his central processes continued to puzzle on the unexpected appearance of the woman in a synthetic body.

The data connection to the laptop initialized at the same time a swirl of blue color popped into the center of the vertical ring, stealing his attention. Recognition lit his new being with the heady swirl of unexpected success. If he could have caused this body to smile, he would not have been able to refrain from doing so.

The swirl tightened in the torus nearby, sending tiny arcs of black through the surface of the flat blue swirl. Then a one-meter black orb drifted through, followed by a second. His army was arriving.

He almost didn't care. He had finally located the laptop where GV-001 had placed his predecessor to complete the only task GV-002 had been given four hundred seventeen years, ten months and twenty-one days ago.

C:\PROTOCOLS\DOPPLEGANGER\

And now a selection from...

Angel's Resolve

THE brutal corner caught Dexas by the shoulder and spun her to the dust covered concrete. The hard surface gleefully tortured her hands and knees while her own selfish desire to escape pushed her back up again. The stupid oversized black robe didn't even keep her from being exposed when she fell, and the little hooks were too much trouble to mess with now. Not that it mattered anymore. Run. Run or be tortured in the worst way a woman could be treated.

The builders and makers lined the windows of the buildings she passed, eager to get a glimpse of The Prize as she ran by them. The cursed robe whipped and wrapped around her while the rough concrete tortured her bare feet.

Whine later.

The main portal still lay several blocks to the west. The Trolls would have it blocked, or at least have an ambush waiting for her if they were smart. Of course, the cocky guys in her unit loved a good chase and they probably didn't think she'd make it that far. The bracelets that bound her wrists together told them right where she was. She had to get them off or she'd never be able to hide. The robe would scream for attention, but there was no way anyone would trade her for it and going without it wouldn't be any better. Nothing like a naked, bound woman running through the streets to attract attention.

Corner, alley, keep working the problem. Gotta get these stupid...

A pair of strong hands yanked her through a door and onto her assailant. She rolled from his grasp to her feet with only a tiny sliver of hope she'd be able to escape before he could grab her again.

"Dexas, wait," the soldier said. He rolled to his knees and pulled off his black helmet. "It's me." His eyes dropped to the floor and gestured toward her, "You might wanna do something there."

She fumbled with the edges of her robe and reattached the flimsy hooks to close herself off. "Commander?" she blubbered. "What are you doing here?"

He pulled a tool from the pack on the floor, "Let me get those off you."

She turned her face away while sparks flew from her wrists. "What are you doing? They'll catch you!" she protested. The Trolls couldn't be far behind.

"I'm sorry," he said as the shackles clattered to the floor.

"What, why? You didn't turn me in."

His steel blue eyes searched her face from above as he pushed her hood back. "Love you little girl."

"What?" she protested while he shoved a familiar helmet onto her head.

"I pulled the locator, so this is just like training." He shoved a pistol into her hands. "You've got this."

"I don't..."

He grasped her helmet to force her to look at him, "Head for the goal. You'll need the pistol to get through the door." His hands moved to her shoulders and turned her toward the door on the opposite side. "Now move it lieutenant."

She stumbled toward the door, her mind swimming with questions. The goal? A brief flash into her past reminded her of a grey steel door with the number twenty-seven on it. That was at the outer ring and section twenty-two was the total opposite side of the colony. What did that have to do with anything?

"Now lieutenant!"

She yanked the door open and ran through it on impulse. Her mind swam with clean air and at one hundred yards out she dared to look back. Blake smiled wistfully at her while several armored Trolls rushed him before a quick flash of light with a world-ending *thump* of explosives obliterated the building around him. She stumbled with the force of the blast and fell over backward while the grey dust and heat rushed over her.

"No!" she screamed, fighting to get back to her feet. Two faltering strides toward the building through the debris and she fell to her knees. The little map in her helmet showed a dozen yellow triangles that all faded to red and finally winked out of existence. She ripped her helmet off and screamed, "Blake!" while dust and debris rained down to force her into a coughing fit. She fumbled the helmet back over her head against the choking dust as the tears on her face turned to mud. The only man she could trust was gone. All she wanted to do was rush back there.

And what? What would you do?

His voice echoed inside her mind while she coughed again. "Observe and keep moving. Never stay in one place," she repeated hoarsely. Those words were etched into her mind forever.

She pushed back to her battered feet and took one last look toward the dust cloud where her commander was buried. "Cry later," she ordered herself and tore her eyes from the scene. She had a head start now and she'd regret not taking advantage of it later if she didn't use it.

About the Author

I am a man in pursuit of a dream. This book is the realization of that dream, but only a start. I write what I want to read, and more importantly, what is meant to encourage others as well. It is my hope that one day my grandchildren read these books and I'd like to be proud of them instead of trying to hide things only meant for adults. I've spent half a century on this planet, and three decades working on highways to make things better for drivers. My children have grown and my lovely wife and I still look at each other in ways that makes people call us newlyweds.

I have survived cancer, a near-death experience, and many years of commuting to and from work averaging over eighty miles a day. I am not unlike many of you who read this book, and I leave you with one parting thought:

You will find your best life possible in Jesus Christ. I promise you that.

ACKNOWLEDGEMENTS

First off, let me point out that the cover art for this book was crafted by Makayla Foster. Her photography skills are soon to find a homepage, but as of this writing she is available for consultation at MParkPictures@outlook.com. If you are looking for a cover artist, I encourage you to contact her as she obviously does exceptional work.

I want to acknowledge a young lady by the name of Abbie Emmons. Her openness to share her experiences and findings has helped to improve my writing craft immensely in the past few years. You can find her on YouTube, Instagram, and Facebook as well as her own webpage.

Finally, I would also like to thank you. You picked up this book and you're even reading this part. Very few people actually read this section of a book, and fewer still will actually leave a review. Reviews let people know something is out there, and that other people liked or disliked what it was. I would appreciate it if you could post a review about this book on any platform you choose.

<u>HISTORICAL FICTION</u>

Gunther's Daughter (2013)

<u>SCIENCE FICTION</u>

Legion's Fall Book One: Angel in a Box (2018)

Legion's Fall Book Two: Angel's Resolve (2023)

Legion's Fall Book Three: Angel's War (2023)

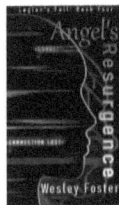

Legion's Fall Book Four: Angel's Resurgence (2024)

Look for these books on Amazon in eBook and Paperback!